TABLE MANNERS

Also by Mia King

GOOD THINGS
SWEET LIFE

TABLE MANNERS

Mia King

BERKLEY BOOKS, NEW YORK

THE BERKLEY PUBLISHING GROUP
Published by the Penguin Group
Penguin Group (USA) Inc.
375 Hudson Street, New York, New York 10014, USA
Penguin Group (Canada), 90 Eglinton Avenue East, Suite 700, Toronto, Ontario M4P 2Y3, Canada
(a division of Pearson Penguin Canada Inc.)
Penguin Books Ltd., 80 Strand, London WC2R 0RL, England
Penguin Group Ireland, 25 St. Stephen's Green, Dublin 2, Ireland (a division of Penguin Books Ltd.)
Penguin Group (Australia), 250 Camberwell Road, Camberwell, Victoria 3124, Australia
(a division of Pearson Australia Group Pty. Ltd.)
Penguin Books India Pvt. Ltd., 11 Community Centre, Panchsheel Park, New Delhi—110 017, India
Penguin Group (NZ), 67 Apollo Drive, Rosedale, North Shore, 0632, New Zealand
(a division of Pearson New Zealand Ltd.)
Penguin Books (South Africa) (Pty.) Ltd., 24 Sturdee Avenue, Rosebank, Johannesburg 2196,
South Africa

Penguin Books Ltd., Registered Offices: 80 Strand, London WC2R 0RL, England

This is a work of fiction. Names, characters, places, and incidents either are the product of the author's imagination or are used fictitiously, and any resemblance to actual persons, living or dead, business establishments, events, or locales, is entirely coincidental. The publisher does not have any control over and does not assume any responsibility for author or third-party websites or their content.

The recipes contained in this book are to be followed exactly as written. The publisher is not responsible for your specific health or allergy needs that may require medical supervision. The publisher is not responsible for any adverse reactions to the recipes contained in this book.

ISBN-13: 978-1-61523-385-4

PRINTED IN THE UNITED STATES OF AMERICA

A taste for simplicity cannot last for long.

EUGENE DELACROIX

Manners maketh man.

WILLIAM OF WYKEHAM

ACKNOWLEDGMENTS

There are several special people I'd like to take this opportunity to thank:

My cofounders of the Debutante Ball (thedebutanteball .com): Kristy Kiernan, Tish Cohen, Jennifer McMahon, Anna David, and Eileen Cook. It was great to kick off our writing careers together; I'll always appreciate the support and synergy.

My fellow authors who believed in me early on, offering blurbs and words of wisdom: Jane Porter, Catherine Spangler, Jessica Inclán, Laura Caldwell, Justina Chen Headley, Susan Wiggs, Jill Marie Landis.

Christine Hustace, who helped keep me sane with her twelve-step friendship program, especially after Luke's birth. You're his fairy godmother, and ours, too. Monika Kwon was there whenever we needed an extra hand around the house, helping me meet deadline after deadline—we're so very grateful, thank you.

Pat Hopkins, my certified nurse midwife in shining bioidentical progesterone armor.

My girlfriend Elaine Ng Huntzinger fielded question after question about Paris, and my sister-in-law Evette Gee did the same for Seattle. Kay Chang Blackburn read drafts, rallied her book group behind me (officially called the Good Things book group!), and helped me lose the baby weight. My dear brother, Lawrence Hsu, updated my website and put up with all my annoying calls and emails about said website. His wife, Annie, offered insight and awesome care packages. Big hugs to all of you.

My hard-core beta readers, Nancy Sue Martin and fellow author Patricia Wood, who read whatever I give them at the drop of the hat. Thank you for the honest feedback while always cheering me on. My husband gets high marks here, too, for reading everything I write in addition to watching the kids and doing midnight runs to the grocery store so I can have the necessary "brain food" to finish my work. I love you all.

The recipe contributors: James Boudreau, Ivy Chan, Amy Chen, Kristi Drake, Lisa Dupar, Clotilde Dusoulier, Scott Harberts, Sean Hartley, Susan Kaplan, David Lebovitz, Stephane Lemagnen, Thierry Mougin, Thierry Rautureau, Peabody Rudd, Daniel Thiebaut, Jess Thomson, Molly Wizenberg, Lan Wong. You're amazing, talented, and passionate individuals. I've loved learning about what you do and I'm grateful to have your recipes in the book.

The recipe testers: G. Bisbjerg, Dee Carney, Amy Froehlich, Tres Hatch, Sally Marie Krantz, Jennifer O'Rafferty, Lynn Salisbury, Amy Sebestyen, Lynn Utsugi. Thank you for rolling up your sleeves and opening your kitchens so I could write a better book.

Charles Purdy, etiquette evangelist extraordinaire.

I'm lucky to be supported by such a great team of people at Berkley Books. My editor, Wendy McCurdy, who keeps saying yes; assistant editor, Allison Brandau; copy editor Jessica McDonnell; publicist Angela Januzzi; the art department who come up with the best covers for my books; the amazing sales team; and everyone else in between. Jenny Bent was always there to offer her support and an encouraging word. You've all had an important hand in getting my books to the shelves and I appreciate it more than you know.

My children—Maya, Eric, and Luke—who pushed me to pursue my dream now rather than later. My husband, Darrin, who has been the best kind of friend, partner, and husband I could wish for. I am grateful.

And last, but never least, to my readers, who make this all worthwhile. Thank you.

CHAPTER ONE

You should never assume anything.
—Charlotte Ford, *21st-Century Etiquette*

Deidre woke up in a tangle of sheets. She checked the clock, and then let out a happy sigh.

Bliss.

The May sun streamed into her bedroom, sunlight dancing on her bare legs. There was a sound from the kitchen as the coffeemaker turned on. Moments later the aroma of fresh-brewed coffee filled the condo.

Her condo. After years of renting, Deidre McIntosh was officially a homeowner.

She gave a luxurious stretch. A quick shower would wake her up, and then she'd roll into her day. Meetings in the morning, a quick lunch, then a walk through the production floor to see how things were coming along with Sweet Deidre, her line of branded baked goods that was scheduled to launch in a few short months.

She grabbed a pillow and gave it a punch, fluffing it up to

fullness. Then she sank back against it and reached for her BlackBerry, scanning the day's headlines and checking her e-mails.

There was the typical high volume of junk mail and spam, along with meeting agendas and pending appointments. Deidre was about to close out when she noticed a text message from Kevin, sent just after midnight.

AT FRANKFURT AIRPORT, ABOUT TO BOARD – BACK IN SEATTLE BY MID-AFTERNOON. DINNER? LOVE YOU.

Deidre quickly tapped back her response.

I LOVE YOU, TOO. MY PLACE, 7:00.

She hit SEND. He would get the message once he landed.

She took her time showering and dressing, choosing a simple but classy outfit: a pink tailored cotton wrap shirt, dark gray pinstripe slacks, black heels with a pointed toe. She'd pull the look together with an oversized braided silver mesh bracelet and her favorite pair of pearl earrings, a gift from Kevin. She took one last look in the mirror and nodded, satisfied. All that was left was to grab one of her breakfast muffins and fill her travel carafe with coffee, and she'd be good to go.

The commute was only half an hour, and traffic moved along at a clip. If the rest of her day continued like this, she'd have plenty of time to pick up something special for dinner. Lamb shanks, maybe. She made a mean osso buco, and it was one of Kevin's favorites. A fresh beet and goat cheese salad would be an easy accompaniment. They could choose a bottle of red from her modest wine collection and she'd have her pick of desserts from work.

She hummed along with the radio as she considered the sweet possibilities before setting on a favorite: a Florentine Tart with almonds, candied cherries, and orange peel, drizzled liberally in chocolate. She made a quick call and was pleased to hear that one would be put aside for her.

Perfect.

She pulled into the parking lot of Jamison Cookies and Confections. She entered the building and walked to the bank of cubicles that housed the Sweet Deidre team. Her assistant, Amber Olson, handed her a stack of messages.

"Good news," Amber said. She was a bubbly redhead fresh out of college, anxious to begin a career in food management. "We found those dried cherries you like. Organic, and they're willing to wholesale them. They cost a little more, but the company's local and can deliver them quickly. I put all the information on your desk."

"Excellent." The cherry almond shortbread cookie was the star of Sweet Deidre's starting lineup. "Can you send the information to Gary in production as well?"

"Sure. Oh, and that reporter from *Taste* magazine is waiting for you in your office."

"What?" Deidre frowned, puzzled. "But it's Monday. We're not supposed to meet until Friday."

Amber shrugged. "Well, she acted like it was today. I thought maybe you'd changed it."

"No, I didn't." Deidre scanned her calendar. She'd have to move some things around, but it wasn't the end of the world. "Let's push off the marketing meeting until right after lunch.

Can you stall the reporter for a few more minutes? Maybe give her a press packet and one of the Sweet Deidre samplers? I'm going to freshen up."

"No problem, Deidre."

In the ladies' room, Deidre checked herself in the mirror. She was having a good hair day, fortunately, even though she was overdue for some highlights and the occasional gray hair stood out among its brunette counterparts. Well, that was forty-one for you. There was no turning back the clock, and Deidre knew better than to try to fight it.

She smoothed her blouse and touched up her lipstick, then ran through the short list of talking points in her head as she headed toward her office.

High quality, all natural ingredients—sourced locally when possible—the latest addition to the JCC family of products . . .

The reporter was waiting patiently in one of the chairs next to Deidre's desk, her notebook resting in her lap. She stood up promptly and offered her hand when Deidre walked in.

"Hi! I'm Rosemary Goodwin."

"Rosemary Goodwin?" Deidre shook her hand. "I thought I was meeting with Rebecca Ellison. And weren't we supposed to meet on Friday?"

"Huh? Oh, there were some last-minute editorial changes." Rosemary pulled out a small digital camera. "Do you mind if I get a quick picture?"

"Sure, but—"

"Say cheese!" The flash went off. Rosemary glanced at the display, a pleased look on her face, and quickly tucked the camera back into her bag. "Wow, perfect—we don't even need another take. You're incredibly photogenic, Deidre. But you probably already know that, having been on TV and all."

"Well, I—"

She placed a handheld recorder on Deidre's desk. "Can we tape this? I find it's easier for me to have my notes transcribed later." She glanced at Deidre, then jotted something down in her notebook.

Uneasy, Deidre moved the piles of paper that crowded her desk to one side. "Can I offer you some coffee or bottled water?"

"Oh, I'm fine." Rosemary beamed brightly at Deidre. "Now, this must be a *very* exciting time for you, with the new cookie line and all!"

Deidre nodded, her confidence returning. "Absolutely. Everyone at Jamison Cookies and Confections is excited about the upcoming launch of Sweet Deidre. As you may know, JCC prides itself on being a local leader in baked goods and confectionary retailing. Sweet Deidre represents an opportunity for the company to move into the gourmet specialty foods market . . ."

"Yes, yes, I got that all from the press packet." Rosemary held up a glossy white folder with the Sweet Deidre logo embossed on the cover, then shoved it into her bag. She leaned eagerly toward Deidre. "But what about *you*, Deidre? This must be *such* a huge change from where you were less than a year ago!"

Deidre paused, uncertain of where this was going. "Well, it's true that we moved very quickly once we decided to create the Sweet Deidre line . . ."

"I mean, first there was the unexpected cancellation of your show, *Live Simple with Deidre McIntosh*, and then being evicted from your apartment. In fact . . ." Rosemary looked down at her notepad and tapped her pen. "You were broke, weren't you?"

Deidre squirmed. "Um, I'm not sure . . ."

"I have a quote here from Theodore Shepard of Open Investments. I believe that's your cousin's brokerage firm, where you were a client? He says that you had no idea about the state of your financial affairs, and that your idea of making a capital investment was to go on eBay and bid on a pair of gently used Manolos." Rosemary looked up. "Is that true?"

Deidre grit her teeth. This wasn't an interview about her new line of baked goods. This was an interview about her and the disastrous year she'd had last year. "Did you say you were from *Taste* magazine?"

Rosemary's smile didn't waver. "I didn't say, actually." She reached into her pocket and pulled out a business card. "Rosemary Goodwin, *The Seattle Scoop*. Can you comment on your relationship with millionaire Kevin Johnson?"

Deidre snatched the card and stood up. "No. I'm sorry, but this interview is over. I'd appreciate it if you'd leave now."

Rosemary gave Deidre a sympathetic smile. "Deidre, think of this as an opportunity to tell your side of the story. You're a hero to women everywhere. You pulled yourself up by your bootstraps, landed the most eligible bachelor in Seattle, produced a comeback documentary series, *and* signed a deal for a line of branded cookies under your own name. I mean, it's quite incredible, if you think about it!" Rosemary blinked innocently.

Deidre didn't say anything, but went to the door of her office and held it open.

"Fine." Rosemary put her things into an oversized messenger bag and hefted it onto her shoulder. "I'll also be writing something on my blog about you and Kevin, in case you want to leave a comment. We could even arrange a live chat with our readers, if you're interested."

"I'm not," Deidre said flatly.

"Well, maybe Kevin would . . ."

"He's not either." Deidre kept her eyes on Rosemary as she gestured to her assistant. "Amber, please help the reporter from *The Seattle Scoop* find her way out of the building."

"You have my card," Rosemary called over her shoulder as she was escorted down the hallway. "Call me!"

"Deidre, I'm *so* sorry!" Amber was wringing her hands and looked close to tears. "I just assumed she was your Friday interview. She made it seem like you were expecting her."

"That's okay." Deidre was still put out by Rosemary's visit. Technically Rosemary hadn't lied, though she had lied by omission to let them think that she was someone she wasn't. "In the future let's just ask for a business card up front. That should clear things up right away."

Amber nodded, sniffling. "Okay."

Deidre gave the young woman a reassuring pat on the arm and watched her leave, still distraught. Deidre felt guilty. Unfortunately this wasn't the first time they'd had a run-in with the tabloid media. The buzz had barely died down after the unexpected cancellation of Deidre's lifestyle and cooking show, *Live Simple with Deidre McIntosh*, and now the press was clamoring over the news that Deidre and Kevin Johnson were a couple.

In this case, it was less about her and more about him. Kevin came from old Seattle money and had a successful venture capital firm. Throw in the fact that he was tall, handsome, single, *and* a genuinely nice guy—well, even Deidre wasn't so sure she could blame them for wanting to get the inside story.

But she did feel bad that it was starting to affect her staff and their productivity at Sweet Deidre. Rosemary's visit had cost them an hour, and the media kits averaged ten dollars apiece. Plus, a perfectly good cookie sampler had gone to waste. Deidre grimaced at the thought of Rosemary driving back to her offices at *The Seattle Scoop*, munching on a Sweet Deidre cookie.

Amber buzzed her. "Deidre, I have Manuela on the line. She wants to meet with you. Are you available?"

"Sure. Tell her I'll be up in ten minutes."

"Actually, she's on her way down and says she'll be here in less than five."

Great. Deidre looked at her disheveled desk. She liked things neat and orderly, but lately that just didn't seem possible. There was always something going on, something that needed attention or revision. She'd come up with a brilliant color-coded system, something she'd borrowed from one of her old *Live Simple* episodes, and it had worked for all of two days before the piles starting creeping up on her desk again.

"Knock knock!" Manuela stood in Deidre's doorframe, beaming. Manuela Jamison was a portly woman whose love for food and sweets was evidenced not only by the company she ran but also by her large and generous frame. Despite weighing in at more than two hundred pounds, Manuela wasn't someone Deidre considered overweight. She was just a big personality in more ways than one.

"Hi, Manuela. Come on in."

"Deidre, honey." Manuela approached Deidre with her arms outstretched and planted a maternal kiss on either cheek. "I just have to say, again, that I am so positively *thrilled* you came on board. You know that, right?"

Deidre wasn't an employee—technically she had a contract with JCC that paid her a consulting fee and royalty off the sales of Sweet Deidre—but she knew what Manuela meant. She nodded.

Manuela sat down on the couch in Deidre's office. "I see a real future for you and JCC. Not just with Sweet Deidre, but with other products, too. The custom cupcake line? Brilliant. You have so many good ideas, and you're just so wonderfully creative, I still can't believe you're under our roof!"

"Thank you, Manuela."

Manuela continued to gush. "And you're *such* a hard worker. *Committed.* I like that about you, Deidre. I told Frank yesterday, 'That girl has an enviable work ethic. She's a keeper!'" Frank was Manuela's husband and COO of Jamison Cookies and Confections.

Deidre blushed. "That's very kind of you to say."

"I just *know* Sweet Deidre will be a huge success; I'm not worried in the least. Which is why I know you won't be fazed by what I'm about to tell you."

Deidre felt the smile fall from her face. "What do you mean? Tell me what?"

"Well, it appears that those qualitative focus groups out in Pasadena and Bakersfield didn't care much for the Sweet Deidre line of cookies and baked goods we sent them. Didn't care much for them at all." Manuela turned her head and called, "Elliot! You can bring them in!"

Manuela's assistant entered Deidre's office, pushing a hand truck. He was skinny with erratically cut black hair, a recent University of Washington journalism graduate who had mastered the moody grunge persona. He deposited four large boxes by her desk and then left.

"Fortunately, I convinced the company to provide us with *all* of the original documentation and evaluation forms. I find it's so much more useful than a neat summary, don't you? By going through each one you'll be able to get a real feel for what our customers want." Manuela was nodding fervently, agreeing with herself.

Deidre had been staring at the boxes and now turned to stare at Manuela. "Each one?"

Manuela stood up to leave. "I remember you told me you were a fast reader. Didn't you once finish seven books in three days?"

"Actually it was three books in seven—"

"I am envious, I can tell you that!" Manuela shook her head in wonderment. "But that skill will certainly come in handy for you now. Just take a look, digest the information, and let me know what the new lineup of Sweet Deidre products will be."

"The new lineup?" Deidre felt her chest tighten. It was May, and the Sweet Deidre cookies were supposed to be rolling off the production line in September. "Manuela, with all due respect, it'll take me a while to go through all these boxes and process the information. Then I need to meet with the Sweet Deidre team and come up with some new recipes. We'll need to test them, tweak the formulation if necessary. I'll need a couple of months, at least."

"A couple of months? Oh, Deidre!" Manuela laughed. "I'll need something by *Friday*." She gave Deidre a friendly wave and was gone.

Deidre lowered herself into her chair in stunned disbelief. Manuela's original timetable had been aggressive—nine months from conception to the shelf. Even if Deidre worked twelve-hour days and late into the night, there still wouldn't be enough time to get it all done.

Five days. Suddenly feeling weary, Deidre pressed the intercom button on her desk.

"Yes, Deidre?"

"Amber, clear my calendar for the rest of the week. I'll also need you to reserve the test kitchen for Wednesday and Thursday. And I'm sorry, but it looks like the entire Sweet Deidre team will be working overtime until further notice. Can you let everyone know?"

"I'll send out a memo right away. Oh, and they're sending over the Florentine Tart you ordered from the JCC retail store."

Kevin. Deidre had completely forgotten that he would be flying in tonight.

"Great," Deidre said, thinking quickly. "And can you find someone to move these boxes out to my car? I'll be working from home for the rest of the day. Thanks, Amber."

Friday, indeed.

So it wasn't a home-cooked meal, exactly. Okay, so it wasn't a home-cooked meal at all, but Deidre had done what she could under the circumstances, and the Jade Palace did make one amazing orange chicken.

It was just shy of 7:00 p.m. when she heard the tinny sound of her doorbell.

"It's open!" Deidre called out, feeling her heart give an excited little jump. She got up from the dining room table and hurried to meet Kevin, a smile already on her face.

Her front door opened and then he was there, right in front of her. A second later she was in his arms, covering his face with kisses.

He responded by kissing her back, a long, deep, lingering kiss that told her he'd missed her, too. Deidre inhaled the scent of him—one part Burberry, one part airport—then laced his fingers with hers, pulling him into the apartment, closing the door behind him.

He was casually dressed in a lightweight sweater and slacks—his typical travel clothes—and he sported a hint of stubble. With brown hair and brown eyes, Kevin Johnson was classically handsome. He had the height and the presence of someone who was comfortable in his own skin. Part of it was pedigree—Kevin knew how to carry himself, and did so with an air of confidence, not arrogance, a trait Deidre found immensely appealing and even sexy.

"I missed you," she told him, wrapping her arms around his waist.

"I can tell," he replied with a smile. He nipped an earlobe. "Nice earrings, by the way."

"Thanks. Some guy gave them to me."

"That guy has good taste." They grinned at each other until Kevin looked over her shoulder. He looked back at her, his eyebrows raised. "Doing a little paperwork?"

"Very funny." Deidre didn't turn around. She knew her once-immaculate condo was now a complete mess. She'd opened up each of the boxes and her living room was now littered with paper. Piles were stacked on the floor, on the couch, on the coffee table, on the dining room table, anywhere Deidre could find a free space. "The focus groups had issues with the Sweet Deidre line. Manuela wants me to figure out what went wrong and then come up with a new line. I've been reading evaluations and transcripts all afternoon."

"Wow, I'm sorry." Kevin rubbed her back. "Are you okay?"

"Yes. And no. Mostly no." She went into the kitchen and emerged with a platter of Sweet Deidre cookies. She picked up a creamy molasses sandwich cookie and offered it to him. "I know you've tried this a million times, but try it again and tell me: Does this seem like an overpriced Oreo?" She kept her voice even, masking the irritation she felt.

Kevin obligingly took a bite and chewed, thoughtful. "No," he said. "Although now that you mention it . . ."

Deidre stared at him. "What do you mean, now that I mention it? The cookie wafers are hazelnut, not chocolate, and the filling is molasses, not vanilla cream!"

"Right." Kevin polished off his cookie. "That's what I meant. It must be the coffee they served on the airplane. Lousy stuff; completely ruined my palate."

"What about this one?" She handed him another cookie. "Several people said it was too exotic. Too exotic! Since when did white chocolate and macadamia nuts become exotic?"

"Er . . ."

She ranted through two more—the spiced sugar coins ("too seasonal") and Meyer lemon bars ("been done before")—before holding up the Sweet Deidre signature cookie.

The cherry almond shortbread cookie.

"They loved this," she said simply. "Someone even called it *sublime*. But guess what?"

"What?" Kevin hazarded.

"They thought the price point was too high. They loved it,

but said it wasn't worth it. Not worth it!" She was about to toss the cookie back on the plate but thought better of it and took a bite instead.

It really *was* sublime. Mollified, she felt her shoulders start to relax.

Kevin helped himself to another cookie. "Deidre, these cookies are amazing. But when you bring a product to market, it's a different ball game. You need to anticipate what's happening with your customer. It's about them, what they need, what their experience is with your product. Think back to when you would develop a show for *Live Simple*. You chose topics that you thought your viewers would be interested in and would benefit from, right?"

Deidre nodded.

"This isn't any different. If anything, it's more difficult because they're making a decision solely by looking at a box sitting on a shelf. It's not a multisensory experience like TV, where they can hear you and see you. You don't have that same kind of influence over a package of cookies. People are comparing it to all the others on the shelf and then weighing cookies over other forms of snacks or treats. If it wasn't on their shopping list, then they may be thinking about their budget. What are they willing to give up in order to buy a package of Sweet Deidre cookies?"

Discouraged, Deidre let out a heavy sigh. "And here I was, all worked up at the thought of having to come up with a handful of new recipes. Instead, now I have to try to anticipate the American consumer's eating and buying habits. No problem."

Kevin offered an encouraging smile. "That's what you have focus groups for. Even food manufacturers who have a long history in the industry haven't figured it out. You don't want to find out that there's a problem *after* the cookies have hit the shelves, so consider this a good thing."

Deidre knew he was probably right, but that didn't mean she had to like it. "Manuela's giving me until Friday to come up with something."

"*This* Friday?" Kevin barked a laugh. "Are you kidding?"

She gave a sigh. "It's impossible, isn't it?"

He shook his head. "Ambitious, yes. Impossible, no. And if anyone can do it, it's you." He gave her a kiss.

"I'm not so sure about that, but I'll certainly try." *As if I have a choice.*

Deidre took a deep breath. "Well, now that it is absolutely clear that I have so much more to do than I originally thought, we'll need to eat quickly so I can get back to work." She gave his hand a tug and led him down the hallway toward the bedroom.

Kevin followed her, perplexed. "Isn't the dining room that way?" He pointed behind them.

"Yes, but it looks like a hurricane hit it and there isn't any place for us to sit." Deidre pushed open the door to her bedroom. Michael Bublé crooned in the background. The lights were off and candles were lit, giving the room a cozy, sensual glow. A picnic blanket was laid out on the ground with containers of Chinese takeout and a bottle of wine.

"Interesting," Kevin said. He gave a mischievous grin when he took in the plate of fortune cookies that sat invitingly in the middle of the bed.

"Dinner first," Deidre said, returning his mischievous grin with one of her own. "And then dessert."

CHAPTER TWO

Etiquette in its true sense serves to make our dealings with
other human beings, if not always pleasant, at least bearable.
—Charles Purdy, *Urban Etiquette*

Marla Banks, Seattle's prominent fiftysomething socialite and star of *At Home with Marla Banks*, arched a perfectly plucked eyebrow at her station manager, Juliette Farquahar. "I'm sorry, but do I look totally insane to you?"

Juliette gave a small, tolerant sigh, crossing her arms as she leaned against the door frame of Marla's dressing room. "No, Marla, you do not."

"That's right." Marla tossed back her head as she pretended to consider her nail polish. "Do I look desperate?"

"No . . ."

"Because, I can assure you, I am *not*."

Another sigh. "I know you're not, Marla. It's just . . ."

"So, that being said, there is *no way* that I'm going to have Deidre McIntosh on my show." Marla stood up. Her driver would be waiting outside, and she had several stops to make before meeting her parents, Edward and Beverly Johnson, for dinner at Lampreia. The topic of discussion would no doubt be her father's upcoming eightieth birthday celebration.

Juliette moved swiftly to the center of the door frame, blocking Marla's exit. "Not so fast, Marla."

Marla stared at Juliette, her surprise quickly replaced by irritation. "Juliette!"

"I'm sorry, Marla, but this is important. With sweeps week almost upon us, I've taken a closer look at our programming. As much as I adore the 'Seattle Socialite Weddings' concept . . ."

Marla held up a hand. "Before you say anything, I want to make something clear. First off, you know this is local cable, right?"

"Marla . . ."

"And that *At Home with Marla Banks* is probably the best thing to ever hit local cable, correct?"

"Well, actually . . ."

"And that the people who actually watch local cable have slim pickings to begin with, which means that a show of my caliber"—and here Marla rested a hand on her chest dramatically—"is spectacular before we even hit the first commercial break. Did I miss anything?"

Juliette looked annoyed. "This as an opportunity to not only ace sweeps week but to bring some new viewers to the show. Enter your special guest, Deidre McIntosh. She hasn't been in front of a camera since *Live Simple with Deidre McIntosh* went off the air. I really think her viewers would tune in to see her again."

Marla looked at her scornfully. "*At Home* is not Betty Crocker, Juliette. What's she going to do, cook up one of her little concoctions on the set? My set is a *bedroom*, not a kitchen!"

Juliette gasped. "Marla, that's brilliant. A cooking demonstration! Her fans will eat it up. She could even make that orgasmic corn fritter, the one that got so much great press last year."

"FORGET IT."

Juliette continued, undeterred. "Her fans will love you for bringing her back. You'll come out the better woman in this."

Marla dismissed the thought with a wave of her hand. "Do you really think I care what anybody else thinks?"

"Well, what do you think about adding twenty to thirty thousand more viewers? A third of Deidre's viewership hasn't switched to *At Home*. This might be one of the first times they see the show, and with your charm, I'm sure they'll be hooked."

Twenty to thirty thousand new viewers? Marla felt herself waver as she chewed on her lip. "Well, that's probably true . . ."

"I'm confident we could get a premium advertiser for the episode, maybe even a sponsor. You could be decked out in diamonds . . ."

"Diamonds?"

Juliette leaned in for the kill. "And, don't forget, this is *your* show," she said. "Deidre will be *your* guest. You get to call the shots, maybe even have a little fun with it."

Now that was definitely appealing. An opportunity to publicly taunt Deidre *and* boost ratings? Ever since Marla learned that her brother, Kevin, was dating Deidre, she'd been hoping for an opportunity to make Deidre's life a living hell. She'd be a fool to pass this up.

Marla leisurely reapplied her lipstick before gathering her purse, a limited edition Tod's handbag in a silver matte calfskin finish. "First of all, I'm not doing any cooking. I don't cook at home; I see no reason why I should cook on the show."

"Fine. Noted."

"Second of all, this is a one-time deal. I'm doing this as a favor out of the goodness of my heart. After we shoot the segment, I don't want anything to do with her."

Juliette looked innocent. "Who?"

Marla smiled as she swept past her. "Exactly."

Deidre cradled the phone between her ear and shoulder as she measured flour into a mixing bowl. "Juliette, can I call you back some other time? I'm in the middle of—"

"A minute of your time, Deidre. That's all I ask. By the way, I heard you bought a condo. Good for you!"

Deidre sighed and wiped her floured hands on her apron. Juliette Farquahar, the station manager for Channel Five, had been the only station manager in town willing to give Deidre a chance after *Live Simple* had been pulled off the air. Deidre had come up with an idea for a comeback show, an NPR-esque documentary series entitled *Seattle Revealed*, which Juliette had agreed to air. After three episodes, the Biography Channel bought the rights to the concept. The royalty had been enough for Deidre to put a down payment on her condo, and Juliette knew it. "All right, Juliette. What can I do for you?"

"Actually, it's what *I* can do for *you*. How does a guest spot on *At Home with Marla Banks* sound?"

Terrible, Deidre wanted to say, but she didn't. She opted for a more diplomatic answer instead. "I'd love to, Juliette, but I can't right now. Sweet Deidre is a few months away from launch and we're having some last-minute glitches. Maybe we can talk about this later in the year." *Or never,* she added to herself.

"Are you sure? Because I *really* think it'd be good for Sweet Deidre, too. Generate some early buzz, get you back in the public eye. We're talking a couple of hours, max. You'll be in and out of the studio in no time. And think about your fans— they'll be ecstatic to see you again!"

Deidre considered this. Some early publicity for Sweet Deidre might not be a bad idea. "What about Marla?"

"Marla?" Juliette sounded like she didn't know who Deidre was talking about. "Oh, well, she's just *thrilled*, of course!"

Deidre knew better. Marla and Deidre had their professional differences, but when Deidre started seeing Kevin, things had gone from uncomfortable to unbearable. Deidre sometimes found it hard to believe that the two were related.

"And I have the *perfect* episode for you," Juliette continued exuberantly. "Right up your alley. I'll send you an e-mail with all of the details. I have a good feeling about this, Deidre. We'll see you in a couple of weeks!" She hung up the phone before Deidre could respond.

A couple of weeks? Deidre looked at the calendar. Ah, sweeps week. That was typical Juliette, doing whatever was necessary to get more viewers to tune in.

Deidre slipped the phone back into its base with a sigh. There was no point in calling her back. Deidre did owe her, and she knew that Juliette had no intention of letting Deidre off the hook. That was all right—a few hours on the air wasn't a big deal, and might even be fun.

Deidre peered into her mixing bowl. Had she finished measuring the flour? Was it six cups or eight? Her thoughts cloudy, Deidre put the bowl aside and picked up the phone again.

She had less than three days. She was going to need some serious help.

Deidre's oldest and closest friend, William Sen, stared dubiously at the ten-pound bags of flour lined up on Deidre's kitchen counter. "I don't know about this."

"It'll only take an hour," Deidre promised. At William's raised eyebrow she hastily corrected herself. "Maybe two."

"*Deidre.*"

"Okay, fine—three. But this is an emergency, William. Please?"

William let out a long breath, running a hand through his meticulously cut hair. He was trim and fit, with boyish good looks and perfect skin tone thanks to his Chinese heritage. He looked more like a model or an actor than a surgeon, but what really set him apart was his mastery in the kitchen. And right now Deidre was desperate.

"Don't you have a twenty-five-person research and development team at your disposal?" he asked.

"Yes, but I worked with them before and look where we ended up. Besides, I'm more creative in my own space. Once I figure out what I'm doing, I'll take it to the JCC test kitchen." She offered him a set of measuring spoons but William shook his head.

"Deidre, you have people who actually get paid to do this kind of work. In case it escaped you, I already have a full-time job." William worked in the cardiothoracic division at King County General Hospital. He glanced at his watch, a top-of-the-line trainer that had a heart rate monitor, chronograph, and more memory than Deidre's laptop. "I have exactly eleven hours before I need to make my rounds. If anything, I should be at home, sleeping."

She gave him a pointed look. "William, I happen to know you only need seven hours of sleep. Which leaves you with four hours to help me." She began bringing out containers of salt, baking soda, and sugar.

He crossed his arms indignantly. "For your information, I now need the recommended eight hours to function at my optimum," he told her. "Besides, any free time I have is supposed to be spent helping Alain plan our commitment ceremony." William and his partner, Alain Rousseau, were planning to exchange vows over Labor Day weekend.

"What do you have left to do?"

William wrinkled his nose. "Everything. We still haven't been able to find a venue. We really want to do something outdoors, to take advantage of the weather before it turns. But apparently everybody else has the same idea, too."

Deidre selected several jars of spices from the pantry: cinnamon, cloves, nutmeg. "Are you going to letterpress your invitations?"

"I wish, but it's not exactly in the budget." William sighed dejectedly and made a big show of reaching for his keys. "Well, I should get going."

"William, wait. Help me for a couple of hours and I'll give you a batch of cookies to take home for Alain."

"A batch of cookies?" William was unimpressed. "I just experimented with every cookie recipe in last month's *Martha Stewart Living*. I'll have leftovers for weeks."

"Okay, okay. What about dinner? I'll buy you guys dinner tonight, alcohol included."

William shook his head. "I'm making sole saltimbocca

and Alain will probably pick up a bucket of KFC on the way home." Alain was also a doctor at the hospital. He was French, a sweet and affable guy with a passion for reality TV shows and junk food. It was completely appalling to William, who was obviously a bit of a gourmand and preferred foreign films and Broadway musicals.

Deidre thought hard, then snapped her fingers. "I've got it. I'll help you find a venue for your ceremony."

William pretended to consider this. "Now that you've reminded me, I *do* have several cake tastings scheduled over the next couple of weeks . . ."

"So I'll go with you, give you my expert opinion."

William raised an eyebrow and looked at her expectantly, then gave his keys a jangle.

Deidre put her hands on her hips. "Fine. I'll negotiate any contracts, if it comes down to that. I should be able to get you some sort of deal—not everyone in Seattle has forgotten who I am."

"Done. I'll give you three hours." William tossed his keys aside and plucked the recipe card from the top of the oven, scanning it critically. "I really think you should swap out the golden sultanas for some Zante currants."

Deidre grinned, feeling a boost of energy. "I like that. I was thinking about adding flax meal to boost the nutritional value, too." She busied herself by pulling out a nest of metal mixing bowls, then sidled up next to him and gave him a nudge. "William, you know I'd have gone with you to the tastings anyway, even if you weren't able to help me."

"I know." William gave her a grin as he flipped through her CDs in search of the perfect baking music. "I just like giving you a hard time. Besides, I already told Alain I'd be here for the rest of the day. Now pass me an apron, will you? I just got this shirt from Bossi & Ich Ky and I don't want to get anything on it."

It took a solid forty-eight hours, dotted with cat naps and lots of caffeine, but by Thursday evening it appeared that Deidre had managed the impossible.

After getting a jump start with William, Deidre recruited the help of her small staff. Together they had prepped, baked, burned, tasted, and tweaked over twenty-two cookie recipes. More than four hundred cookies had slid in and out of the ovens at the JCC test kitchen, with a few mishaps and the occasional miracle. It was now up to Deidre to choose the final five recipes.

Her staff was out getting dinner, taking a much-deserved breather. Deidre sat alone in her office, bleary-eyed and exhausted, staring at the remaining recipe cards. She flipped through the cards, mulling over each one, willing herself to stay awake.

The chai tea cookies, she finally decided with a yawn. She was about to toss the index card to the side when she hesitated, suddenly unsure.

Or the cherry pinwheels.

Maybe the chocolate mint meringues?

Deidre tried to concentrate on her notes, on the ratings and collective scoring of the remaining recipes, but the names swam before her eyes, blending into one another. Why was this so difficult?

Her cell phone rang and Deidre reached for it, grateful for the break. She pressed the speakerphone button and leaned back in her chair. "Hello?"

"Deidre, it's Lindsey." Lindsey Miller's crisp, no-nonsense voice carried clearly over the din of clanging plates and laughter in the background. Lindsey was the owner of the Wishbone, a diner in Jacob's Point, where Deidre had lived the previous year when Seattle proved to be temporarily inhospitable. Lindsey was a down-to-earth, tell-it-like-it-is kind of person, someone who hadn't let Deidre wallow in the misery of losing her show. Deidre cherished their friendship, and immediately felt her spirits buoy.

"Lindsey! How are you?"

"Oh, for . . . Take me off the damn speakerphone, will you?"

Deidre hastily pressed the button as she brought the phone up to her ear. "It sounds busy at the Wishbone."

"Busy enough. Listen, who's this Rosemary Goodwin person and why is she pestering me?"

It took Deidre a moment before she placed the name. She made a face. "Rosemary Goodwin is a reporter with *The Seattle Scoop*, a tabloid paper here in Seattle. Why? Did she call you?"

"Call me? I wish. No, she came down here and parked her behind in a four-person booth. She then proceeded to bug all of my customers, asking questions about you. When I told her that she needed to order something or leave, she ordered a muffin. A muffin! And during my lunch rush!" Lindsey's voice was thunderous.

"I'm sorry, Lindsey."

"What are you apologizing for?" Lindsey sounded more annoyed with Deidre than with Rosemary. "She was asking all sorts of questions: how well did we know you, how long you were down here, where did you stay, what did you do, what's happening with you and Kevin . . ."

Deidre felt alarm bells go off in her head. Jacob's Point was a small town, and its handful of residents were both chatty and curious. "What did you tell her?"

"Not a thing. Just that you came in here from time to time, minded your own business. She cornered Bobby from the hardware store and he said the same thing. Ditto for Doc Hensen."

Deidre smiled in relief, grateful for the loyalty. God knew there were certainly stories to tell if they wanted to tell them.

"So when are you and that handsome boyfriend of yours coming down, anyway?" Lindsey loved to tease her about Kevin, who frequented the Wishbone whenever he was staying at his place on Lake Wish.

"I don't know. Work has been a little intense. And Kevin's been traveling a lot, but whatever free time we have, he's got business dinners and parties and other engagements we have to attend."

"Hard life." Lindsey was probably rolling her eyes.

Deidre looked at the index cards in front of her. Lindsey wasn't her target market exactly, but she was sharp and Deidre valued her opinion. "Hey, maybe you can help me, Lindsey. I have to choose five recipes for the Sweet Deidre line."

"Huh? I thought you already did that."

"I did. It's a long story. Can I read them all to you and you tell me what you think?"

"Sure, I'm on my five-minute dinner break. Shoot."

Deidre was only halfway through when Lindsey said, "Get rid of that chai one and the butterscotch-raspberry torte thingy—"

"Really? But it melts in your mouth and has the most wonderful aftertaste!"

"Well, that's great, Deidre, but I'd never spend my money on something like that. It's too hard to imagine how it'll taste and I have better things to do with my time and money. Get rid of it."

"But—"

"I've got to go. Got some customers wanting their checks."

Deidre reluctantly pulled the cards out of the pile. "Thanks, Lindsey."

"Don't be a stranger now. And look out for that Rosemary Goodwin person. I didn't like her, and I sure as heck don't trust her."

The next morning, in a quiet conference room at JCC, a silver tray holding five different plates with five different types of cookies was placed in front of Manuela Jamison. The elegant presentation was made by Amber, whose youth made her look spry and chipper, unlike the rest of the Sweet Deidre team, who wore a uniform look of exhaustion.

Deidre sat next to Manuela, her pen poised over a notepad, ready to jot down any notes. She prayed she wouldn't have to. She didn't feel like she had it in her to come up with something else if the new line failed to pass Manuela's muster.

"Hmmm." Manuela took small nibbles, chewing thoughtfully. When she was finished sampling each cookie, she took her time dabbing the corners of her mouth with a napkin, then looked around the conference room.

Everyone held their breath, Deidre included. After what seemed like forever, Manuela gave a slight nod of approval.

"Well done. Send it off to Gary in production so he can source the ingredients and figure out the production line.

I also want samples sent out to the market research firm that's organizing the focus groups so we can get another round of feedback immediately."

There was a collective sigh as everyone relaxed and began to gather their things. They gave Deidre a congratulatory pat on the back as they left, anxious to get home and get some sleep. Deidre thanked everyone as she watched them file out, ready to go home and crawl into bed herself. Kevin was on the road again, this time on a quick trip to Tucson for a couple of days. She stood up, only to have Manuela grasp her arm and pull her back down.

"A moment of your time, Deidre," Manuela said, nodding to Deidre's chair.

Deidre sat back down. "Is everything all right, Manuela?"

Manuela gave a slight, so-so nod. "You could say that, yes. In fact, that's the problem." She picked up a cookie and held it up to the light. "Everything is just all right. But I don't want 'all right.' Jamison Cookies and Confections doesn't want 'all right.' We want excitement. We want promise. We want Deidre McIntosh in a package." She dropped the cookie back on the plate and looked at her protégé.

Deidre tried to hide her confusion. "I'm sorry, Manuela, but I thought you just said the new line was well done."

"Yes, it was well done. You had less than five days to come up with something new, and you did. But what I tell your staff and what I tell you are two different things entirely. Even if the focus groups like this batch better, I'm telling you that something is missing. Something important." She waggled a finger.

"What?"

Manuela gave a shrug as she pushed herself up from her chair. "I don't know."

Great.

"But I do know that in this economy, people aren't going to take risks on a new brand unless it holds a promise. A hope for the future. Do you understand?"

They're just cookies! Deidre wanted to shout, but instead she said, "Well, I can sit down with the marketing team and come up with some new slogans or a stronger platform—"

Manuela shook her head. "No, no, Deidre. When I brought you in, I wanted the Deidre McIntosh product. Not something fabricated or dreamed up to sell more cookies, but the real thing. A reflection of you, of who you are. These cookies are good, and they may even sell well, but they're not Deidre McIntosh." She headed for the door.

Wearily, Deidre followed her. "Manuela, I think that, under the circumstances, these cookies will do just fine. They may not be perfect, but they're close enough. I'm happy with them."

"I suppose that's it." Manuela looked at her somberly. "I don't settle, Deidre. Never have and never will. And I didn't think you would, either." She turned on her heel and disappeared out the door.

THE SEATTLE SCOOP

COOKIE QUEEN AND SEATTLE DREAM ARE HOT ITEM!
A *Seattle Scoop* Exclusive! By Rosemary Goodwin

For Deidre McIntosh, Seattle's lifestyle-TV maven turned cookie queen, her "pie-in-the-sky" dreams have literally become a reality!

When Channel Five unexpectedly ended its run of *Live Simple with Deidre McIntosh* last year, the TV star was devastated. But it was the appearance of Seattle's newest day-time talk show, *At Home with Marla Banks*, that pushed this once-merry first lady of craft and kitchen over the edge.

The sensational host of *At Home* declared Deidre "a Suzy Homemaker" who had "worn out her welcome in Seattle." Marla Banks was only too happy to see Deidre head for the hills as her own show rapidly climbed in ratings.

Shunned by the media and evicted from her apartment with hardly a penny to her name, Deidre left Seattle for some R&R at an undisclosed location in the country. It was rumored that she changed her hair color in an effort to remain incognito.

But it was Deidre who had the last laugh. Months later she was dating Kevin Johnson, Marla's only brother and Seattle's most eligible bachelor. This young millionaire has been seen with some of the most gorgeous society gals around, but it's Deidre who seems to have gotten a hold on his heart!

And if that wasn't enough, Deidre returned to Seattle armed with a new show. *Seattle Revealed*, the original documentary featuring local businesses, was bought by the Biography Channel. While industry insiders say Deidre should have held out for more, this lucky gal was on a roll. Days later, Jamison Cookies and Confections announced a partnership with Deidre McIntosh. Sweet Deidre, a line of gourmet cookies, will be in select stores later this year.

Deidre certainly seems to have the perfect life. When asked about the recent changes in her life, including her whirlwind romance with Kevin Johnson, Deidre admitted, "It's true we moved very quickly." Are wedding bells in this couple's future? Log on to our blog and tell us what you think!

CHAPTER THREE

You can't be truly rude until you understand good manners.
—Rita Mae Brown

"Today I have no words to describe my special guest."
The camera panned on Marla Banks, who offered a wry smile while holding her signature martini in one hand and her miniature chow chow, Fred Astaire, in the other. Marla was dressed in a fitted, one-shoulder Swarovski crystal mesh gown by Giorgio Armani Privé. A stunning diamond cuff and matching dangle earrings completed Marla's ensemble. Fred Astaire wore a glittering dog collar with a brilliant cut diamond in the center.

Off camera, Deidre was filled with a mix of trepidation and dread. Why had she agreed to do this? Sure, she owed a favor to Juliette. Sure, it was a great opportunity to get some early publicity for Sweet Deidre and hopefully appease a disgruntled Manuela. And then there was Kevin, who was optimistic that Deidre and Marla could forge a relationship of some kind.

In the end Deidre had agreed because there were more reasons to do it than not to. Now, however, she was feeling the heavy weight of regret as the makeup artist applied a final dusting of powder to Deidre's face.

Marla would be showcasing three Seattle socialite brides-to-be: a twentysomething former debutante (first marriage), a thirtysomething heiress (second marriage), and a fortysomething society hostess known for her exclusive, high-class soirees in her fifteen-bedroom mansion (fourth marriage, plus one highly publicized annulment). The women were accompanied by their own entourage of assistants, makeup artists, and hair stylists. It was a bit overwhelming, but Deidre didn't have time to get nervous—she was already being waved on to the set.

"She needs little introduction," Marla was saying, "and so without further ado, here is Deidre McIntosh."

The studio audience whooped and stood up as Deidre steeled herself and walked out onto the set, waving.

"Hello, Marla," Deidre said, her smile bright and her eyes fixed on the audience. She was miked, but her trained voice carried clearly throughout the studio.

Marla let her eyes flicker down Deidre's body, clearly unimpressed by Deidre's choice to wear an apron over her clothes. "What a lovely . . . smock," she said, somewhat derisively.

Deidre smoothed the Sweet Deidre monogram cheerfully. "Thank you. It's one of our commemorative aprons in honor of the launch of my gourmet baked goods line, Sweet Deidre, which will be in select stores and bakeries across the country early this fall."

Marla smirked, her voice flat. "How delightful." She took a sip of her martini.

Deidre smiled. "I'm glad you think so, Marla, because I brought one for you, too. In fact, I have a Sweet Deidre apron for every member of the studio audience."

The audience began clapping wildly, and Deidre saw Marla flush in annoyance before tipping her nose and turning back to the camera.

"We'll be right back after the commercial break, and first-time bride Georgette Dean Newburg, of the Seattle Newburgs, will be joining us to talk about her upcoming wedding to millionaire entrepreneur Alex Stuart."

The red light on the camera turned off, and Marla tossed Fred Astaire onto his plush pillow before downing her martini and gesturing for a refill. She ignored Deidre as her makeup was touched up and the set refreshed.

Well, that was to be expected. Deidre certainly wasn't under the illusion that they'd be doing much bonding, on or off camera. Besides, she had more than enough to keep her busy during the short commercial break. She took a step back as a portable oven and kitchen island were rolled onto the set, then quickly began checking her ingredients to make sure everything was in order.

"What the hell is this?" Marla narrowed her eyes and pushed away her assistant, Tommy, who was handing her a fresh martini. The drink sloshed on the ground and Tommy, looking flustered, quickly began to mop it up.

Puzzled, Deidre stared at Marla. "It's the temporary kitchen set for Georgette's charm cake," she said.

"*What?*"

The cameraman held up a hand. "Thirty seconds!"

Marla spun around. "Juliette!" she screamed.

As if out of nowhere, Juliette appeared. "Marla, there was

a last-minute change in the programming. Georgette was so excited to be on the set with Deidre that she asked for ideas about her bridesmaids' luncheon. Deidre came up with the charm cake idea, so we're going with it. Have fun, you two—you'll do great. Ten seconds!" She hurried off the set.

Deidre felt a pang of sympathy for Marla. This was exactly the sort of thing that Deidre didn't miss about the business: executive decisions that weren't conveyed until it was too late to do anything about it. It was tacky and unprofessional, but that was show business, like it or not, and Marla seemed to know this, too.

"She is *so* fired," Marla muttered with a scowl as a fresh martini was quickly placed in her hands.

The red light went on, and both Deidre and Marla pasted smiles on their faces and turned to the camera.

"Welcome back to *At Home with Marla Banks* and our special Seattle Socialite Weddings episode. One of my adorable brides, Georgette Dean Newburg, is here in preparation for her first wedding. Georgette?" Marla beckoned.

A young, bouncy blonde sailed onto the set wearing a dress with a square neckline, a pleated bodice, and a bubble skirt. Simple, exquisite, clearly expensive.

"Hi, Marla! Hi, Deidre!" Georgette was trying to keep her cool but was bubbling over with excitement. Her left hand went up to her face to brush away a loose strand of hair, revealing a huge emerald-cut diamond engagement ring.

Marla's eyes honed in at the size of Georgette's diamond before turning to Deidre. "And what are we doing for young Georgette today?"

"Well, Georgette told us that she wanted ideas for her bridesmaids' luncheon, so we came up with a variation of the traditional charm cake." Deidre reached below the counter and pulled out a prepared double-layer cake with ivory meringue buttercream icing and trimmed with daisy filigree appliqués. Yellow and white satin ribbons flowed from between the layers of the cake. There were *ooh*s and *aah*s from the audience as the camera zoomed in.

Deidre smoothed a ribbon as she explained. "The idea behind the charm cake is that each bridal attendant chooses a ribbon and gives it a pull. Each charm is different and, as the legend goes, reveals a person's future."

"Each charm comes with its own explanation," Georgette added. "And a bracelet, so they can wear their charm until they get what they want."

"Marla?" Deidre gestured toward the cake, encouraging Marla to choose a ribbon so they could demonstrate how the charm cake worked.

Marla gave Deidre a glare as she yanked a ribbon. Three figures holding hands—a father, a mother, and a child—dangled from the end of the ribbon with bits of frosting clinging here and there.

"Ooh!" Georgette squealed, excited. "That looks like a family. Maybe you'll get married again and have a baby!"

Marla gave Georgette a look that Deidre prayed wasn't caught on camera. Hurriedly, Deidre turned to face the audience.

"Charm cakes are simple enough for you to make at home." Deidre brought out a chocolate Bundt cake with soft satin pastel ribbons emerging from the center. The cake was capped with edible fresh flowers. "Today I'll show you how to make a delicious Bundt charm cake. The recipe can be found on www.athomewithmarla.com."

"Do I get an apron, too?" Georgette asked eagerly.

Deidre nodded and motioned for someone to bring a Sweet Deidre apron for Georgette, who, after struggling to put it on ("Where do my arms go?"), looked ecstatic.

"Marla, you should wear yours, too!" Georgette said encouragingly.

Marla deftly responded by taking a long draw on her drink.

Deidre began mixing the ingredients, explaining each step with Georgette as her keen assistant. Whenever there was a short lull, Marla asked Georgette questions about her upcoming wedding. Deidre was a bit surprised to find that everything was going so smoothly. She and Marla actually seemed to have a natural rhythm that wasn't always easy to achieve on air.

Deidre had just finished mixing the batter when she heard Marla suck in her breath. Deidre nodded enthusiastically as Georgette continued to wax on about her wedding dress as she discreetly followed Marla's gaze. What she saw surprised her, too.

Kevin and his parents, Edward and Beverly Johnson, were off camera, waving and beaming proudly.

Georgette glanced over as well and let out an exclamation. That was the problem with live television—you couldn't control what was going to happen on the show. Georgette turned excitedly to Deidre.

"Deidre, I *have* to ask. Are you and Kevin planning your own special event in the future? I read something about it the other day in *The Seattle Scoop!*"

Damn that Rosemary Goodwin. Marla's eyes went wide before narrowing into dangerous slits. Deidre kept her composure as she handed the bowl of batter and a spatula to Georgette and motioned for her to fill the Bundt pan. "Well . . ." she started.

"Don't be ridiculous!" Marla said sharply. She put down her drink and took a step toward the two women, wobbling as she lost her balance. Before Deidre could grab her, Marla slipped and fell to the ground, taking Georgette and the bowl of batter with her.

Alarmed, Deidre offered a quick smile to the camera, knowing that there would be a hasty cut to commercial. Someone held up a cue card to let Deidre know what was coming up next. "Well, we're going to clean up a bit over here and when we come back, we'll decorate our Bundt cake and take a tour of Seattle's most exclusive wedding venues."

The red light went off, and Deidre quickly bent down to help Georgette get up. The set was soon flooded with people, including a concerned Kevin and his parents.

"Whew," Georgette said good-naturedly, looking down at herself. "It's a good thing I wore this apron! I don't think I got anything on my dress!"

The same, however, couldn't be said for Marla. She was covered in batter. Kevin was quick to help his sister stand up, and beneath the chocolate, Marla was livid.

"Looks like there was some water on the ground," someone observed.

A stagehand bent down and bravely took a taste. "Not water," he said. "Vodka."

Upon hearing this, Marla's assistant, Tommy, paled. "Oh," he stuttered. "I must not have mopped all of it up when Marla . . . I mean, when I . . . spilled the drink earlier."

A furious Marla stormed to her dressing room, trailed by an apologetic Tommy and a concerned Beverly Johnson. Edward

Johnson seemed unperturbed and was chatting with one of the studio's engineers. Juliette glanced at Deidre. "You still good to go?"

Deidre nodded. There was a finished Bundt cake waiting in the oven, and she could forgo the ganache frosting. All that was left was to place the charms inside the center of the Bundt cake and cover it with flowers, and they could move on with the programming.

Kevin was wiping his hands on a dish towel when he came up behind Deidre and gave her a quick kiss on the cheek. "I was having lunch with my parents and my mom wanted to stop by. Never a dull moment, eh?"

She smiled, happy to see him. "Not on my watch."

Kevin's eyes skimmed the set, which had been dolled up to look like a wedding reception. "So I guess an on-air proposal would be anticlimactic now?"

Deidre's heart skipped a beat even though she knew he was joking. "If you want your sister to serve my head on a platter to the audience, be my guest. She might even be willing to wear a Sweet Deidre apron while she does it." Deidre could feel a slight shine on her forehead. "Powder, please," she called out.

"Ten seconds to air!"

Kevin gave her another kiss before leaving the set. The studio audience was now being distracted (or, as Deidre liked to say, "entertained") by one of the show's production assistants. Some members of the studio audience had proudly donned their complimentary Sweet Deidre aprons. Deidre made a mental note to offer the remaining charm pulls to a few lucky people after the show. Sometimes the post-show could be as much fun as the show itself.

Although, grinning secretly to herself, Deidre wasn't sure it could get any better than this.

The next day Deidre took a break from work to meet William and Alain at the Hanging Ivy, one of the last venues they were considering for their commitment ceremony. It was all-inclusive, which sounded ideal in theory but proved to be just plain awful in reality.

"I'm sorry, guys, but . . ." Deidre looked at the expectant faces of William and his partner, Alain, before reaching for a napkin and spitting out the remains of an undercooked, soggy German chocolate cake. She took a long drink of water before delivering the bad news. "It's practically batter, for starters, and the coconut-pecan frosting is way too sweet."

"I know." William looked miserable, the cake on his plate untouched. "But they said it was their bestseller. They'll give us a discount if we order this cake *and* choose the chicken instead of the fish as the entrée."

"What? No." Deidre beckoned them close and kept her voice low. "Do you guys have to use this place? I mean, there are so many other nice venues in the city . . ."

William shook his head. "Like I told you, it's too late. Everything is booked up."

"What about changing the date? You shouldn't have to settle for something you don't want." She flicked an unidentifiable crumb off the table and shuddered.

"I know, but we really want to have the ceremony over Labor Day weekend, before the weather starts to turn."

"And we really want to have it outdoors," Alain added.

"Yes, but . . ." Deidre gestured to the space around them, to the rickety tables and chairs with their tired centerpieces, to the bushes of dead rhododendrons in the entrance. "Surely you can do better than this!"

The two men stared at her, then shook their heads.

"You know I want to open my own practice next year," William said. "And Alain is still paying off his student loans. Money is tight."

Deidre stared at the cost sheet in front of her. "But this is ridiculous. You only have twenty people on your guest list. This shouldn't have to cost an arm and a leg."

Her phone chimed, reminding her that she had a meeting in one hour. Her afternoon was packed, and on top of that she needed to find a dress for the birthday celebration honoring Kevin's father. It was only a couple of days away and she still had nothing to wear. "I'm sorry, guys, but I have to run."

"Deidre, what should we do? If we want to hold the date, we have to give them a deposit today." William looked at her, pleading.

"*Merde*, it would be easier just to have it in our backyard," Alain mumbled, frustrated. "We can fit over a hundred people back there."

"The whole point of having it somewhere else is so that we don't have to worry about all the setup and cleanup," William argued. "It's supposed to be easier for us if we don't have to worry about all of the details."

"I hate to break it to you, but regardless of where you have it, you're going to be worried about the details. Obsessing, in your case." Deidre took a moment to picture William and Alain's home in Belmont, with its spacious backyard. The trees would provide the perfect canopy, and there was plenty of room for both the ceremony and reception.

"You know, I think Alain is on to something. Your backyard is gorgeous. Having it at home won't be that much more work, and then you can have it exactly the way you want it. After all, it *should* be your perfect day. You'll have your closest friends and family with you, and it won't be a big deal to rent tables or have it catered. It certainly won't cost more than *this* place." Deidre cast another disdainful look around her.

The manager called over to them, her voice forced gaiety. "And how are we doing? I don't mean to rush you, but we have another couple coming in soon."

Deidre gave the woman a polite smile and then whispered, "Plus, I don't think I can bear to have this woman overseeing your ceremony. I just don't think she gets it, and you're going to end up with those little plastic containers of bubbles wrapped up in tulle."

"Actually, she mentioned fortune cookie favors," Alain said. William let out a groan.

"Oh, God, it's just getting worse." Deidre shook her head. "I can't let you go through with this. We're moving the ceremony to your house, and I'll do what I can to help." Her voice was firm.

"Really?" For the first time since they arrived, Alain and William looked hopeful.

"Yes, in fact . . ." She looked at the two men fondly, William especially. They'd been through so much together, and he was one of her oldest and dearest friends. "I don't know why I didn't think about this sooner, but I'd love it if you would let me coordinate the whole thing. It'll be my gift to you."

"Are you serious?" William grabbed her hand and gave it a squeeze.

"Absolutely. Twenty guests? I've had dinner parties for more people than that. This will be a walk in the park. Besides, I've had a million ideas racing through my mind since being on Marla's show. I'd love to be able to put some of them to use. What do you say?"

She laughed as both men enveloped her in a hug.

"I'll take that as a yes."

It was just past eight o'clock at night when Deidre finally walked through the doors at Nordstrom on the corner of Fifth and Pine. She knew she had less than an hour before the store closed, so she quickly took the escalator to the second floor.

A display of evening gowns caught her eye, and Deidre made a beeline for them, her eye on a one-shoulder black gown. She skimmed through the row of dresses until she found her size, then hurried to the dressing room to try it on.

When she stepped out to gaze at herself in the three-way mirror, the saleswoman gave an exaggerated gasp. It was a full-length gown with taffeta rosettes wrapping around her left shoulder. Deidre knew the ruched empire bodice looked good on her, giving her a little room to breathe while draping gracefully to the ground. Better yet, the price was reasonable and within Deidre's budget. She even had a pair of heels at home that would be a perfect match.

"Going somewhere special?" the saleswoman asked as she started to ring up Deidre's purchase.

"My boyfriend's father is celebrating his eightieth birthday this weekend," Deidre said, still marveling over her good luck at having found the perfect dress. And in fifteen minutes, no less.

"Well, you look like a million bucks. You'll be the belle of the ball, I'm sure." The woman beamed at her as she accepted Deidre's credit card. "Where's the party?"

"At McCaw Hall."

The woman hesitated as she was about to swipe the card. "You're not talking about Edward Johnson's eightieth, are you?"

Surprised, Deidre nodded. "Yes. Why?"

"Well, it's just that all the ladies that have been buying gowns for the event have bought them over there." The saleswoman nodded across the floor. "In our Collectors and Couture department. All the high-end designer evening wear is there. Maybe you want to take a look before we run this through?"

Deidre knew that any dress in that department would start at $2,500. While she did own a handful of high-end designer clothes and shoes, they'd all been bought on sale or, as the reporter from *The Seattle Scoop* had learned, from eBay. Buying a gown from the Collectors and Couture department would require paying retail that would rival a mortgage payment.

"No, that's okay," she told the saleswoman. "This dress will be fine."

"Are you *sure*?" The woman gave the gown a critical once-over, frowning now, and suddenly Deidre didn't feel so confident. "I think maybe you should just take a look. It can't hurt, can it? You say you're the girlfriend of his son?"

Deidre nodded, knowing where this was going.

The woman cancelled the transaction and handed Deidre her credit card. "I'll just hold this dress here, but I think you'll find something much more appropriate over there. They just got in a new collection from Oscar de la Renta. Come, we don't have much time."

Deidre clutched her credit card in the palm of her hand, feeling the bumps of the embossed numbers as they crossed the floor. Thank goodness there'd be a nice chunk of money when Sweet Deidre launched. She was going to need it.

CHAPTER FOUR

*It certainly is easier to be a good host when
there are ample funds available.*
—Letitia Baldrige, *Taste*

The luminous five-story serpentine glass grand lobby of the Marion Oliver McCaw Hall was a fitting venue for Edward Johnson's eightieth birthday gala. The expansive space had been artfully ornamented with large black-and-white photographs of Edward printed on canvas, displaying his youth, his travels, his friendships with foreign dignitaries and heads of state, his family. It was an impressive tribute to an accomplished businessman.

As Deidre walked through the doors, her arm looped through Kevin's, she could hear similar murmurs of admiration from the other guests as well.

"Apparently they spared no expense," someone said behind them, awestruck.

"That's Edward for you," someone else chuckled.

"It's not particularly original," a woman sniffed. "I expected more."

More? Deidre couldn't believe it. She wanted to turn around and tell the woman that, despite Deidre's genuine affection for the Johnson family, if there was any "more," they could probably fund a small country. Kevin, sensing a potential confrontation brewing, quickly guided Deidre through the crowd.

"You look beautiful," he told her. His hand was warm on the small of her back.

Deidre softened, and she smiled. "Thank you." She had finally decided on a black Chanel linen and silk cocktail dress that was the least expensive in the collection but still cost Deidre an arm and a leg. Worse, she'd had to buy a pair of shoes to match, which cost almost as much as the first gown she had liked.

Kevin kept Deidre close by his side as they made their way around the lobby. She marveled at how easily and effortlessly he mingled with everyone, how he remembered names and small personal details. He introduced her to everyone, raising a few eyebrows here and there as people considered her. She wasn't a part of the elite social circle Kevin and his family tended to travel in, and everyone seemed to know this.

They spotted Kevin's mother and Marla standing beneath an immense hanging glass mural. Edward was off to the side, handsomely dressed in a tux, a drink in hand as he chatted animatedly with someone who looked suspiciously famous. As they got closer, Deidre could see that Beverly's forehead was puckered in a frown.

"Mother, you look stunning as usual," Kevin said by way of greeting. He gave her a kiss.

"That is a lovely dress," Deidre agreed admiringly.

"Thank you. It's Celine," Beverly said offhandedly, clearly distracted.

"Hello, Marla." Deidre forced a smile as Kevin greeted his sister and gave her a kiss.

Marla grudgingly offered a cheek to her brother while her eyes took in Deidre's dress.

"Ready to wear." She smirked. Kevin shot his sister a warning look.

Beverly was smiling and nodding as people walked by. "Marla," she said under her breath, "I really think you should check with André and see if he's come up with a solution by now."

Marla was acknowledging people as well, the smile on her face fixed as photographers came by and took their pictures. She replied through clenched teeth, "Mother, the whole reason we're paying André to manage this event is so that he can take care of problems like this. Kenneth, how are you?" Marla crooned, giving a man a kiss on the cheek as he walked by.

Kevin frowned. "What's going on?"

"The cake. It's completely ruined." Beverly shook her head, blinking rapidly as if to hold back tears. "I can't believe this is happening. Your father will be so disappointed."

"I really don't think he gives a damn about the cake," Marla said, motioning for a waiter to refresh her flute of champagne.

"That's not the point!" Beverly snapped, looking annoyed. "I spent an inordinate amount of time looking for the perfect cake. I paid perfectly good money to have *that* cake delivered to *this* venue for your father's birthday. *I want that cake!*"

"Well, that's obviously *not* going to happen, since most of it is on the floor of the kitchen!" Marla snapped back. Another couple passed by and both Beverly and Marla pasted smiles on their faces again.

"Ginny, Leslie, it was so good of you to come," Beverly enthused. As soon as the couple had passed, mother and daughter were at it again.

"Okay, stop," Kevin said, holding up a hand. "Deidre and I will go back and see what's going on."

Deidre touched his Kevin's arm. "No, it's your dad's party. You need to stay here with your family. I'll run back and see what's going on."

Beverly looked relieved. "Oh, Deidre, would you?"

"Are you sure?" Kevin asked. "I can run back there with you. It'll only take a second."

"No, don't worry. I'll be fine." It would actually be a relief to step away for a moment. Deidre felt like she had been holding her breath from the moment they'd walked in. "I'll be right back."

It took Deidre almost ten minutes to make her way through the crowd to the kitchen facilities. When she entered the kitchen, everyone looked up suspiciously.

"Ma'am, the event is that way," a sous chef said, pointing to the door.

"I know," Deidre called out over the clamor of the kitchen. "I'm actually here to see if there is anything I can do to help with the cake."

At the mention of the cake, there was a subdued hush. Finally a waiter pointed in the direction from which Deidre could hear frantic murmurings.

"Thank you," she said. She was about to walk away when a young woman, most likely a kitchen assistant, offered Deidre an apron. "Watch your step," the young woman whispered, her voice foreboding.

Deidre tied on the apron as she walked. Soon she saw

several people huddled around the remnants of what was once an ambitious, five-foot-high, seven-tiered birthday cake.

"Oh dear," Deidre said, slowing down. It didn't look good.

A slender man in a black tuxedo frowned. "Who are you?" His nose seemed to twitch and he had an accent Deidre couldn't quite place.

"Deidre McIntosh, a friend of the Johnsons. And you are?"

"André Houghton. The event coordinator." His chin quivered as he gave Deidre an insolent look.

Getting rid of him would be Deidre's first order of business. "Ah," she said. "And where is the cake designer?"

"Right here." A petite woman stepped forward. Deidre recognized her immediately.

"Sugar!" she exclaimed. Sugar Templeton was a well-respected pastry chef turned premium cake designer and sugar artist. She was a highly coveted professional who did excellent work.

Deidre turned to André. "I'm sure you have a laundry list of things to do," she said. "Your banquet event order must be an inch thick."

"Three inches," he said importantly. "And God knows what else may be going wrong. But instead I'm stuck here, trying to salvage this mess. I can assure you that the Johnson family is *not* happy with this situation. Not happy at all." He glared at the group.

Deidre finally placed the accent. It was English, and it was fake. She'd bet her dress that at one time André was Andrew. He probably went by Andy. She would have loved to call him on it, but she needed to resolve the cake matter first.

She surveyed the mess in front of her. "Well, I definitely think it's salvageable and that there's probably not much you can do, André. Why don't you go outside and let the Johnsons know that everything's under control?"

André sputtered. "Under control? Do you have *eyes*? Because I know we're not looking at the same thing here! What are you going to do, scrape the cake off the floor and serve it to them?"

Not to them, Deidre thought hotly, *but maybe to* you.

Instead, she decided to pull her trump card. She fastened a sweet but firm smile on her face. "André, my *boyfriend*, Kevin Johnson, and his family just want to make sure everything is going smoothly for their father's eightieth birthday celebration, and I'm telling you that the cake is under control. So I'd appreciate it if you could convey that message to them and then turn your attention to your many other responsibilities. I'll be sure to let them know that you're doing an excellent job."

André gave a sniff before turning on his heel and walking away. Deidre could hear him yelling at the kitchen staff over some trivial detail.

"Deidre, I am *so* relieved to see you." Sugar rubbed her temples. A pair of bejeweled spectacles was perched on the top of her head. "I'm on the verge of a nervous breakdown. Seriously."

"Don't be. What happened?"

"Catastrophic structural failure, what else? We were late coming in and feeling rushed. The client was panicking. One of the lower dowel rods slipped while we were carrying the cake in, and in trying to save that tier, one of my assistants tripped and the whole thing toppled backward. We took out half of the base tier in the process and the cake collapsed." Sugar leaned wearily against the wall. "My team salvaged what they could but reconstruction is impossible. I always carry plenty of extra frosting and piping, and of course I have my repair kit, but this is beyond even me. I can't see straight anymore."

"When did you sleep last?"

"Three nights ago." Sugar looked exhausted. "I had a huge wedding cake gig yesterday and I foolishly thought I could pull both off. The wedding went off without a hitch, thank God, but tonight . . ."

"Is not over," Deidre finished for her. "Accidents happen, Sugar, even to the best of chefs. You and I know that better than anyone."

"Well, this cake is supposed to roll out in two hours. They want it on display for half an hour before we cut and serve. I've called everyone but it's too late. There's just not enough time to have enough cake baked and delivered for four hundred and fifty people. I've sent two assistants off to get several sheet cakes, but I don't think the client is going to be pleased." Sugar closed her eyes. "I think I'm just getting too old for this business."

"Well, now is not the time to be planning your retirement," Deidre said kindly but briskly. "Let me see what you managed to save, and let's get someone to clean up this mess on the floor. It looks like you salvaged what you could. I don't see anything else you can use."

Sugar nodded for someone to follow Deidre's instructions as she led Deidre to the stainless steel table that held several large vats of what was left of the cake.

It was a mess, no doubt, but even Deidre could see that it had once been a work of art. "Tell me about the cake," she said, hoping to shift Sugar's energy while she came up with a plan.

Sugar sighed. "It's an orange Grand Marnier chiffon cake filled with Grand Marnier buttercream. Gilded in edible gold leaf. And we made two thousand white icing roses, if you can believe that."

"The roses seemed to have held up well." Deidre took a small piece of the cake and tasted it.

"A lot of them did, thank goodness."

"Well, it's delicious. And you're right; you definitely don't have the time to get anything other than plain sheet cake to substitute." Deidre thoughtfully gazed into space, considering the flavors in her mouth. She turned to Sugar. "How much are you willing to spend?"

Sugar shrugged. "At this rate, you tell me." Sugar's business was a lucrative one, and Deidre figured that she would be willing to do whatever was necessary to turn the situation around.

"Call your assistants and have them pick up enough Grand Marnier for one shot glass per guest, give or take. We'll serve it on the side of each individual slice. And have them pick up another five full-size sheet cakes, if they can. On second thought, make that eight. We're going to rebuild the cake. And I think I can get my hands on enough chocolate truffles from JCC to round out the plate." Deidre pulled out her cell phone to call Amber.

After a brief conversation, Deidre gave Sugar the thumbs-up and snapped her cell phone shut. "Even better. Six hundred pieces of dark chocolate ganache covered in dark chocolate with edible gold leaf. It'll be here within the hour."

Sugar nodded, revived. She rapidly gave orders and got on the phone to her assistants. She sent someone to look for the banquet manager to arrange for the shot glasses. As everyone scurried off, Sugar looked at Deidre.

"I've had problems before, but I have to tell you—no pun intended—that this one takes the cake."

Deidre laughed. "Really? I envy you. I could regale you all night with the horrendous mishaps I've had. But you just needed some fresh horses, Sugar. Don't be too hard on yourself."

Sugar smiled and touched Deidre's arm. "Deidre, thank you."

"Don't thank me yet. We still have a lot of work to do."

"Deidre, how can I ever express my gratitude?" Beverly Johnson caught Deidre in a grateful hug. "I thought for sure it was over!"

Deidre was tired but exhilarated. "Well, I've learned that it's never really over until it's over. Besides, I was just an extra pair of hands. Sugar was the one who pulled it off in the end."

It was true. Once all the pieces started to fall into place, Sugar seemed to snap back to her old self. With Deidre's help, they were able to reconstruct the cake and rebuild the ruined tiers, then frost and reapply the roses just in time. Sugar was a master with the icing and piping bag, working faster than two of her assistants put together. She even incorporated the extra JCC chocolates with some last-minute sugar work. The result was not what Beverly Johnson had originally envisioned and paid for—it was better.

Beverly was still gushing. "Really, I wouldn't have believed it was possible."

"Good cake," Edward agreed, picking his teeth with a toothpick. "Is there any lobster left?"

Beverly threw her husband an exasperated look before turning back to Deidre and beaming. "You're a godsend, Deidre. My son is one lucky man."

Kevin whispered in Deidre's ear, "Well, *I* know that."

Deidre smiled as she whispered back, "And don't you forget it." She gave him a quick kiss and tried not to be flustered as Marla looked on, suddenly interested.

"Deidre, I just realized that you must be *starving*," she crooned. "You missed dinner!"

"No, I'm all right," Deidre said. "I had something to eat in the kitchen." The truth was Deidre felt more comfortable back in the kitchen with Sugar and the waitstaff than she did out front with Edward's guests. She had intentionally delayed coming out until Kevin had texted her several times and left repeated phone messages on her cell phone, wondering where she was.

Marla pretended to fan herself. "Well, *that's* a relief! Still, you didn't have a chance to really meet anyone. I know everyone is dying to meet the woman who seems to have captured my brother's heart. Come on, I'll take you around."

"Oh, that's all right, Marla . . ."

Marla waved away Deidre's protests. "Come, come. It'll be fun. The press will have a field day. We mustn't let them down now, hmm?"

"Er . . ." Before Deidre could think up an excuse, Marla had looped her arm through Deidre's and was leading her into the crowd. Deidre looked back helplessly at Kevin, who had an amused smile on his face and gave her an encouraging nod.

"You saved my mother from having a major conniption fit," Marla said as they glided through the crowd. "I can't tell you what a feat *that* is." She patted Deidre on the arm. "Good job."

Was it her imagination or had Marla just paid her a compliment?

"Sometimes I can get a little short with my family," Marla

confessed. "Hell, with everyone. But watching you tonight made me realize that even in the direst of situations, there's no reason we can't handle things with a little compassion and grace." She gave Deidre a benevolent smile.

"Thank you, Marla." Deidre was genuinely touched. This was a watershed moment. "And I have to say, I know we've had our differences in the past, but I've come to admire . . ."

"Ah, Sabine!" Marla exclaimed, pulling Deidre forward before she could finish. "Darling, how *are* you?"

Before them stood a sleek, stunning woman in her midthirties. Her dark hair was pulled back into a tight chignon, and she looked as if she'd stepped out of the pages of a high-gloss fashion magazine. "Marla," she crooned, giving her an air kiss on each cheek. "I'm doing fabulous, thank you. What about you?"

Marla touched one of her diamond earrings modestly. "Oh, I can't complain, but I probably will anyway. You know how it is."

Sabine nodded knowingly, and then looked questioningly at Deidre.

"Oh, my manners!" Marla rolled her eyes. "May I present Deidre McIntosh? Deidre, this is Sabine Durant. She's an old family friend. We go *way* back. She flew in especially for Daddy's party."

Deidre offered her hand. "Sabine, it's nice to meet you."

"Likewise." Sabine leaned forward to give Deidre a peck on both cheeks. Deidre caught a whiff of expensive perfume. "So this is the famous Deidre McIntosh. I've heard so much about you. It's a pleasure to finally meet you."

Sabine had heard about her? Intrigued, Deidre asked, "How . . . ?"

Marla interrupted her with a light laugh. "Oh, Daddy's waving me over. I'll be right back." Marla excused herself and hurried back to her table.

"Always on the go, that Marla," Sabine observed dryly. She fumbled in her bag and brought out a gold cigarette case. "I was about to step out for a smoke. Join me?"

"I don't smoke," Deidre said. "But I'd be happy to join you. It's a bit stifling in here."

Sabine let out a laugh. "I know what you mean."

The two women made their way out onto the promenade. It was a beautiful night, clear and crisp, the sky full of stars.

"We don't get many nights like this in London," Sabine said with a sigh. She opened her case and chose a cigarette. As if on cue, two men showed up, lighters in hand.

Sabine thanked them with a sultry smile as she produced her own lighter and lit her cigarette. Crestfallen, the men retreated. Sabine blew out a thin stream of smoke and shook her head, a smile on her lips.

Deidre tried not to stare at Sabine, who looked even more luminous in the moonlight. "So what do you do, Sabine? Are you a model?"

"A model?" Sabine exclaimed with a laugh. "I *do* like you, Deidre McIntosh! No, I . . ."

"There they are!" Marla sailed onto the promenade with Kevin in tow. "We've been looking *everywhere* for you two!"

As they approached, Deidre noticed a look of surprise on Kevin's face when he registered the woman standing next to her.

"Kevin!" Sabine ground out her cigarette and stepped forward. "I was wondering when you were going to come by and say hello. It's been ages, hasn't it? You naughty boy!"

Naughty boy? Deidre turned to look at her boyfriend, who had turned slightly scarlet.

"Tabby," he said finally, and gave her a quick kiss on the cheek.

"The *cheek*?" Sabine laughed. "*Really*, Kevin."

Deidre was suddenly filled with trepidation. Tabby . . . Why did that name ring a bell?

"I see you two have met," Kevin said. He came to Deidre's side, slipping an arm around her waist. He cleared his throat.

Sabine cocked an eyebrow. "Now I've made you uncomfortable, I see. I'm sorry."

Deidre noticed that Sabine didn't look that sorry as she kept her gaze steady on Kevin.

"What? I'm not uncomfortable, Tabby." Kevin tried to laugh it off and glanced at Deidre with a wobbly smile on his face.

Tabby. Suddenly Deidre remembered. Kevin had once been engaged to a woman named Tabby. It had been years ago, and it hadn't worked out. Deidre hadn't cared to know much beyond that, and it hadn't bothered her.

Until now.

Marla pretended to scoff. "Oh, come, come! We're all old friends here." She turned to Deidre as if to confide in her. "Sabine—well, my brother affectionately calls her by her nickname, Tabby—is the daughter of publishing magnate Malcolm Dominic Durant, founder of the Durant Media Group. Sabine here is president of Durant Magazines International."

"Wow," Deidre said. Durant Magazines International published some of the most prominent home and lifestyle magazines, including one of Deidre's favorites, *Adoré*. While Sabine had the air of someone who was accomplished, this was more than Deidre had expected. "Wow," she said again, somewhat daunted.

Sabine gave a nonchalant shrug. "It's not as glamorous as it sounds." Then she laughed gaily. "Okay, well maybe it is, but it's just business." She opened her cigarette case again, this time offering a cigarette to Marla, who naturally accepted.

"This is just like old times," Marla said happily as she took a deep draw on her cigarette. She leaned toward Deidre. "We're as close as two families can be, but unfortunately we just don't see as much of Sabine as we'd like. She insists on living part-time in Europe and part-time in New York. She hardly ever makes it to the Pacific Northwest. But we catch up with her now and then when we fly to New York, don't we, Kevin?"

Kevin had been staring sheepishly at Sabine. "What?" he said.

"I said, we try to catch up with Sabine and her family when we can." Marla shook her head and gave Deidre a theatrical sigh.

Kevin didn't respond until Deidre gave him a nudge. "Oh, right."

There was a beep from inside Sabine's sequined clutch. Sabine checked her watch and tossed her cigarette. "I have to go. My jet's waiting for me. We have a photo shoot in Belize and, well, it's a long, boring story, but I have to be there. I'm going to say good-bye to your parents. Deidre, it was lovely to meet you. Marla, a pleasure as always. And Kevin . . ." Sabine gave him a playful wink before heading inside.

Kevin's eyes followed Sabine thoughtfully as she glided back to the grand lobby.

"Lucky for you Sabine gave back the ring," Marla said to

her brother as she finished her cigarette. "Though I noticed my engagement present was never returned. If I remember correctly, it was a Christofle limited edition silver serving tray. Oh, I probably shouldn't be saying this in front of Deidre, should I? Forgive me, Deidre. That was *so* tactless."

Deidre wanted to strangle her.

Kevin shook himself from his reverie and pulled Deidre close to his side. "Marla, Deidre knows about my engagement to Tabby," he said simply. "She knows it ended over ten years ago. It's a thing of the past."

"Of course." Marla nodded accommodatingly. They began to walk back to the party. When Kevin opened the door to let the women walk in first, Marla gently touched Deidre's arm and whispered coyly, "Except you and I know that it's never really over until it's over. Is it?"

THE SEATTLE SCOOP

SHE'S NOT IN KANSAS ANYMORE!
A *Seattle Scoop* Exclusive! By Rosemary Goodwin

It wasn't a pair of ruby slippers, but a pair of brand-new Jimmy Choos.

Deidre McIntosh, who was seen at Edward Johnson's eightieth birthday gala at McCaw Hall this past weekend, is keeping up with the Johnsons. She wore Chanel, bought off the rack at Nordstrom. The saleswoman attending her confessed that Deidre had been initially reluctant to spend the money, opting instead for a mass-produced gown that would have certainly been her downfall had she chosen to wear it. Still, it didn't take much to get Deidre to cross over from

Special Occasions to Collectors and Couture, where she had her pick of the latest designer collections.

"She's a diva in disguise," said another Nordstrom employee, who preferred to remain anonymous. "She whipped out her credit card and spent almost $4,000 in less than twenty minutes, without even batting an eyelash!"

It must have been worth it, because apparently Kevin Johnson couldn't keep his eyes off of his date, even when his former flame and ex-fiancée, Sabine Durant, made an unexpected visit to the Emerald City. Does anyone remember how that one went down? Yikes! We can only hope that Deidre will have better luck! Log on to our blog and tell us what you think!

Chapter Five

Good manners are made up of petty sacrifices.
—Ralph Waldo Emerson

Mother, did you see this?" Marla Banks threw the newspaper onto the table at Rover's, where she and her mother always had lunch on Fridays. "I can't believe she's dragging our family name into this trashy tabloid. It's completely humiliating!"

"Though you have to admit, she does look lovely," Beverly commented, peering at the article with interest. "And if memory serves, haven't you made an occasional appearance in *The Seattle Scoop* as well?"

Marla snatched the paper back. "That's not the point." A waiter approached them with a bread basket but Marla waved him away impatiently. The last thing she needed was empty carbs. "Deidre clearly has no idea how to carry herself in good company."

Beverly unfolded the napkin and placed it in her lap. "Well, as much as I'm fond of Deidre, I'm afraid I have to agree."

Marla looked at her mother, surprised. Beverly had been partial to Deidre ever since she and Kevin had started dating, a fact that irritated Marla to no end.

"Really?" she asked cautiously, reaching for her wineglass.

"Yes. She seems a little . . . I don't know . . . nervous, I suppose. Which is why I think you should help her find a dress for the K Ball."

"What?" Marla sputtered. "Deidre is going to the K Ball?"

The K Ball was one of Seattle's most prestigious fundraising events. The K stood for Klondike, in honor of the Alaskan gold rush that ended the depression in Seattle back in the late 1800s. It was invitation only, at $25,000 a table, and the Johnsons always had a table.

Beverly gave her daughter a slightly exasperated look. "Well, of course, Marla. Kevin's going, and he's invited Deidre. I gave her the last seat at our table."

This was becoming a never-ending nightmare. "Mother, you can't give that seat to Deidre. I already offered it to . . . to . . ."

She was coming up empty. Her mother looked at her patiently, ready to call her bluff.

Then it came to her.

". . . to Wedge Franklin. I've already offered the seat to him." That should do it. Her parents were huge fans of Wedge Franklin, her mother especially. He was in his midfifties but still single, having never married. He'd had a crush on Marla for years, lavishing her with gifts and compliments, even though she'd made it clear that she was *not* in a courting sort of mood, especially not by a man of diminishing stature with a crooked toupee.

"Wedge? Really?" Beverly looked at her daughter with interest. "You haven't had a guest at our table in six years. And that's not counting the years you didn't even bother to show up yourself."

Marla coughed. "Yes, well . . ."

"And doesn't Wedge usually buy a couple of tables himself? He's on the board of the K Foundation, isn't he?" Their appetizers arrived, sautéed sea scallops with baby beets in a shellfish broth. Beverly daintily cut herself a small piece as she waited for her daughter's response.

Damn, Marla obviously hadn't thought this through. Brooding, she poked at a scallop. Wedge was known as Seattle's most lovable philanthropist (the most generous being Bill and Melinda Gates), a title Marla found completely off-putting. It was one thing to make the occasional donation or to earmark funds for a new library wing—which would of course bear the name of the gift giver—but Wedge seemed to constantly be involved with one charity or another, setting up trusts and foundations at the drop of a hat, even making substantial anonymous donations. What was the point of that?

"Regardless, Wedge is a gentleman," Beverly declared. "I'm sure he'll be happy to give up his seat for Deidre."

Marla scowled and studied a nail. What was the point? Her parents were always siding with Deidre, even though they barely knew her.

Beverly dabbed the corners of her mouth with a cloth napkin, careful not to muss her lip color. "Oh, come on now, Marla. If Kevin's happy, I'm happy. And Deidre makes him happy. I was the same with you and your husbands," she reminded her daughter. *"All three of them."*

That stung. The irony was that Marla didn't even care that much for marriage. She'd just been tired of her parents' jocular conversations, wondering if she'd ever meet her match and settle down. So Marla's response was to pursue the richest and most famous of men. As it turned out, finding someone to marry wasn't difficult at all. Staying married, however, was. It was without a doubt more trouble that it was worth, so keeping her own company now suited Marla just fine.

"That was different," Marla sniffed. "I married those men. Kevin and Deidre are just dating."

"Well, who knows? Maybe Kevin and Deidre will . . ."

Marla stiffened. "Don't say it!" she said sharply.

"Really, Marla." Beverly surveyed the restaurant, nodding and smiling decorously at a few familiar faces. "There's no need to get so worked up."

"Mother, do I need to remind you what happened the last time Kevin was serious with someone? And what happened to the Johnson family ring?"

Beverly continued to eat, unperturbed. "Marla, Sabine found the ring and returned it. No harm done."

Marla stared at her mother, aghast. "No harm done? She lost it in a bar in Brazil! A *topless* bar!"

Beverly looked remorseful at the memory but said firmly, "Marla, I know you're partial to that ring, but you know it passes to Kevin for him to give to his future spouse. It's the family tradition. We're just going to have to trust his judgment and, like I said, Sabine did return the ring."

"With the help of a $50,000 reward and half of the Brazilian civil police force." Disgruntled, Marla tossed her napkin on the table.

"I have to say I was surprised to see her at your father's party. You seemed to be quite chummy with her, in fact."

"It's all water under the bridge," Marla said, though it clearly wasn't. If she'd known that Kevin would go from Sabine to

Deidre, she might have made a greater effort to keep Kevin and Sabine together. The devil you knew was always better than the one you didn't, which was why Marla was willing to forgive—but not forget—Sabine's imprudence with the ring. "As it turns out, Sabine and I have more in common than I realized."

"I'm glad to hear that. The Durants are close family friends, and it was incredibly stressful for me to have you at odds with Sabine while she was engaged to Kevin." Beverly frowned as she sipped her water.

"Well, we get along quite well now," Marla said carefully, not wanting to give anything away. "We help each other out from time to time."

"Good," Beverly said approvingly. "Well, you may want to extend that same courtesy to Deidre, too. I don't think she's yet found a gown for the K Ball."

"What a surprise," Marla drawled. "And how does that concern me?"

"Because you happen to have a closet full of gowns, some of which you've never worn and probably never will wear. I'm sure that there's at least one in there that's unique and original and would suit Deidre just fine."

Marla waited for her plate to be cleared before responding. "Possibly, but it doesn't suit *me* just fine," she retorted. "Anything I loan her she'll just stretch out of shape. I'll have to throw it away by the end of the night!"

"Well, you've been known to do that anyway, so I can't see how this would be any different." Beverly glanced at the dishes being served at the next table. "That hamachi tartare does look delicious. I think I'm going to change my order from the foie gras. What about you, Marla? Hamachi tartare as well?"

Marla shook her head. She'd lost her appetite.

The idea of finding something for Deidre to wear from her closet—what was her mother thinking? What incentive could Marla possibly have to help Deidre out? What was in it for her?

Marla watched her mother call to a waiter, tugging impatiently on her fitted trompe l'oeil jacket. That was the problem with high fashion; it came at a price. The jacket was gorgeous but left little room for Beverly to move comfortably about.

A small smile played on Marla's lips as the answer revealed itself.

"But Kevin, I insist." Marla gave her brother a sweet smile as he regarded her with slight suspicion. She had stopped by his office to pay him a surprise visit. "My closet is her closet. True, she's a bit heavier than me, but I'm sure a tailor could add an extra panel if necessary."

Kevin's phone rang and he pressed a button, silencing the call. He reached for his mug of coffee before tilting back in his chair. He took a sip. "Marla, come on."

"What?" She feigned innocence.

"You never share *anything*. Do you honestly expect me to believe that you'd let someone go through your closet, much less Deidre?" He gave a chuckle.

She knew he wouldn't be easily convinced. Pretending to be offended, Marla stood up. "Kevin, I am just trying to do you a favor. You're my brother, after all, and let's be honest. You don't want her showing up in some outfit she picked up from just anywhere, do you?"

Kevin picked up a pen and began to flip it over his fingers.

Marla had no idea where he'd learned that skill—prep school, most likely—but she found it mesmerizing as well as annoying. She let her eyes skim the walls of his office until she came upon a tranquil framed photograph of Lake Wish. She pursed her lips in irritation.

It was one of Uncle Harry's silver gelatin black-and-white images. A bit of a recluse, their uncle Harry had once been a photographer for National Geographic. His photos had won awards and were displayed in some of the most prestigious galleries around the world. Even now, Uncle Harry refused to sell his work ("An annoying purist," she'd overheard her father once say in exasperation), and Marla was quite aware that she was the only Johnson family member that didn't own one of his prints.

The thought rankled Marla. If Uncle Harry was going to be giving his work away, it was tasteless to overlook a key member of the family, even if the proffered photograph ended up hanging in the garage. True, Marla preferred paintings over photographs, but that was primarily because the walls of her Fairfield Hills mansion required large, splashy canvases that cost an arm and a leg. It wasn't her fault that she had twenty-foot ceilings.

"Marla, give Deidre some credit," Kevin finally said. "She can hold her own, and hold it well. I'm not worried about her."

Marla sniffed. "That may very well be, but let me ask you this: Has she bought a dress for the K Ball?"

His long silence was answer enough.

Marla shook her head mournfully. "The night of the ball will be here before we know it. She'll be lucky if she can find something at the *mall* at this rate."

"Marla, you're exaggerating and we both know it."

"Am I? I don't think you'll disagree that our social circle is a new experience for her. She's going to have to step it up quite a bit, especially in the fashion arena. Under the circumstances, helping her will be helping me: I certainly don't need the potential embarrassment."

Kevin didn't like the insinuation and he frowned disapprovingly. "Marla . . ."

She quickly changed her tack. "All I'm saying is that for the K Ball, Deidre needs something special, and it just so happens that I have a closet full of special."

"I don't think that will be necessary, although . . ." Kevin's voice trailed off as he mulled something over. His office overlooked the waterfront and Marla could see the Seattle-Bainbridge ferry making its way across the choppy water. "I mean, she's got a lot on her plate right now with Sweet Deidre . . ."

"Of course she does," Marla said in a soothing voice. "She must be *very* busy."

"And she is attending all these events because I've asked her to . . ."

"She must really care for you." Marla kept a straight face and tried not to gag.

Kevin jotted something down on a piece of paper. "You know, you're right. It would be one less thing on her mind."

"Then it's settled. Tell her I'll have some gowns sent to her within the next week."

Kevin nodded and gave his sister an appreciative nod. "Thanks, Marla."

Marla gave a serene nod and picked up her purse, slinging it over her shoulder as she sauntered toward the door. "Oh, believe me. The pleasure's all mine."

* * *

True to her word, Marla had six stunning gowns delivered to Deidre's condo the following week. Deidre had been surprised to get the phone call from Marla, and practically went into shock when she heard Marla's offer.

"Six or seven gowns," Marla had said blithely. "Some I haven't worn, but they're already last season. You don't mind, do you? Ha, what am I saying? Of course you don't. And you can find shoes to match, I assume. I'd send some over, but your feet are so much bigger than mine."

While Deidre still didn't trust her, Marla *was* Kevin's sister, and the bottom line was that Deidre needed something for the K Ball. The Chanel cocktail dress had burned a hole in her pocket and she was loath to spend more money on another dress she'd wear only once. "Marla, thank you. That's very generous—"

"Escada, YSL, Versace, Christian Dior. Just choose whichever one will work and get rid of the rest, donate them to charity or whatever. I'll have them sent over." Before Deidre could say good-bye, Marla had hung up.

"Maybe she's trying to make it up to you," William suggested now as Deidre signed for the delivery. He was at her place, trying to make some decisions about the commitment ceremony. He popped a handful of soy nuts into his mouth. "You know, for being such a—"

"I'm sure she's doing this for Kevin," Deidre said, interrupting him. "Although, I wouldn't be surprised if there was something wrong with them."

William's eyes grew wide with mock horror. "Maybe they're booby-trapped."

"Maybe. Stand back." She tentatively unzipped the first gown bag that had an Escada Couture logo emblazoned on the front.

A gorgeous beaded gown with a fitted black velvet bodice and square neckline tumbled out. The full skirt had an ivory silk and black velvet diamond pattern and was elegant and quite heavy in Deidre's arms. It even smelled nice, and in a matter of moments Deidre's living room reminded her of the inside of a designer boutique. Hands down, this had to be the single most expensive item in her condo, barring the condo itself.

"Wow," Deidre finally managed, running her fingers over the intricate bead and sequin work. "I've never seen anything this incredible close up."

"This is like Fashion Week," William said, his voice full of awe. He held up a stunning bias cut silk evening gown in a shimmery blue. "Vera Wang, Deidre. *Vera Wang!* And look . . . Christian Dior! Yves Saint Laurent! And . . ."

"Cut it out," she told him. "You're making me nervous. And since when did you become so interested in women's fashion anyway?" William's magazines of choice were *Bon Appétit* and *Gourmet*, not *Vogue* or *Vanity Fair*. Okay, maybe *Vanity Fair*, but Deidre wasn't used to seeing him worked up over clothes he couldn't wear.

William was checking the tags on one of the dresses and didn't bother looking up. "Alain totally got me hooked on *Project Runway*. But come on, Deidre, these are *the* names in high fashion—you don't have to be gay to know that, for pete's sake!"

"Sorry, sorry."

"I thought for sure she'd send you junk, but this is the real deal." He looked at her eagerly. "So which one are you going to try on first?"

"None." She gently eased the gowns back into their bags and carefully zipped them up. "It's going to take me a while to go through them, and I want to focus on your commitment ceremony first. You're tying the knot in a little over three months. The big day will be here before you know it."

Deidre brought out a large box from underneath the dining room table. The box was overflowing with magazine clippings, wedding favor samples, menu choices, place settings, and other bits and pieces she'd been collecting for William and Alain.

"Now, I haven't had a chance to sort through everything, so some of this stuff may be completely out of left field," she warned him. "Still, inspiration comes from the oddest of places, so I wouldn't throw anything out just yet."

William picked up a wedding magazine and flipped through it glibly. "No . . . no . . . pass . . . no . . . no . . . Oh, my God, look at that centerpiece!" He started cracking up.

Deidre snatched the magazine from him. "Like I said, it's just to give you some ideas." She brought out some color swatches. "Now, I was thinking floral wreaths on some of the trees, maybe anchoring strings of paper lanterns from the fence posts . . ."

William wasn't paying attention and had picked up a catalog of wedding supplies. "Did you see these cheesy insulated bottle holders dressed up in little tuxedos and wedding dresses? Puhlease!"

"William!"

"I just think it's funny how women are always getting caught up in all this stuff. It must be in your genes or maybe its hormones, I mean . . ." He stopped as he opened a book of cake designs. "*Whoa*. Did you see this stacked cherry blossom cake? It's gorgeous!"

She considered it. "Yeah, I like that. It sort of has an Asian theme coupled with a classic European elegance."

He turned the page and gasped. "Look at the detail on this cake!" He turned the page again. "I *love* those borders!" William was practically salivating.

Deidre would give him a week to become just as "hormonal" as the giddy brides he'd criticized only seconds ago. "And don't forget, you get to register," she reminded him.

He looked at her, his eyes wide. "Register?"

"Of course. Just decide which store and they can tell you how to set up a gift registry—"

"I know how to set up a gift registry; it just completely slipped my mind that we'd get to!" William was now bouncing in his chair, unable to contain his excitement.

"Well, you get to. Now, we're probably going to want to tent everything in case of inclement weather, although—"

"Deidre, I'm sorry, but I've got to run. Can we finish this later?"

She gave him an exasperated look. "William, we have to make some decisions!"

"I know, I know," he said as he gathered his things. "But I forgot I need to be at the hospital. They've been paging me."

Deidre crossed her arms and looked at him suspiciously. "How come I didn't hear your pager go off?"

"It's on vibrate." He gave her a quick peck on the cheek then headed for the door. "You're the best," he told her.

She gave him a knowing look. "You're going to Williams-Sonoma right now, aren't you?"

"No." He looked guilty. "Okay, yes. I just want to get some ideas, that's all!"

She laughed. "Fine, go. But don't do anything until you talk to Alain first. Registering is something you do *together*."

"But . . ."

"Together," she said firmly, and shooed her friend out the door.

With the dresses safely tucked away and William on the hunt for Le Creuset cookware, Deidre turned her attention to preparing a fabulous dinner for Kevin. He was leaving for Boston the next day, and while he'd only be gone for three days, he had another big trip planned right after the K Ball. Deidre was determined to spend as much time with him as possible until then.

She prepared shrimp with a basil spinach and prosecco sauce along with a tomato and chickpea quinoa. For dessert she made several poached pear tartlets. She put candles on the table, uncorked a bottle of wine, and placed a small vase of fresh flowers in the center.

Kevin soon arrived, using the key Deidre gave him to let himself into the condo. He told her about his day, about a new nanotechnology start-up he was funding. *Advanced semiconductor wafers . . . nanowires . . . market applications . . . technology bottlenecks.* Deidre didn't understand a lot of it but she listened anyway, captivated by Kevin's enthusiasm for his work. When they finished eating, they went to sit in the living room, taking their time as they finished a bottle of pinot gris.

Deidre snuggled closer to Kevin on the couch. "This is nice." She sighed, resting her head on his shoulder.

"It is," Kevin agreed. He kissed the top of her head. "That was a great dinner, by the way. Thank you."

"You're welcome," she said. "It's just so relaxing to be at home, isn't it? To not have to rush around or worry about client dinners or cocktail parties or fancy balls . . ."

Kevin looked at her, taking the hint. "It's a bit much, isn't it?"

Deidre gave him a smile. "I just have to *look* at my calendar and I'm exhausted."

"I know," Kevin said sympathetically. He reached for a lock of Deidre's hair and twirled it around his finger. "And it doesn't help that I'm traveling all of the time. I think that's why I haven't really gotten serious with anyone since Tabby."

Tabby. Deidre hadn't made a big deal about Sabine, but if ever there was a chance to talk about her, now would be it.

Deidre reached for the bottle of wine. "So Sabine obviously didn't mind all of the business dinners and parties . . ."

Kevin broke out in laughter. "Tabby? Are you kidding? She *lived* for those moments." He gave a slight snicker but his voice was affectionate. "Seems like she still does."

Deidre took her time pouring some more wine into their glasses, carefully forming her thoughts. "So did you ever regret that things didn't work out with her? Since you have so much in common and everything?"

"Tabby and I don't have as much in common as you'd think," Kevin told her. "Being able to sync up your BlackBerrys will only get you so far." He chuckled at some distant memory and shook his head.

"But wasn't it easier?" Deidre pressed. "You have so much history together, you travel in the same circles, plus it doesn't hurt that she's easy on the eyes . . ."

"Deidre, I know what you're getting at and I'm telling you, you have nothing to worry about," he assured her. "I have a history with Tabby, yes, but that's all in the past. We're just friends now, if you can even call it that, and I rarely ever see her. Which, quite frankly, is fine by me."

That was fine by her, too. Relieved, Deidre donned a look of indifference. "Who said I was worried about anything?"

"Good." He took both her hands in his and gave them each a kiss. "Did Marla set you up with a dress for the K Ball?"

Deidre nodded. "She set me up with several. They're all so gorgeous, I'm almost afraid to try them on."

Kevin cleared their wineglasses and dessert dishes from the coffee table. "Well, the K Ball is next week. I say we dim the lights and have ourselves a fashion show."

"What? No way. I need to do this on my own, in the privacy of my bedroom." Deidre had held up one of Marla's gowns against her body, noting the snug-fitting bodice with concern. She was in good shape, but Marla was stick-thin and svelte.

"Even better." Kevin held out a hand to help Deidre up. "I'll give you a head start. I'll finish cleaning up out here and then I'll meet you in the bedroom."

Deidre gave him a serious look. "I'll be honest and tell you that I'm not sure if I can get into them. Your sister has the waist of a geisha."

Kevin pulled Deidre to him and gave her a long, deep kiss, a promise of what was to come. "How about this: If you can get into them, I'll help you get out of them. Deal?" His voice was low, sexy, and suggestive.

Deidre's lips tingled from the kiss and she could fell the blood rushing to her head. She could probably squeeze into one dress, maybe even two. It took her a moment before she was able to respond, and when she did she was already half-way to the bedroom. "Deal."

Chapter Six

Without good manners, romance is almost impossible.
—Charles Purdy, *Urban Etiquette*

The K Ball was a different sort of opulence from Edward Johnson's birthday party. Held in the Spanish Ballroom of the Fairmont Olympic Hotel, it boasted a more spirited, playful occasion equivalent to a red carpet affair.

Deidre wasn't prepared for the swarm of beautiful and moneyed people striking poses as photographers and media figures staked out the lobby and ballroom foyer. Kevin was in his element, keeping Deidre close to his side as he greeted people gamely and deftly deflected any questions about his personal life. A few people lobbed questions at Deidre—"How long have you been together?" "Where do you see this going?" "What are you wearing?"—but it was clear that she didn't carry much weight with this crowd. Her level of celebrity had been restricted to local cable, and while her fans loved her, it was never anything like this.

At least she knew she looked good. Deidre had chosen an

elegant Joanna Mastroianni green brocade gown from Marla's collection. Aside from being the most flattering dress on her, it was also the only one she could actually zip up. Marla's other dresses were so snug that Deidre could barely shimmy them past her waist.

Beverly was dazzling yet regal in a red iridescent ball gown. Marla had appeared a few minutes after they had arrived, looking dramatic in an embroidered one-shoulder silk sirene dress with a heavy crepe satin train. She reluctantly introduced Deidre to her date, Wedge Franklin.

Deidre liked him immediately. He was affable and kind, a far stretch from the sort of man she expected to see hanging around Marla. He seemed genuinely pleasant and Marla let them talk for all of two minutes before impatiently whisking him away under the pretense that they had other people to meet.

Beverly beamed as Kevin and Deidre approached their table and took their seats. Kevin introduced Deidre to the other guests. Everyone looked so immaculate and perfect that she was relieved she'd decided to spend the money on having her hair and nails done right before the ball.

The ballroom slowly filled up as people found their tables. Only one seat next to Kevin remained empty.

Marla's.

"Where is she?" Beverly wondered aloud, looking around the ballroom as everyone took their seats. "They're going to start dinner service soon."

"Ah, leave her be," Edward said, loosening his tie. Deidre wished she could do the same with her dress. "You know Marla. I'm sure she'll be joining us soon."

They were in between their salad and entrée when Marla appeared, a smug look on her face.

"Marla, where have you been?" Beverly admonished as the men at the table stood up politely. "We're almost halfway through dinner!"

"Mother." Marla gave her a pointed look. "Wedge invited me to join him at his table, and since I couldn't have a guest at ours, I figured the polite thing to do would be to accept his invitation."

"Marla." Beverly was clearly displeased. "You could have told me. Now this seat will go to waste!"

"Oh, don't worry," Marla assured her with a wave of the hand. "I found someone to take my place. She's just like family, too. She should be here any moment." Marla scanned the ballroom until her face broke into a smile. "There she is. Sabine, darling!"

Deidre stiffened as Kevin looked up with interest. Sure enough, Sabine Durant was gliding toward them, resplendent in a strapless midnight blue chiffon gown that Deidre was certain was pure silk. The bodice was fitted with gold tone embroidered detail, and her long dark hair was loose and hanging sleekly down her back.

"Look at what the cat dragged in," Marla exclaimed, delighted. "You look fabulous, Sabine!"

Sabine smiled demurely, catching Deidre's eye. "Hello, Deidre. It's so nice to see you again. And Kevin . . . Oh, don't get up." She bent down to give him a kiss on the cheek, lingering, Deidre thought, a moment too long. A glossy red imprint from Sabine's kiss remained on Kevin's cheek.

"Tabby," Kevin said. "What brings you to this neck of the woods? Twice in one year?" He looked amused. "This has to be a record."

"Kevin," Sabine countered coquettishly. "I *love* Seattle.

I just don't have enough reason to come here anymore. You know that."

Kevin raised an eyebrow. "Since when have you loved Seattle? If I remember correctly, you called this a city of over-caffeinated underachievers."

Sabine's smile didn't waver but Deidre thought she saw her nostrils flare ever so slightly. "I meant that affectionately, silly boy."

"Introductions, introductions," Marla said gaily, quickly leading Sabine around the table. By the time Sabine had returned, Kevin stood up to pull out the empty chair next to him.

"Do take care of her, Kevin," Marla clucked. "She flew in today and has to catch the first flight out tomorrow. Poor thing doesn't know which way is up."

"I'm not that helpless, Marla," Sabine said sweetly as she sat down.

"Just making sure you're attended to, darling. Have a lovely dinner, everyone." Marla gave a little wave and disappeared.

Kevin cleared his throat. "Tabby, can I get you a drink?"

Sabine gave him a glittering smile. "That would be lovely. The usual."

The usual. Deidre didn't appreciate Sabine's familiarity with Kevin, even if they had been engaged once. She didn't consider herself a jealous person, but Sabine's intimate, almost proprietary attitude was rubbing Deidre the wrong way.

Kevin seemed oblivious. "Deidre? What about you?"

"I'm fine," she said. "Thank you." She tried to catch his eye but he'd already turned to signal a server.

The men at the table were enthralled by Sabine, and much of the dinner conversation revolved around Durant Media Group and Sabine's extensive travels. Call her crazy, but Deidre could swear that Sabine was intentionally talking about every place she'd ever visited with Kevin, purposely drawing him into the conversation.

"Oh Kevin, remember that all-night bar in Mooréa?"

"We were in Athens for six days, and didn't once leave the Amphitryon!"

"And then he bought these ridiculous leather shoes in Buenos Aires. Remember?"

"The gondola broke down when we were twelve hundred feet above ground!"

If Deidre hadn't been so taken by Sabine's tales herself, she would have been offended. To the naked eye, it seemed as if Sabine and Kevin were still together. Even Edward and Beverly were at ease with Sabine, laughing and reminiscing along with her.

"And yet," Kevin interjected nonchalantly, "for all our travels, I still couldn't get you to come out to my house on Lake Wish, in Jacob's Point." He swirled the ice in his empty glass.

Sabine didn't respond at first. "Really?" she finally managed. "I thought I'd gone out there once or twice."

"No, you didn't."

"I'm pretty sure I did."

"Oh, I'm pretty sure you didn't." Kevin refused to be swayed. "Trust me: I'd remember."

"Well." She gave the table a smile. "There are only so many hours in a day, aren't there? And you know my work keeps me busy. Besides, I don't think United flies to 'off the beaten path.'" She gave a little laugh.

"You fly by private jet," he pointed out. "And there are several private air strips close by."

Sabine didn't say anything, her smile frozen on her face.

Finally, she said, "Well, I'm open for an invitation any time." Her expression was suddenly serious, the casual flirtation gone. She locked eyes with Kevin, challenging him.

Deidre had enough. It was clear that this woman was making a move on her boyfriend. As much as she hated to do it, Deidre felt she didn't have any other choice. She gave Kevin a discreet kick under the table, smiling as she did so.

It was a solid kick, and it hit the mark. Kevin winced in surprise, shaken from his reverie.

"Kevin." Beverly discreetly tapped her cheek. "You may want to go freshen up."

"What?" He looked mystified.

"Lipstick," Deidre said under her breath.

"Oh, I'll get that," Sabine said, dipping her napkin in her water and raising it to Kevin's cheek.

Kevin held up a hand. "No, that's all right. I need to pay a visit to the men's room anyway." He got up hastily, giving Deidre a guilty smile in the process.

"I don't know how you stand it," Sabine said to Deidre once Kevin was out of earshot. "He's a handful, isn't he? Stubborn."

"I don't think so," Deidre said tightly. "He just knows what he wants." *Take that!*

Sabine's eyes narrowed. "Does he now?"

Deidre grit her teeth. This was like high school all over again. An uncomfortable hush descended over the table as everyone suddenly focused on their food.

Beverly cleared her throat. "Deidre is quite the businesswoman, too," she said, steering the conversation in another direction. "She has a cookie line that will be launching in a few months."

"A cookie line?" Sabine arched an eyebrow. "What's it called?"

Deidre smiled gratefully at Beverly and lifted her chin. "The line is called Sweet Deidre . . ." she began.

"Cookies," Sabine repeated slowly, her lips curled in amusement. "*Named after you*. How utterly charming!" She gave a condescending laugh.

Deidre sucked in her breath, biting her tongue. She felt on the verge of saying something she knew she'd regret later. A quick trip to the bathroom would be the wisest move.

Deidre excused herself from the table and stood up. There was a tug on her gown, and then the unmistakable sound of fabric ripping.

The conversation at the table came to an abrupt halt.

"Oh, dear," Beverly said, her hand to her mouth.

Six inches of the left seam on Deidre's gown had split open, revealing a little bit of skin and the nude Spanx waist shaper that was keeping Deidre tucked inside her gown.

Sabine handed Deidre several napkins to cover herself, her lips pressed together as she suppressed a laugh.

"What's going on?" Kevin asked, appearing beside a red-faced Deidre.

Deidre was too mortified to speak. It was Sabine who came up with an answer.

"I think sweet Deidre will be calling it a night," she said silkily.

Kevin escorted Deidre out of the ballroom, his jacket draped over her shoulders. It hid the offending tear in her dress but Deidre could feel the night air on her skin as they walked.

Fortunately there was only a light trickle of photographers remaining, most of whom were smoking and couldn't be bothered to look up as Deidre and Kevin headed toward the valet to pick up Kevin's car.

On the drive home, she stared out the window, still humiliated beyond belief. She wished she could put the night in rewind and start over again. Kevin had quickly made their excuses but Deidre sensed a frisson of disappointment and embarrassment emanating from Kevin's parents.

Despondent, she mumbled, "Kevin, I'm sorry you had to leave the K Ball. I know there were some people you needed to talk to . . ."

"Are you kidding? I'd much rather rent a movie anyway." He smiled at her gamely for a moment before returning his eyes to the road. "In fact, I don't know why we didn't do this in the first place."

Deidre knew the answer. For most people there were business engagements, social engagements, and family engagements. For Kevin and his family, they were all one in the same. The K Ball, like everything else, was just one more thing that Kevin was expected to attend, like a birthday party for a family member or an anniversary.

"Kevin, come on. I know the K Ball is important to you and your family . . ."

Kevin pulled into a parking space at her building and cut the engine. "Maybe," he admitted. "But you're important to me, too. I'm just sorry that I've always got something going on and now I'm leaving tomorrow for two weeks . . ." His voice trailed off as he frowned, looking out over the dashboard. "It's not really fair to you."

She didn't like the regretful look on his face. "What? No,

Kevin, that's not it. We just need to find some balance or something. It's been a busy year for me, too. It won't always be like this."

"Deidre." He looked at her almost pityingly. "I'm not having a busy year. I *have* a busy life. That's not going to change."

"But . . ." Deidre stopped herself, unsure of what to say next. Kevin was right.

He reached out and tenderly touched her cheek. "We don't have to figure this out tonight, Deidre. Look, I'm already packed for my trip, so why don't you change your clothes and we'll go out somewhere fun, get a drink or something? Or we could just stay in, if you want."

If I want. Deidre tried to quash the rising sense of panic in her chest. What had she been thinking, complaining about Kevin's commitments and obligations? It was a part of his life—a big part of his life—and if she wanted to be a part of his life, too, she'd have to be okay with that.

"No, I'd love to go out," she lied, forcing her voice to sound light and cheerful. When Kevin regarded her dubiously, she leaned over to give him a quick kiss on the cheek. "Really."

Later that night, Deidre lay in bed with a sleeping Kevin next to her. They'd stayed out late, much later than Deidre would have thought wise since Kevin had an early flight, but it didn't seem to bother him. They hit several popular martini bars before ending up at the Palace Kitchen for a late-night bite.

While her body was weary, her mind was racing. Despite Kevin's reassurances, all she could think about was Sabine.

She knew things were over between Kevin and Sabine, yet

she couldn't help but wonder about what could have been. After all, he'd known her practically his entire life. Their families were close, and it was assumed that they would end up together.

Early in their relationship, Kevin had told Deidre about his one and only engagement. He had been in his late twenties and Sabine in her midtwenties when he'd "proposed." The proposal had been somewhat contrived and was hardly a surprise to anyone who knew the couple—the venue for the proposal having been secured six weeks in advance, charged to Sabine's credit card—but Kevin and Sabine enjoyed the attention and initial giddiness that came with getting engaged.

After a few weeks, however, the excitement began to wear off. It was Sabine who panicked first, unsure of whether her dress was right, if the invitations were right, if the timing was right. And it was only a matter of time before the real issue came up: whether the man she was engaged to marry was right.

Kevin had been toying with his doubts as well, but had chosen to honor his commitment to wed. He liked Sabine well enough, and they'd been good friends for so long that he didn't see why they couldn't eventually fall in love. And even if they didn't fall in love per se, they had more in common than most people. They could probably craft a marriage that had a chance of making it, at least for a couple of years.

They never made it to the altar. Two months before the wedding, Sabine disappeared. It was rumored that she'd retreated to her family's property in Lausanne, Switzerland, presumably on a spa holiday. Kevin chalked it up to pre-wedding jitters and gave Sabine some private time to collect her thoughts. But a few days later a tabloid snapped several racy photographs of Sabine partying it up in São Paulo, Brazil. Aside from being drunk and scantily clad, Sabine wasn't alone. She was flanked by several young Brazilian men, one of whom was reported to be her newest flame. Kevin and Sabine called off the wedding but remained friends.

Deidre lay in the dark, anxious. Her mind flashed to a point earlier in the night, at the K Ball, when Sabine had managed to coax a smile from Kevin, and then a laugh. Maybe that was what was bothering Deidre, that Sabine could so easily break through his defenses, Kevin's initial annoyance giving way to playfulness, even indulging in Sabine's banter.

What if something had changed? Kevin and Sabine were cut from the same cloth. The money, the legacies. They didn't think twice about a $500 bottle of wine or a $2,500 dress. They owned property all over the world, had multimillion-dollar businesses. Deidre, on the other hand, still had a mortgage on her modest condo.

Kevin turned over in his sleep, his arm coming to rest over Deidre's side. He pulled her close to him. Seconds later he was snoring again.

You need to sleep, she told herself. She wanted to wake up early and fix Kevin a quick breakfast before he left, even though he'd said it wasn't necessary. It wasn't necessary for him, maybe, but it was necessary for her. It would help quell not only her anxiety about Sabine, but also about Sweet Deidre—the feedback from the focus groups would be in any day now.

Deidre felt her own eyelids grow heavy at long last. *Sleep,* she willed herself again, and this time, she did.

THE SEATTLE SCOOP

DEIDRE REVEALED!
A *Seattle Scoop* Exclusive! By Rosemary Goodwin

Partygoers at this year's exclusive K Ball got an eyeful when Deidre McIntosh's gown tore during dinner service at the $2,500-a-plate affair.

"She was beet red," said one source, who asked to remain anonymous. "She tried to play it off, but you have to wonder if she did it intentionally, for the attention."

Deidre and her boyfriend, local millionaire Kevin Johnson, were not available for comment.

Log on to our blog and tell us what you think!

CHAPTER SEVEN

*When major setbacks occur, the most important
thing is to remain calm. The situation will
only get worse if you act irrationally.*
—Charlotte Ford, *21st-Century Etiquette*

Deidre walked into the JCC offices on Monday morning, determined to stop obsessing about Kevin and Sabine. Kevin loved her and adored her, and he had told her so right before he left. He hadn't seemed to mind that Deidre wasn't as perfectly put together as Sabine, or that she only spoke one language instead of five. Deidre was an accomplished woman, too, and she had a gourmet cookie line that was about to launch. She was making herself crazy over nothing.

As she neared Amber's desk, she saw the young woman hastily shove something into her drawer before offering Deidre a bright smile.

"Good morning!" Amber seemed more animated than usual. "You had a few calls already. I put them right into your voice mail."

"Great, thanks. Anything important?"

"Not that I can tell."

Deidre skimmed her schedule. "Okay. We have a team meeting this morning. Let's get an assortment of pastries from the shop and have the conference room stocked with fresh coffee and tea. See if you can sneak a few chocolates in as well—I know everyone likes those amaretto truffles that just came out."

Amber was scribbling furiously onto a pad of paper. "Sure, Deidre. That's a great idea!"

Deidre looked at Amber. It wasn't *that* great of an idea. "Is everything all right, Amber?"

Amber's cheeks pinked before she gave a laugh. "What? Yes, everything's fine, Deidre!"

Deidre surveyed the young woman doubtfully. "Are you sure?"

Amber hesitated for only a second. "Positive!"

"Okay. Well, I'll be in my office."

"Great!"

That was weird, Deidre thought as she stepped into her office. What was Amber being so secretive about?

She sat down at her desk and powered up her computer. There was a beep and then rows of gibberish began running across her screen. Deidre tried to type something on her keyboard but to no avail. She loved JCC but they seriously needed to upgrade their computers. At least once a month there was a crash or bug of some kind, putting everything on hold for a couple of hours.

Deidre went to the doorway and saw Amber staring intently at her computer screen. "Amber, is your computer working? Mine's all jacked up."

The young woman looked startled as she quickly turned off her monitor display. "Um, mine's working fine. Do you want me to call the tech department and have them send someone over?"

"That would be great. I've got all sorts of junk up on my screen."

"Oh, that happened to me last week. Maybe I can take a look." Amber got up and headed into Deidre's office. Deidre was about to follow her when she paused, tempted.

She slipped around to Amber's desk and pressed the ON button for the monitor. The screen flicked and turned on.

The desktop was empty, and only Amber's e-mail program was opened. Deidre was about to turn away when she saw a Word document that had been reduced to a thumbnail at the bottom of the screen.

AMBER_OLSON_RESUME

Was Amber looking for another job?

"Deidre, you just needed a clean reboot—" Amber emerged from Deidre's office and froze when she saw Deidre hovering over her desk. "Oh."

Deidre looked at her guiltily. "God, Amber, I'm sorry to be a snoop, but are you planning on leaving?"

Amber looked guilty. "No. Not exactly, anyway."

"Why are you being so secretive, then?"

Amber let out a sigh before coming around to her desk. She opened a drawer and pulled out a newspaper. She handed it to Deidre. "I just thought, well, that maybe I should look around. You know—just in case."

Deidre looked down at the paper in Amber's hands. It was *The Seattle Scoop*, along with a shot of her at the K Ball, gaping at the tear in her dress.

"Oh! Sorry." Amber grabbed the paper out of Deidre's hand and replaced it with another, then made a big show of crumpling up *The Seattle Scoop* and throwing it in the trash. "I found it in the break room . . ."

"It's not a big deal, Amber." Deidre used to enjoy indulging in the occasional tabloid herself until she started appearing in them.

The Seattle Scoop had been replaced with the classified section of *The Seattle Times*—the want ads, to be exact. Several ads for food and beverage jobs had been circled with a red pen. Deidre felt a little hurt. "I thought you liked working here, Amber."

"I do!" Amber replied quickly. "I love it here, Deidre. Honest. I just thought I just should be prepared, that's all."

"Prepared for what?"

"Deidre!" Manuela sailed down the hallway, a cloud of perfume leading the way. She embraced Deidre in an exuberant hug then looped her arm through Deidre's. "Oh, you look just adorable this morning. Doesn't she look adorable, Kimber?"

"It's Amber . . ." Deidre tried to correct her, but Manuela wasn't listening.

"*Such* a gorgeous day! Much too nice to stay inside, don't you think? Come, let's go have lunch. I know the most charming place!"

"Lunch? Now?" It wasn't even nine.

"You know that it's healthier to eat earlier in the day, don't you?" Manuela waggled a finger. "Gives you the rest of the day to burn those calories off. Shall we?"

Manuela had a car waiting outside. Deidre didn't get a word in as Manuela chatted animatedly about her weekend and her husband, Frank, who was an avid hunter. "Deer and elk," she was saying. "I think it's completely inhumane but I love to eat fresh game, so therein lies the dilemma as you can see."

The owner of the famous Pike Place eatery knew Manuela well, and was obviously accustomed to Manuela's early lunches. They were shown to a table where Manuela promptly ordered several items before they'd even had a chance to take their seats. Soon their table was covered with plates and bowls filled with food.

Manuela's fork hovered indecisively over a dish of marinated morels. "So, the feedback from the focus groups came in this morning." Manuela speared a mushroom and braised celery heart, then popped it into her mouth, chewing with great gusto.

Deidre hadn't expected the results to come in so soon. She was suddenly nervous, her fingers tightening around the water glass in her hands. "What did they say?"

"Oh, not good. The response was only marginally better than before." Manuela rolled her eyes in a *can you believe it* sort of way as she stabbed at another mushroom.

Deidre felt her stomach drop. "What?"

"Consumers are so fickle, aren't they? You practically need a degree in psychology to figure these things out." Manuela turned her attention to several platters of fish before deciding on the cedar-planked salmon. She took a bite and practically swooned. "Delicious! Deidre, you really must try this." She offered Deidre a generous forkful.

Deidre shook her head. She forced herself to keep her voice level and calm, despite feeling a rise of panic. "So what happens now?"

Manuela waved her fork in the air. "Well, I've spoken with

Frank and Gary. As you know, these are trying economic times, Deidre. People are being very careful with their money. Everyone's cutting back, shrinking disposable income. Well, you read the papers. My point is, it's a tough time to launch a new brand."

Deidre grimaced. This wasn't the kind of discussion she wanted to have with Manuela right now. All of her time and creative energy these past few months had gone into Sweet Deidre. She had a mortgage and a car payment, not to mention her daily living expenses. Though she was currently on retainer, the big payoff would be when the line officially launched.

"Frank is a chocolatier at heart and has been dying to put our attention more on the chocolate side of the business. You know my family's history with the business, correct?"

Deidre nodded. Jamison Cookies and Confections had been founded by Manuela's grandparents Wallace and Abigail Jamison. What started as a simple bakery with a single butter cookie grew into a production facility producing thirty different varieties of cookies and handcrafted premium chocolates that were sold directly to customers and area supermarkets.

Over the years the company had gone through several reinventions: upgrading formulations, opening and closing different divisions, changing their distribution model. In the mid 1980s, JCC made the strategic move to expand into the nongrocery sector. It was a smart business move, ensuring the company significantly greater distribution through chain drugstores, superstores, and the food service segment. But they also lost some of their panache along with the change. Deidre knew that since Manuela had become CEO after her father's passing the previous year, she had been anxious to reclaim a share of the gourmet specialty foods market.

"In my mind, Sweet Deidre is the perfect marriage for both sides of the business," Manuela continued. "So, despite the pressure from Frank and Gary to turn our attention elsewhere, I've negotiated for some more time for you. You'll have ten more days to come up with something viable. I have confidence in you, Deidre. Third time's the charm, I'm sure!"

Deidre let out a sigh of relief. "Great, Manuela. I'll go back right now and start on this right away—"

Manuela held up a hand as she took a long drink of sparkling water. "Oh, and before I forget, I took the liberty of jotting some notes down, some guidelines if you will, to help you with this next batch of cookies." Manuela reached into her briefcase and pulled out a thick binder. On the cover was the Sweet Deidre logo, only it wasn't the Sweet Deidre logo. This logo had a boring type with a gingham border, a far cry from the lovely pink Sweet Deidre script resting on a mossy green square that was on their letterhead and marketing materials.

Deidre swallowed. "You just did this?"

"Actually, no. After that first round of feedback, I got a few people together to try their hand at it. Just for fun, to see what they would come up with. Now, with this second round of feedback being so poor, I really think you should take a look." Manuela nodded toward the binder encouragingly.

Deidre opened the binder. There was a table of contents, color-coded and tabbed, and slick images of mocked-up packaging and cookies in glossy sheet protectors. "Oh," she said. Her eyes skimmed the first few pages.

Value coupled with a healthy treat . . . Less indulgent sweet treats, more home-style feel . . . Fresh from your grandmother's oven . . .

It was almost identical to so many other JCC product offerings. Deidre didn't know what to say. This wasn't her line anymore, was it?

As if reading her mind, Manuela quickly assured her. "Now, I know this isn't what you had in mind, but clearly we need to try something different. And, given the financial state of the country, we need raw materials and ingredients that are lower in cost, so we can pass on those savings to our customers. *'Fresh from the kitchen, home-baked goodness!'* Let's give people a sense of security. People want the familiar. Chocolate chip, oatmeal, but with a twist. A Deidre McIntosh twist." Manuela poked through the bread basket until she found a roll that met her satisfaction.

"But chocolate chip and oatmeal have been done to death . . ."

"Deidre." Manuela put down her butter knife, her normally ebullient personality gone. In its place was the sharp and serious businesswoman who was at the helm of Jamison Cookies and Confections. "My family has built this company up from a small bake shop to a nice-sized business. We're profitable. We post twelve to fifteen percent increases in sales every year. We know what we're doing." This last sentence was spoken with an air of finality.

Deidre didn't disagree. JCC was a solid company that performed well in the industry, and as much as she trusted her instincts, she didn't have the same kind of on-the-ground experience as Manuela and her team. She was new to the business, and it seemed she still had a lot to learn.

"No problem, Manuela," she said. "I'll read through this and come up with some recipes that are more traditional and budget friendly."

Manuela held up a finger. "Not budget friendly," she corrected. "*Value friendly.*"

Deidre forced a smile. "Right."

"I'm so glad you see it that way! I'm confident you'll make it work. And remember that I don't want just any cookies, but Deidre McIntosh cookies. Give me that excitement and pizzazz that you used to bring to your shows. Deidre McIntosh in a package—*a promise for the future!*"

And all for $1.99, Deidre added sardonically to herself.

Manuela looked pleased as she let out a dainty burp. "Now, let's look at the dessert menu, shall we?"

Deidre went back to the office to break the news to the Sweet Deidre team. Oddly enough, none of them seemed particularly surprised, not even when she held up Manuela's binder with the homely Sweet Deidre logo.

"Why do I get the feeling that everyone already knew about this?" Deidre muttered once everyone had filed out of her office.

Only Amber remained and she looked guilty. "There were rumors," she confessed. "I think Manuela's assistant, Elliot, started them. It didn't take long before everyone knew that something was up."

"Everyone except me."

"Sorry, Deidre." Amber went to the door. "Do you want this open or closed?"

"Closed, please."

In the quiet of her office, Deidre flipped through the binder.

There was a computer-generated image of her in a frilly home-maker apron à la *I Love Lucy*, not the tasteful and contemporary chef's apron she'd worn on Marla's show. She had a toothpaste-commercial smile and a cartoon bubble floated above her head: "Fresh-baked goodness for your pocket *and* your stomach!"

God, it was horrible.

She looked at the clock. It was 8:00 p.m. in London. Deidre picked up her phone and called Kevin, disappointed when the call went right to voice mail.

She started to leave a message, summarizing her meeting with Manuela. She was still talking when there was a beep telling her that her time was up. She hesitated before pressing the number on the keypad to delete the message so she could start fresh. Another annoying beep midway through. She tried one more time, only to run out of time again, and finally gave up trying to leave a message at all.

William was next on her list, and he picked up almost immediately. "Hey, Deidre, we were just talking about you!"

"Really?" God, it was good to have friends. "Oh, William, I'm having the most awful—"

"Alain and I are having a disagreement. I want to register with Dean & Deluca in New York and he wants Home Depot. Can you talk some sense into him, please?"

"Well, actually—"

"Deidre." Alain was on the phone now. "I tried to tell him that we already have dishes and pots and pans in the house but no decent tools."

"Alain, anything with Teflon doesn't count as real cookware," William tried to explain.

"I don't even know what you're talking about!" Alain argued

back. "Deidre, what we really need is a sawhorse or a work-bench so I can build a deck out back—"

"Ha, that'll be the day! You haven't even finished those bookshelves you promised me!"

"That's not my fault! *You* can't decide on what color paint I can use. What's wrong with white?"

"White? There is no 'white,' Alain! There's 'dogwood' or 'marshmallow' or 'whitetail' or 'ivory lace' . . ."

The two continued to bicker. Out of the corner of her eye, Deidre caught a glint of sunlight bouncing off a framed picture sitting on her desk. She picked up the photograph, a close-up of her and Kevin taken several months ago. They'd taken the picture on a clear day, the camera set on a timer atop a pile of rocks. Lake Wish was shimmering in the background. They were laughing, happy and relaxed, far away from the demands and distractions of the city.

She ran her finger over the outline of Kevin's face.

"Deidre, are you listening?"

"Sorry, boys, but you're on your own." Deidre replaced the photograph on her desk and began to gather her things. "I have to go out of town for a couple of days."

William and Alain stopped quarreling. "A couple of days?" Alain asked. "Where are you going?"

She didn't answer, but said instead, "I love you both. I'll call you later."

Deidre headed out of her office, pausing only to turn off the light and close her door.

She was going to the only place that felt like home.

CHAPTER EIGHT

Friends and good manners will carry
you where money won't go.
—Margaret Walker

Deidre stopped by her place to load up her Volvo SUV then headed southeast on I-90 toward Jacob's Point. The trip would take almost four hours.

Jacob's Point wasn't home, exactly, but it was where her heart and soul felt most at peace, something she never felt in the city even after years of living there. In Jacob's Point Deidre felt that she could be herself—her honest, flawed self—and right now that sounded really good.

Jacob's Point boasted a small population with a handful of stores and one local eatery, the Wishbone. Everything else was miles away. Deidre liked driving through the small towns with their rustic charm, a precursor for what was to come. Away from the hustle and bustle of the city, it seemed easier to catch a breath, to slow down her pace and take in what was around her. With the windows down, the wind blowing in her hair, and her stereo playing John Coltrane, Deidre didn't know why she'd let so much time pass since her last visit.

At the heart of Jacob's Point was Lake Wish. The name was a derivation of Skitswish or *Schitsu'umsh*, the name for a tribe of Coeur d'Alene Indians that had passed through the area. It literally meant "the ones that were found here." For Deidre, this had certainly been true.

The lake was nestled deep in the woods and tucked out of sight. Most tourists didn't know about it, or if they did, had difficulty finding it. There were no signs or markers. It is almost too easy to drive right by the town, unaware of the beauty hidden within.

Both Kevin and his uncle Harry had places on or near Lake Wish. Uncle Harry's place was a small, two-bedroom cabin that had seen better days. At first glance it didn't even look habitable, at least not by humans. Deidre had transformed it into a cozy home away from home when she'd mistakenly stayed there the year before.

Kevin's handsome, more palatial seven-bedroom property was something that might be found in the pages of *Architectural Digest*, a lovely, pale gray lake house with white trim that blended seamlessly with the tall evergreens. Deidre missed the large stone fireplace that opened into both the kitchen and the living room. She looked forward to curling up in front of the fireplace with a glass of wine and a good book. Unwinding was exactly what she needed to help her find inspiration and get Sweet Deidre back on track.

She dialed the number for the Wishbone, looking forward to telling Lindsey that she'd be seeing her good friend in a matter of hours. If anyone could help her get perspective on the situation, it was Lindsey.

"I'm sorry, Deidre, but Lindsey isn't here." The voice on the other end of the line belonged to Mary Martin, one of the waitresses at the Wishbone. "She actually hasn't been in for a couple of weeks."

Deidre turned off the car stereo. It wasn't like Lindsey not to be at work—the woman was a workhorse. She never took a sick day, even when she was sick.

"Is she all right?" Deidre asked.

"I don't know. She just called one day and said that she wasn't able to come in, and that if we needed anything, we should talk to her husband. We're only open a couple of days a week until Lindsey can hire a cook."

Hire a cook? Lindsey was very particular about her kitchen, and Deidre couldn't believe that she would willingly invite someone else to run it.

"Is she planning to retire?" Even as she asked the question she knew it was unlikely. Lindsey was in her early fifties, still several years away from retirement. She still had to pay off the mortgage for the diner, plus she'd been excited about several new side projects she'd started, such as the *Wishfull Eats* cookbook.

"I don't know, Deidre. No one knows what's going on. Everyone's worried but Lindsey isn't saying anything. Hannah's gone by her place twice but nobody answered the door. Lindsey's truck was in the driveway, too."

Deidre didn't know what to think. Lindsey and her husband, Sid, had three school-aged children whom they home-schooled. Sid and Lindsey traded off being with the kids, and their oldest son, Caleb, was a big help with his two younger siblings. Somebody was usually at home.

"What about Sid and the kids?"

"Sid came by the other day for lunch and he brought the kids. Everyone looked good, but kind of quiet. He said that Lindsey was working on getting some people to help out, but in the meantime we'd just have to do the best we can. Said he would help us if we had any questions, but to be honest, he looked pretty ragged. The kids seemed kind of gloomy, too. You know Daisy—a regular little chatterbox. Even she didn't have much to say." Someone murmured in the background. "I'm sorry, Deidre, but we're swamped and I have to go. You can try her at home, but she probably won't pick up."

"Okay. Thanks, Mary."

Deidre was frowning as she tried Lindsey's number at home. The phone rang three times before the machine clicked on.

"Hi, you've reached the Millers—Sid, Lindsey, Caleb, Brandon, and Daisy. Sorry we're not here to take your call . . ."

Deidre hung up, her mind clouded with worry. What was going on?

She tossed the phone into her purse and put her foot on the gas pedal, intent on getting to Jacob's Point as quickly as possible.

It was nearing dusk when Deidre pulled into Lindsey's gravel driveway. She was exhausted from the drive, unable to enjoy herself as she mulled over what Mary had told her.

But now that she was finally there, she wanted to laugh with relief. There was Lindsey in her front flower garden, pulling weeds and tossing them into a Hefty lawn bag, which was already three-quarters full.

Deidre glanced at the clock on her dashboard. What was Lindsey doing home? Deidre knew she preferred to be in the kitchen, and it was almost dinnertime at the Wishbone.

Normally Lindsey would be busy prepping the food and thinking aloud, planning the next day's menu. What was she doing here, on her hands and knees, when it was almost dark out?

Deidre cut the engine and got out of the car. Lindsey stood up and turned slowly as Deidre approached.

"Well, I'll be damned," Lindsey drawled, hands on her hips. She brushed a stray strand of hair away from her face.

"What does it take for you to answer your phone these days?" Deidre asked jokingly, hugging her friend. She stepped back when she realized that Lindsey wasn't hugging her back.

Lindsey's face was drawn and pale, her hair unwashed. Her roots had grown out and it looked as if she'd lost some weight. Lindsey wasn't a vain person but she took great pride in her appearance. The woman standing before Deidre was disheveled and gaunt, the playful glint in her eye gone.

"Are you on some kind of new diet?" Deidre tried to chide.

"Diet?" Lindsey brushed the dirt off her hands. "Yeah, the have-a-major-heart-attack diet. You'll lose ten pounds, just like that." She grasped the corners of Hefty bag and moved to lift it.

Deidre's mouth went dry. "What?" She grabbed the Hefty bag out of Lindsey's hands. "Lindsey, what are you talking about? *When?*"

"About three weeks ago. Not long after you called." Lindsey handed her a twisty tie. "You can leave that there. Sid will be home soon. He took the kids over to a friend's house to give me a break." She turned on her heel and headed into the house.

Deidre tied up the bag and put it to the side, then followed Lindsey. She didn't know what to say. Lindsey wasn't even fifty-three. While she wasn't model thin, Lindsey was in good shape and as healthy as an ox.

Lindsey walked into the kitchen, putting a kettle of water onto the stove to boil. "Well, spit it out. It's not like you not to have something to say." She turned on the kitchen faucet and started to wash her hands.

Deidre stammered. "I don't know what to say, Lindsey. You're so young! How could you have a heart attack?"

Lindsey dried her hands on a dish towel. "Well, it's not like I had much choice, Deidre. It kind of picked me."

"What happened?"

Lindsey sat down at the table. "I was at the Wishbone serving Sunday brunch when it felt as if someone had punched me in the middle of my chest. I started sweating and Hannah told me I looked funny. I didn't pay her much attention. I was more uncomfortable than anything, so I took a rest in one of the booths, and then finally called it a day and drove home."

Deidre stared at her incredulously. "You were having a heart attack and you drove yourself home?"

Lindsey looked irritated. "Well, Deidre, I didn't *know* I was having a heart attack. I thought it would be one of those clutch-your-chest-and-keel-over kinds of things, like the way it is on TV. Later I found out that the symptoms for women are different from men. Did you know that heart disease is the number one killer of women? And that it kills more women than the next six causes of death *combined*? I mean, it even beats out cancer. Do you know how many people I know who have cancer? *A lot*. And still, heart disease is taking women down left and right. How depressing is that?"

Deidre couldn't believe it. "I can't—"

Lindsey continued as if Deidre hadn't said anything. "Anyway, I went home, rested for a bit, but nothing changed. The pain started to get more intense. Sid was worried and insisted that we drive to the hospital, but you know how I am about that. The hospital is an hour and a half away, and I figured I could just wait until the next day to see Doc Hensen. But Sid insisted, so we got the kids and piled into the truck and off we went."

The teakettle started to whistle. Lindsey rose, but Deidre motioned for her to sit down. "I'll take care of the tea. Then what happened?"

"We finally made it to the hospital and the doctor there did an EKG. The next thing I know, they've got me in one of those gowns and in bed with IVs coming out of me. Turns out I was having a heart attack and was lucky to still be conscious. A myocardial infarction is what they called it." Lindsey snorted.

Deidre shook her head. "I just can't believe it. I'm so glad everything turned out okay." She reached for her friend's hand and was surprised when Lindsey pulled away and put her hands in her lap.

"I have permanent muscle damage to my heart, Deidre. They had to put in a stent. If I had gone in earlier, I probably would have come out fine. As it is, I'll be on medications and a restricted diet for the rest of my life." Lindsey sat back in her chair, her eyes avoiding Deidre's. "I don't have the energy to go back to the Wishbone."

"Well, of course not, Lindsey. You just had a heart attack. You still need time to recover . . ."

Lindsey shook her head. "It's not that. I just . . . I just don't care about the Wishbone anymore, Deidre. All that hard work—for what? Another heart attack? Forget it."

Deidre carefully placed the tea bags into the mugs and poured the hot water. "Lindsey, it's too soon. The girls can manage the Wishbone for a little while longer. And I'll help you find some backup in the meantime."

Lindsey blew on her tea, cooling it down. "I don't want backup, Deidre. I want out."

Clearly this wasn't the time to present the pros and cons of Lindsey leaving her business. Aside from the fact that Lindsey still had an outstanding note on the Wishbone, it was unlikely that anyone would step up and buy the business from her. It was a small town and very few people, if any, could do what Lindsey did.

"After what you just went through, you probably want to spend more time with your family," Deidre said.

Lindsey shook her head. "Not really. No. I mean, you'd think I would, but I don't." She sipped her tea, indifferent.

Deidre was surprised and a little concerned. She knew that Lindsey loved her family more than life itself. "Uh, well, how are Sid and the kids doing?"

"Fine. Same ol', same ol'." Lindsey looked around her kitchen. "I know I've got some Ritz crackers around here. I can't eat them, of course, but I guess I should play hostess and serve you something. Interested in some lentil soup?" Lindsey said this sarcastically, her nose twitching. "Doc wants me on this regimented diet—no fat, no sugar, no salt until he says so. Which of course rules out my entire menu at the Wishbone. If I can't eat it, why make it? Now where are those Ritz crackers?"

"I'm fine, Lindsey," Deidre assured her. "I brought some Sweet Deidre treats for you and the family. We're getting rid of this line, too. It turns out I have to go back to the drawing board one more time . . ."

Lindsey smirked. "Bummer."

Deidre wished she hadn't said anything—her situation obviously paled in comparison to Lindsey's. "Well, I'm sure I'll figure something out," she said hurriedly. "But if having sweets in the house isn't a good idea, I can get rid of them."

"What? Don't be ridiculous. Sid and the kids will love them. They still have to eat, after all, and I'm sure as heck not feeding them." Lindsey finished her tea with a gulp.

"You're not feeding them?"

"Well, Caleb and Brandon can fend for themselves—even Daisy knows where all the snack food is. And Sid lived for ten years as a bachelor eating baked beans out of a can. They'll survive." Lindsey got up and shuffled to the kitchen sink. "Everyone will survive just fine without ol' Lindsey."

It took Deidre a minute to realize that Lindsey wasn't just talking about her family, but about the entire town of Jacob's Point. Everyone had come to rely on Lindsey's warm smile and home-cooked meals.

The front door slammed and there was the sound of footsteps. The kids filed in, one by one, their faces anxious until they saw Deidre at the table. "Deidre!" they cried. Caleb was fourteen years old, Brandon was eleven, and Daisy was eight.

"Hey, guys," she said affectionately, giving them each a hug. Lindsey sat back in silence. "How are you?"

The children exchanged a careful glance. "Fine," Caleb said, speaking for all of them. He was very smart, a couple grades ahead of his peers. He was also an excellent swimmer.

Lindsey slapped the table, making everyone jump. "Caleb! Manners!" she snapped.

Caleb turned red and stuttered, "We're fine, Deidre. Thank you for asking."

Deidre turned to stare at her friend, who was jerking her thumb toward the living room. Once the kids were out of ear-shot, Deidre said, "Lindsey, that was unnecessarily harsh." She'd never seen Lindsey treat her children that way.

"Well, the world's a harsh place," Lindsey replied unsym-pathetically.

There was a rustle of paper bags as Sid stepped into the kitchen. His face looked ragged; he was clearly exhausted.

"Got some things from the store for dinner," he said. "Hey, Deidre. I thought that was your car outside." He came over and gave her a kiss.

"Only one like it in Jacob's Point," Lindsey said dryly. Jacob's Point didn't have much by way of luxury cars. Lindsey got up and cast a look around the kitchen. "Well, not that this hasn't been nice, Deidre, but I think I'm going to go to my room. Thanks for stopping by."

Deidre was startled. "Oh. But . . ."

Lindsey disappeared down the hall, then Deidre heard the click of a bedroom door closing.

Sid put the bags on the counter with a sigh. "Sorry about that, Deidre. She's been having a hard time since the heart attack. I assume she told you?"

Deidre nodded. "Yes. I still can't believe it. How are you doing?"

Sid stared out the kitchen window. He was sporting a day's worth of stubble and had bags under his eyes. "Tired. Good, I guess, considering that I almost lost my wife. I think about that when she gets in one of her moods. It's hard juggling the kids and her while trying to make my shift at the plant. They've been pretty understanding at work, but with the econ-omy so tight I don't want to be gone too long."

"What's going on with the Wishbone? Mary said it's only open a couple of days a week."

"Lindsey doesn't want to go back to the Wishbone. Business has dropped because the girls can't make all the shifts and Lindsey's not there to figure everything out. You know me—I've got two left thumbs in the kitchen. I can figure out the books, but it was Lindsey who took care of everything. Lately she's been talking about just letting it go. She just doesn't seem to care anymore."

"Is it the medication?" She got up and helped him unload the grocery bags. Mostly soups and instant meals, she noticed.

"I don't think so. She's got some depression and anger issues, but she won't admit it. Her cardiologist wants her to do some cardiac rehabilitation, but Lindsey refuses. There's the drive, which she hates, plus she thinks it's all a load of crap. They talk about positive lifestyle changes: exercise, education, nutritional guidance. She won't have any of it." His voice was strained as he read the directions on a box of macaroni and cheese. "Shoot. I forgot to get more milk."

Deidre touched his shoulder. "If you don't have anything specific planned for dinner, let me help. I'd love to cook for you all tonight." She was fairly certain that she could put together a jambalaya or something a little more hearty.

Sid shook his head as he rummaged for a saucepan. "Deidre, that's really nice of you, but I don't want to put you out. Plus Lindsey will probably get on me later about it. She doesn't want anybody's help; she won't even let me tell people what happened. It'll just be easier if I take care of it." Worry lines were furrowed deeply into his forehead. "I just . . . I just wish she'd snap out of it. They said depression is not uncommon for the first couple of weeks, but if it goes beyond four weeks, it's serious. It also increases her chances for another heart attack. And with the bills and mortgage and the note on the Wishbone . . ." Sid hung his head. "I'm scared we're going to lose everything."

Deidre cast a long glance toward Lindsey's bedroom. It only took her a moment to make up her mind. "Well, if I can't be of service here, then I think I'd better head to the Wishbone."

"The Wishbone?"

Deidre nodded, determined. She gave Sid a tight hug. "I'm going to take Lindsey's place until you can find someone suitable to take over."

From her bedroom, Lindsey could hear her husband and Deidre murmuring, their voices low. She knew they were talking about her. Well, no surprise there. The lady with the heart attack would always be an interesting subject for conversation, so much better than the weather or latest movie. *What happened? What did the doctor say? What were the causes? Did you have any symptoms? But you're so healthy!*

She might as well get used to it.

Lindsey turned to stare at herself in the mirror hanging above their dresser. She'd lost weight, those damn ten pounds she'd been battling for the past decade and a half. If she'd had a crystal ball, she could've saved herself the trouble of all those Weight Watchers meetings out in Pullman. She could've spent more time playing with her kids or learning to take up knitting instead.

Could've, would've, should've.

There was the sound of the front door opening and closing, and then Deidre's car crunching out of the gravel driveway.

Lindsey was surprised; she hadn't thought Deidre would give up so easily. Then again, what did she expect? Lindsey remembered what it was like when her mother had been diagnosed with cancer. The neighbors had offered their support in the beginning, and then disappeared into the woodwork. Once her mother became terminal, it was as if she'd had no friends left. People acted strange and awkward, unsure of what to say in the presence of someone sick and dying.

She thought about all the tests and cancer screenings she'd gone through over the years. What a complete waste of time. What had been the point if she was going to have a heart attack in the end?

Deidre had her glamorous life, her knight in shining armor, a career, and a future to look forward to. She was still a young thing, forty or forty-one. Either way, she was younger than Lindsey. Lindsey, with her stretch marks and her graying hair. Lindsey, with her beat-up old '83 Durango and rusty Ford pickup that had cardboard and duct tape serving as one of the windows. Lindsey, who hadn't bought any new clothes for herself in ages.

They were only a few years away from paying off the house and the note to the Wishbone. But now a few more years of hard work felt like a lifetime. Sid wanted to put an addition on the house to give them a little more room, but that would take both time and money. The thought of taking on new debt or having to scrimp and save any more made Lindsey want to give up altogether. She hadn't felt that way before, but then she hadn't had a heart attack before.

She knew that there were people who, after a brush with death, developed a new outlook on life. The nurse at the hospital, a heart attack survivor herself, told Lindsey about lists she used to make. Lists about what she was grateful for, lists of her accomplishments, lists of things she still wanted to do in life. One of her lifelong dreams was to write a novel, and she was taking a writing class at the community college. The nurse had also been recently been certified to scuba dive and was saving for a trip to someplace in Australia that had good diving.

Lindsey had listened politely, but she'd hoped the nurse had other rounds to make and would be on her way soon. Lindsey had no interest in lists or writing or learning how to scuba. All she really wanted was to be left alone.

She knew Sid and the kids were worried but, frankly, they were all old enough to figure things out for themselves. She'd done her job, raising her kids and homeschooling them, giving them the tools they needed to make it in this world. They were good kids, and they'd make good lives for themselves. She wasn't worried about them. They would be able to find a way to make things work, with or without her.

And Sid. Well, if anything were to happen to her, another heart attack or cancer like her mother, there was always the small pittance of life insurance from the credit union. It wasn't much, but it would tide Sid over until he could figure out what to do next.

Lindsey looked at her hands, at the dirt caked under her nails. Before the heart attack, she had been meticulous about keeping her nails clean and short—it made her job in the kitchen all that much easier. She thought for a moment of the Wishbone, of her stacks of scuffed, stainless steel bowls, of the dishwasher that needed to be replaced, of the cash register that had taken her a month to master. Her once-coveted walk-in cooler unit now felt like a waste of electricity. The Wishbone was open intermittently, and the girls were doing their best to keep things afloat. She was tempted to tell them to let it go and get on with their lives. It was Lindsey's kitchen and Lindsey's problem, not theirs. If anyone should be there, it should be her.

Except that being in the kitchen was the last place Lindsey wanted to be.

CHAPTER NINE

Manners are the happy way of doing things,
each one a stroke of genius or of love.
—Ralph Waldo Emerson

I really miss you," Kevin said later that evening. It was the first time they had spoken since he'd left for London, and hearing his voice comforted her. "The Chelsea Flower Show is going on right now. You'd love it. I wish you were here."

"Me, too," Deidre murmured. Kevin was always asking her to join him on his travels. When they first started dating it seemed like the perfect opportunity for her to finally see the world. But within a matter of weeks her own schedule filled up with demands from *Seattle Revealed* and then Sweet Deidre, making such trips out of the question. "But I'm also glad I can be here for Lindsey and Sid."

There was a long pause on the other end of the phone. "Tell me again how this is going to work?" he asked, his voice a mix of compassion and concern. "You aren't serious about this, are you?"

Deidre held the phone against her ear and sighed, tucking

her legs under her as she curled up on the couch. She was at Kevin's place on Lake Wish, having just dragged herself through the door. A fire would have been nice to stave off the chill in the air and warm up the house, but it was late and Deidre was too tired to move.

She'd gone from Lindsey's house straight to the Wishbone. It was a busy night for the small town, and the last diner had left at 9:30 p.m. Then there was the cleaning, the cashing out, the prepping for the next day. Lindsey was orderly, so everything was easy to find, but Deidre had never really worked a restaurant on her own, much less run one.

Hannah and Mary had been relieved to see Deidre and were helpful in showing her the ropes. It didn't take long for Deidre to see where corners had been cut to accommodate Lindsey's absence. No more daily specials; the daily cash receipts were not quite matching what was left in the register; food was going to waste due to poor preparation or mistakes. There was a standing order with a food service company that needed to be cancelled or at least revised, and they were running out of cleaning products. The fresh greens had wilted and meat had spoiled and gone bad. The dishwasher was making funny sounds and would probably need to be replaced.

"Ummm . . ." she started hesitantly.

"Deidre, you can't stay in Jacob's Point and run the Wishbone. Who knows how long it will take for Lindsey to assume her responsibilities there? I know you want to be a good friend and help her out, but I'm not so sure this is the best way."

She knew he was right, but she couldn't leave with things being the way they were.

"I know, Kevin, but what do you suggest? Nobody in town can do what Lindsey does. And it's not just about the

Wishbone. If you saw Lindsey, you wouldn't recognize her. She's not being rational. She's distancing herself from everyone, even her family." Deidre took a deep breath. "I'm really worried about Sid. He's running ragged, trying to keep all the balls in the air. They have bills to pay and I just don't think he can pull it off. And the kids—they're scared. They don't know who she is anymore. She doesn't hug them, doesn't encourage them—she's completely indifferent. Lindsey needs follow-up care and treatment, but she's refusing."

There was a long silence. Finally Kevin said softly, "Deidre, I'm sorry to hear that. But it's not your responsibility to make sure Lindsey gets the care she needs. She's a grown woman, and you have to honor her decisions. In the meantime, I'll have my secretary draft a letter to the Millers, letting them know that they don't need to make any payments until the Wishbone is up and running full-time again. Other than that, I'm not sure what else we can do."

Kevin had bailed out Sid and Lindsey when the bank had foreclosed on the Wishbone years ago. He now held the note to the Wishbone but it was more a gesture of support for the community. His lake house had a professional kitchen but he didn't care to use it. Eating at the Wishbone was much easier, plus he liked the people, so saving the Wishbone was as much for himself as it was for Lindsey and the rest of the town.

Deidre stared at the window overlooking Lake Wish, the water as still as glass in the moonlight. "That will be a big help, Kevin, but I don't know if that's enough. Right before I left the house, she was talking about letting the Wishbone go altogether. I can't tell if she's serious or not, but she doesn't seem to have any interest in it anymore."

"Well, if that's the case, then I definitely don't think you should stay down there," Kevin said firmly. "Days will grow into weeks, and your focus needs to be on Sweet Deidre and getting your product ready for market."

Deidre bit her lip. She still hadn't told him about her conversation with Manuela. "Um, about Sweet Deidre . . ."

"Oh, I wanted to tell you that I met a guy last night who used to run Cadbury's. I told him what you were doing, and he was intrigued. He has a consulting firm, and I know he'd love to talk with you after Sweet Deidre gets off the ground." Kevin's voice softened. "I'm just so proud of you, sweetheart. I hope you know that."

Deidre cringed. Well, that cinched it. There was no way she was going to tell him the truth now. Not only would he be disappointed, but he'd probably think she was out of her mind for staying in Jacob's Point when she clearly had her own issues to deal with.

"It's not just the Wishbone," she said, steering the conversation back to Lindsey. "Sid needs help getting Lindsey to go to her cardiac rehabilitation sessions. Right now, every second counts—the longer this drags on, the worse it is for Lindsey."

Kevin didn't sound convinced. "And you're the only person who can do this?"

Deidre knew that Lindsey had a younger sister who lived in Puyallup, a couple of hours away. Deidre had never met her—she didn't even know her name, come to think of it— but Lindsey had mentioned on more than one occasion that they weren't very close. Her sister was what Lindsey called "an artsy type," unable to hold down a steady job and constantly asking Lindsey for money, yet rarely showing any interest in Lindsey's life. Deidre suspected that Lindsey's sister probably wouldn't have much luck getting Lindsey to do anything. "Not the only one, but the best one, next to Sid."

Kevin let out a sigh. "Well, do whatever you think is best, Deidre. I'll be back next week and if there's anything I can do to help, I'll do it."

"Do you still remember how to bus tables?" Deidre asked jokingly. Kevin had helped out at the Wishbone one night last Christmas season. It was the first time he'd ever worked in a restaurant.

Kevin didn't laugh. "If it comes to that, then we're *really* in trouble. Get some rest, Deidre, and we'll talk tomorrow. I'll be catching the train to Amsterdam in the morning, so I'll call you before I go to sleep. I love you."

Deidre smiled at the tenderness in his voice. Her relationship was fine; she had nothing to worry about. "I love you, too, Kevin."

She hung up the phone and looked at the clock. It read half past midnight. Deidre had optimistically told the girls that she would be in at daybreak to open the Wishbone and greet the breakfast crowd. What had she been thinking?

Deidre climbed the stairs to the second floor, slipped out of her clothes and into one of Kevin's old T-shirts and sweatpants. The bed beckoned, and she crawled in between the silky comforter and featherbed. Within seconds she was asleep.

The next couple of days were a blur. In between breakfast, lunch, and dinner at the Wishbone, Deidre was on her laptop, frantically trying to figure out how to save Sweet Deidre. She'd take a basic cookie recipe and then add something—dried fruit or something more adventurous, like a shot of espresso or pralines—only to realize that she'd veered from the directives in the damn binder Manuela had given her. They were concerned about an expensive cookie and didn't want to take a risk with something new or unfamiliar.

But nothing seemed to work. Deidre didn't know how to put a line together that would achieve Manuela's objectives of being value-based while remaining familiar yet distinct enough to stand out in the marketplace. It sounded easy enough, but Deidre knew that very few brands did it with great success, if any. You were either on one end of the spectrum or the other. So Deidre would scrap whatever she was working on and go back to the drawing board, her inspiration waning, until it was time to turn her attention back to the Wishbone or Lindsey.

Manuela often called several times a day, hoping to catch Deidre in a moment of brilliance while not so subtly reminding her that the deadline was looming.

"Frank is chomping at the bit," she said by way of motivation. "I think he's already talked to some of our confectionary producers and planned out a line of holiday truffles."

Great, no pressure. "Manuela, I'm working as hard as I can to come up with a successful redesign," Deidre replied in what she hoped was a convincing manner. "I still have a week, and I'll be working every minute until then." *But,* she added to herself as she cast an eye around the busy diner, *not exactly on Sweet Deidre.*

The girls were revived and excited to have Deidre running the show at the Wishbone, but no one else had stepped up to take over, including Lindsey. Deidre was going to the Millers' house in the early evenings, right before the dinner rush, her arms full of food and chattering about whatever local gossip she'd acquired during the day. She made it sound as if they were having a ball at the Wishbone—"Janet Everett adopted a retired service parrot named César who can tell the difference between decaf and regular!"—hoping that Lindsey would feel that she was missing out. But Lindsey didn't bite, just poked listlessly through her food, her eyes blank and uninterested. She was still refusing to go to her rehabilitation classes or to any follow-up appointments with her cardiologist.

"Lindsey, you've got to help me out here," Deidre pleaded a couple of days later. She could see that her friend was slipping deeper and deeper into a fog of resentment and bitterness. Deidre had been in Jacob's Point for almost a week and was starting to feel that Kevin was right—maybe this was more than Deidre was able to handle. Lindsey needed professional help, medication even, but it was clear that she wasn't going to budge without a fight.

Deidre was helping Lindsey sort a pile of dirty laundry, separating the darks from the lights. Lindsey's movements were slow and lethargic—a far cry from the efficient woman Deidre remembered.

Lindsey gave a grunt. "Deidre, it was your idea to stay, not mine. Quite frankly, I'm not really sure why you're still here. Don't you have a shiny life back in Seattle to get back to?" She punched a button on the panel of the washing machine a little harder than was necessary.

Deidre struggled to contain her frustration. "I'm here because I want to help you, Lindsey." She noticed a ring around Sid's collar and picked up the spray bottle of stain remover.

"Funny. I don't remember asking for your help." She plucked the spray bottle from Deidre. "I've got that."

Deidre grabbed it back and quickly sprayed the collar before

Lindsey could do anything. "Well, you've got my help, like it or not. But you're right. I do have a life I need to get back to." Since that first day, Deidre hadn't said anything more about Sweet Deidre, about what was on the line this time.

Lindsey wasn't fazed. "So go. Who's stopping you?"

"Lindsey, if being belligerent toward me helps, then by all means, go for it. But you've got your family tiptoeing around you, a diner that needs some direction . . ."

Lindsey reached for a box of laundry detergent. "There's always something, isn't there? *I am tired of working so damn hard all of the time, Deidre.* Did you know that Doc Hensen told me last year that my knees were going out?" Doc Hensen was the local GP of Jacob's Point. "My knees! I have a bottle of glucosamine the size of a trash can sitting in my kitchen. And do you think I like yelling at Sid and my kids all of the time? I hate it! But why does everything have to ride on me? The house, the kids, the diner?" She angrily shook some detergent into a measuring cup and poured it into the washer.

"It hasn't been that long since your heart attack, Lindsey. You just need some more time."

"For what, Deidre? To get my strength back so I can run myself into the ground again? No, thank you." The washer had filled with water and was starting to agitate.

"What are you saying?"

Lindsey turned away from Deidre, closing the lid with a bang. "I'm saying that I've decided to put the Wishbone up for sale. I'm done."

Sid arrived at the Wishbone the next morning looking tired and fatigued as he placed a FOR SALE sign in the window of the diner. Deidre was silent as she watched him center it carefully and apply tape to the window. He was about to leave when Deidre pointed to an empty booth.

"Sit," she instructed, though she kept her voice kind. While Sid was a coffee man, Deidre thought that if he had any more caffeine, it would probably put his system into shock. She opted to make him a cup of peppermint tea instead. She put an order in for an egg white omelet with bell peppers and a side of turkey bacon. He needed to keep up his strength.

"I can only stay a minute." Sid slipped his cap off of his head and sat down.

Deidre looked at the back of the sign. "So you're definitely going to sell the Wishbone."

He nodded, his voice low. "Lindsey's not budging, and we all know you can't keep doing this forever. If we can sell the business, we can hopefully have enough to pay what we owe Kevin. If we can even sell it, that is."

Deidre didn't know what to say. It would be hard to find someone interested in buying the business, much less someone who would be willing to pay much for it. While the Wishbone was the only game in town, it was popular in large part because of Lindsey.

Mary brought out Sid's order, and Deidre sat with him in silence as he ate quickly, almost as if he were starving.

"Maybe we should see if Doc Hensen will have better luck than you or me in getting her to go to those rehabilitation sessions," Deidre said. Doc Hensen was a regular at the Wishbone.

Sid shook his head. "We already tried that. She won't even let him come into the house. He stood on our lawn the other day, calling to her to let him in, and she wouldn't do it. Lindsey's got her pride, and it's been hard for her, having to rely so much on me and the kids. Having you here is driving her crazy—she can't stand the thought of you putting your life on hold to help her out."

"I know, I know. She's just a stubborn . . ." Deidre stopped. "Wait. It drives her crazy, you say?"

Sid nodded as he wiped his mouth. "It's all she talks about. She'd give just about anything not to be indebted to you or anybody else."

Deidre didn't know why she didn't think about this before. She found herself grinning. Sid knit his eyebrows and looked at her warily.

Deidre gave him a reassuring pat on the shoulder. "I think I know how to get her to see her doctor."

"How?"

"Don't worry, I have it under control. It's a bit of a long shot, but it's all we've got. I'll see you later tonight."

That evening, Deidre went to the Millers' house as usual. This time, however, Deidre didn't force a happy, cheerful face. She didn't bother to touch up her makeup, either, and even went so far as to muss her hair before getting out of the car. Then, to get herself into the mood, she heaved an elaborate sigh and dragged herself up the walk to the front door.

Brandon opened the door, a smile on his face as Deidre gave him a quick wink and handed him a chocolate chunk cookie. As he stepped aside to let her pass, she donned her gloomy face again and plodded into the kitchen, where Lindsey was sitting morosely at the table.

"Hey, Lindsey," Deidre said. She let out another sigh and began unloading the bag. She readied herself for the usual protest, which she knew was done half-heartedly seeing how the table was already set, awaiting Deidre's arrival.

Lindsey began, "Deidre, I've told you before. You don't have to come by with all this food and—"

"What?" Deidre interrupted her, a distracted look on her face. "Oh, well, it's not much this time." She peered into the bag, pulling out containers and opening them. "Huh. What's this?"

Even Lindsey couldn't hide her curiosity as Deidre frowned and pushed the containers toward Lindsey. Inside were slices and slices of day-old bread, almost twelve containers in all.

"Strange," Deidre said. "I was going to do a cheese and onion soufflé tomorrow with this. I must have left your dinner at the Wishbone. Sorry." She let out a melodramatic sigh. "I just can't keep anything straight anymore."

"Deidre, look. You've already done so much and we appreciate it, we really do. But you've got a life and a business to run. We all just need to let the Wishbone go and get on with our lives."

"No, no." Deidre shook her head adamantly. "I'm here for you, Lindsey. I know you'd do the same for me. Who cares if Sweet Deidre isn't going to happen anymore?"

For the first time, Deidre saw genuine emotion cross Lindsey's face. She looked horrified. "What?"

Deidre waved it off, her face washed in defeat. She gazed out the window, listless. "The focus groups didn't like the new line of cookies, *again*, so JCC is giving me one last chance before they pull the plug on Sweet Deidre. I have to come up with something *completely new* by next week, but I haven't had any time to figure it out."

Lindsey pursed her lips.

"But don't worry about it. You were here for me last year when I needed someone, and I want to be here for you,

Lindsey. That's what matters most, right?" Deidre reached over and gave her friend's hand a mechanical pat before wearily bringing her fingers to her temples. Then she stood up and began to move the containers to the kitchen counter. "Let me see what I can do with this. Do you have any tomato soup?"

Lindsey got up and moved in front of Deidre. "Stop," she said. "You've done enough. I'll take care of dinner. You go get some rest."

"Oh, I've got to get back to the Wishbone." Another sigh.

"Deidre, you've got to go back to Seattle. We both know this. The Wishbone is my responsibility, and I've decided to sell it. There's no point in you staying. You need to go. I just wish . . ." Lindsey looked out her kitchen window. "I just wish there was something I could do to thank you for all you've done."

Deidre hesitated. "Well, there is something . . ." she said, feigning reluctance.

"What? Tell me."

Deidre turned, a determined look on her face as she put her hands on her hips. "I want you to see your cardiologist, and then I want you to start going to those rehabilitations sessions." Her voice was firm.

The initial look of shock on Lindsey's face made Deidre wonder if she'd gone too far. Maybe Lindsey really wasn't ready and needed more time. But then she saw the beginning of a smirk. That was a good sign—Deidre hadn't seen a Lindsey smirk since she'd been back at Jacob's Point.

"Why do I feel like I was just duped?" Lindsey muttered.

Deidre gave a shrug. "I don't know, but I'm not leaving Jacob's Point until you promise. I'll slug it out for however long is necessary, even if it means losing Sweet Deidre." *Not that it would take much at this point anyway*, she thought in a brief moment of despondency. Either way, she hoped Lindsey wouldn't call her bluff.

"Deidre . . ."

"I should probably get back to the Wishbone. We can talk later—I'm not planning on going anywhere for a while."

Lindsey let out a long exhale. "Fine. You win." She got up and moved to the oven, turning the knob 375° F. She filled a large stockpot with water and set it on the stove to boil. She washed her hands then slowly pulled a knife from the knife block. She chewed on her lip.

Deidre watched her guardedly. What was Lindsey up to? Chopped Deidre for dinner, with a side salad and day-old bread?

Lindsey didn't say anything, but after a moment she started to cut the crusts off the bread. She fished out a ceramic bowl and started lining the bottom and sides with the bread.

"Fine," she said again. "If that's what it's going to take to get you to leave, then fine."

Deidre stood up, triumphant, but quickly erased any sign of gloating when Lindsey glared at her. "Lindsey, I'm proud of you. It takes guts to get rid of the likes of me."

"Yeah. Go figure." Lindsey pulled out a box of spaghetti, then went to the freezer for a bag of frozen peas.

"I'll let Sid know of your decision so he can get you in this week to see your cardiologist. And, not that I don't trust you, but I will be driving back down to Jacob's Point to take you to your first cardiac rehabilitation session the day after tomorrow."

Lindsey ferociously clutched a yellow onion. Deidre got up and gently eased it out of her hands. "It won't be so bad,

Lindsey. Try it just once, that's all I ask. If they're a bunch of dopes, you don't have to go back."

Lindsey didn't say anything, but finally gave an imperceptible nod.

Deidre pulled the wooden cutting board toward her. "Now, let me guess: we're doing a pasta bake. Should I finely chop the onions? What else do you need?"

"Get one of those big cans of chopped tomatoes from the pantry." The water was boiling now. Lindsey added the spaghetti.

Deidre wanted to give Lindsey a big hug but decided not to push her luck. Lindsey had agreed to have follow-up care, she was cooking again, and Deidre was finally on her way back to Seattle.

THE SEATTLE SCOOP

IT'S BAKE OR BREAK FOR DEIDRE MCINTOSH
A *Seattle Scoop* Exclusive! By Rosemary Goodwin

Does anyone know where Deidre McIntosh is?

Things have been quiet the past few days at the Sweet Deidre HQ in the Jamison Cookies and Confections building. No one has seen Deidre or her car in the company parking lot for days, prompting industry insiders to speculate if the cookie line is in more trouble than the company is letting on. The company "declined comment," which is another way of saying that Deidre's branded cookie line may be on its last legs.

Log on to our blog and tell us what you think!

CHAPTER TEN

A good mirror is your best friend.
—Peggy Post, *Emily Post's Etiquette*

Ms. Banks! What a pleasure to see you again!" The manager of the exclusive fine jewelry boutique looked ecstatic upon seeing Marla sweep into the store. Her family had been using them for years, but Marla tended to favor the flashier New York jewelry houses. Still, she felt a certain obligation to give them some business, and knew they would be quick to accommodate her, which was always a good thing.

Marla drew a blank and glanced at her assistant, Tommy, who silently mouthed, "Mr. Leroy Grotsam."

"Leroy! The feeling is mutual, of course." Marla gave him a tight smile as she offered her hand. "We're here to have Fred Astaire fitted for another collar. The last one had such small diamonds it almost looked like costume jewelry."

Leroy looked horrified. "Well, we can't have that!" He practically fanned himself.

"No, we absolutely cannot." Marla settled herself on a

settee and handed Fred Astaire to Tommy. One of the sales assistants brought Marla a flute of champagne and she settled back comfortably. "Now, I was thinking of having you design something exclusive for Fred Astaire. His coat is lovely but it's thick, and I want something that's really eye-catching." No point in adorning a dog with diamonds if no one could see them.

Leroy was nodding fervently. "Yes, yes. That is not a problem at all. We have a new designer working on some in-house projects right now. We just spirited him away from Harry Winston." Leroy looked positively gleeful.

Marla gave him a bored once-over. "I know."

Everybody knew. It had been in all the papers and the entire northwest socialite scene had been clamoring for a chance to work with him. Marla knew there was a waiting list over a year long, but her family's long history with the Seattle luxury jeweler meant that she would always be accommodated.

"I'll have him come out in a moment. He is working on a very special piece right now. For your brother Kevin, actually." Leroy looked pleased.

"Kevin?" Marla frowned.

"Yes. He brought in a diamond. Said it was your mother's? A family heirloom?"

Marla narrowed her eyes and handed her champagne flute to the nearest person. "What? When?"

Leroy suddenly looked nervous. "Um, I'm not sure . . ." he tried to backpedal.

"Let me see the diamond," she demanded, fixing Leroy with one of her looks.

Leroy paled as he nodded to an assistant. "Well, technically your brother brought it in, but I suppose it wouldn't hurt if you wanted to take a look. You understand, I'm usually very discreet when it comes to . . ."

Marla held up a hand, silencing him. "Just get the diamond." She walked toward one of the display cases and sat down, drumming her nails impatiently on the glass.

The assistant emerged a moment later with a black velvet box. Leroy took it from her and carefully opened it for Marla's inspection.

Marla caught her breath. Sure enough, it was the diamond from Beverly Johnson's original wedding ring, a beautiful but modest princess-cut diamond handed down from Edward's side of the family. Marla felt a familiar pang as she touched the diamond, remembering how she used to sneak it from her mother's jewelry box when she was a child and dreamily slip it on her finger.

"What did he ask you to do?" Marla asked.

Leroy hesitated but Marla gave him another look. "To resize the band and restore the diamond in its original setting."

Marla didn't like the sound of that. "Did he say why?"

Leroy shook his head.

"When is he supposed to pick it up?"

Leroy hesitated again. This time Marla forced a sweet smile. "Leroy, this is family. Kevin is my brother. He's traveling in Europe and would expect no less from me if I didn't make myself available to help him out."

Leroy checked the tag hanging from the box. "In one week," he answered unhappily.

Marla knew her brother was scheduled to return in a couple of days. What was he thinking? Surely not . . . No. He'd be insane. *Insane.* No one was deserving of that ring, and Marla sure as hell wasn't going to let it go to someone who didn't think twice about wearing the same outfit repeatedly.

Clearly she would need to significantly step up her efforts to get Deidre out of Kevin's life. Marla was through playing games. Yes, she'd had some devilish fun sabotaging the ball gown she'd lent to Deidre. Marla had deliberately selected dresses that she knew would be too small for Deidre, leaving only one rather snug option. She hadn't actually seen the seam split on the Mastroianni gown, but Sabine had told her afterward that it had been priceless. Marla wasn't completely thoughtless—she instructed her tailor to allow for no more than a half a foot of the seam to split, even having him reinforce the stitching to make sure it didn't accidentally go beyond that. Marla just wanted Deidre to be humiliated enough to opt out of the relationship with Kevin on her own.

But that wasn't happening, and it was time to take things to the next level. Marla may not have gone to college, but she was known for thinking fast on her feet. It took her all of five minutes before she knew what she was going to do. She flipped open her cell phone.

Ten minutes later, Marla closed her phone with a satisfied snap, a confident smile on her face.

It was too easy.

Marla's driver drove up the cobbled driveway leading to Marla's house. With over eight thousand square feet of living area, it was more a mansion than a house, boasting twin marble balustrade staircases, a home theater, and a generous infinity pool that overlooked the grounds. Marla wasn't much of a swimmer, but her guests sometimes enjoyed it, and you couldn't have a respectable house without a pool these days. She wasn't much for plants or flowers, either, but there was a conservatory as well. Marla liked to entertain in there, particularly during the winter months when it was cold and wet. She had a small grounds staff that maintained the five-acre property, and she let her house manager, Stanton Gray, tend to those details. She really couldn't be bothered.

The interior of the house, however, was Marla's domain. She'd decorated it herself—not doing the actual work, of course, but she'd spent countless hours with her interior designer. Antique furniture with hand-painted accents, Persian knotted-wool rugs, expensive art adorning the walls. She had ornate crystal and gilt bronze chandeliers from Italy, intricate Georgian moldings from Craigavon in Northern Ireland. Each room had its own personality, an eclectic style that was entirely Marla's own. It was one reason *At Home with Marla Banks* was so popular—her viewers loved her somewhat outrageous sense of style and fashion.

"Are you expecting anyone, Ms. Banks?" Her driver glanced in the rearview mirror, eyebrows raised.

Marla looked up from her compact where she was studying a wrinkle and frowned at the sight of an unfamiliar silver Lexus parked in her driveway. She wasn't expecting anyone, and Stanton knew better than to let an unexpected visitor park out front.

She didn't wait for her driver to come around and open her door. She was marching up the steps, Fred Astaire tucked under her arm, when the front door opened and Wedge stepped out.

"What are *you* doing here?" she asked. She turned to look at the Lexus, her eyes narrowing. "Where's your Bentley?"

"Oh, I got rid of it," was Wedge's offhanded reply. "I thought it was time to simplify, so I sold it. The Bugatti and the Mercedes, too. I gave the proceeds to the Swedish Medical Center for a new HD MRI machine. I got myself the Lexus hybrid instead. Better for the environment."

Here we go. Marla handed her purse and Fred Astaire to Stanton. She glanced again at the car parked outside. It wasn't much of a head turner. "It looks like an old person's car," she sniffed.

Wedge tilted his head as he considered his car. "You think?" he asked, not looking particularly concerned one way or the other. "Well, I guess I'm an old person, so that wouldn't be too far off base." He gave a good-natured chuckle.

Marla glowered. He was the same age as she was, and she was most definitely *not* an old person.

"It's a nice car, though," Wedge continued. "Handles well. I thought maybe you might like to go for a ride."

Marla's eyes looked at him with disdain. "Go for a ride?" He had to be joking.

"Sure. You can even drive." He held out the car keys, the tags from the dealership still on them.

Why would she want to go for a drive, much less be behind the wheel? Marla couldn't even remember the last time she'd driven herself anywhere. "I'm afraid I have a prior engagement, Wedge." She headed into the living room, hoping he'd take the hint and go away.

Wedge followed her, unperturbed. "When?"

"Now." She went to the satinwood Carlton writing desk in the corner of the room and picked up a stack of mail. She rifled through it, putting a few aside and the rest in the trash. She sensed Wedge standing behind her and made a point of turning her back on him.

Wedge gave an appreciative whistle. "Nice mounts," he said.

Marla's cheeks pinked as she spun around. "What did you say?" she demanded.

"I said, nice mounts." Wedge came over to the desk, running his hand along the smooth curves and acanthus leaf carving. "Are they silver plated?"

It took Marla a moment before she realized that he was talking about the damn desk. "I don't know," she replied flippantly. "I picked it up at a Sotheby's auction last year."

He took in the oval panel doors and the short drawers, his eyes lingering on the tooled leather writing surface. "It's a gorgeous piece. Very inspiring."

Marla gave a careless shrug. "It holds the mail."

"This is a formidable piece, Marla. Victorian, right? Late nineteenth century? It could do a lot more than hold the mail. This is one of the most impressive antique writing desks I've ever seen." He gave it one more appraising look. "You have excellent taste."

Despite herself, Marla felt herself soften at the compliment. She *did* have excellent taste; there was no question about that.

She singled out an envelope and slit it open with a letter opener. She pretended to read it while wondering why Wedge was still standing there.

This was partially her fault, she knew. You couldn't give a dog a treat without expecting it to come back for more, and Marla had seen more of Wedge in the past month than she had in three years. It was that damn K Ball that threw her off, her need to come up with a viable excuse to get Sabine closer to Kevin. Wedge had doted on her all evening, and the next day had a huge bouquet of wildflowers sent over to her house.

Wildflowers. *Really.*

"So where are you off to?" Wedge asked.

Marla didn't look up. "I have an errand." She sliced open two more envelopes. There was an invitation to a baby shower—*oh, please*—and some gibberish from a local women's group. Both went into the trash.

The look on his face was annoyingly earnest. "Well, I'm free. I can go with you."

God, he was persistent. Marla was ready to tell him no when it occurred to her that this could actually work out in her favor. It would definitely be better than going on her own.

The only downside was that she would have to put up with his company for another couple of hours. She stared at his beaming face and thought, *Oh, what the hell.* There were worse things.

"I need a few minutes to freshen up," she announced. "And then I'll be ready to go."

"Take your time," he assured her, and he seemed to mean it. He tossed his car keys in the air and gave a satisfied hum as he caught them. "I'll be waiting."

"Marla, Wedge. What a surprise." Deidre answered the door in jeans and a T-shirt, her hair pulled back in a ponytail. The quintessential all-American girl.

"I'd have called, but we were in the neighborhood and thought it would be a good time to pick up my dresses." At the blank look on Deidre's face, Marla explained. "From the K Ball? The ones I lent you? The one you ripped?" She tried to peer beyond Deidre's body to get a glimpse inside the condo.

"Oh, right. I'm so sorry about that, Marla. I thought you told me to donate them, so I did."

Marla didn't really care what happened to the gowns, she'd just needed an excuse to see Deidre. "Fine. Whatever. Darling, we're parched. Could we possibly get something to drink?"

"What? Oh." Deidre reluctantly stepped aside and Marla stepped in, pulling Wedge in behind her.

It was a small place, simply furnished. Unoriginal mass-produced furniture from Pottery Barn or Restoration Hardware. No real artwork to speak of, not until Marla spotted a framed photograph of Lake Wish hanging on the wall.

Uncle Harry had given Deidre McIntosh one of his photographs.

Wedge saw it, too, and strode forward to get a better look.

"What a stunning photograph," Wedge commented, peering close. "I wonder where this was taken. Canada, do you suppose?"

Marla pretended not to hear him. Deidre appeared with two glasses filled with ice and what Marla hoped was vodka. "No, it was taken right here in Washington, just a few hours southeast of Seattle," Deidre said. She handed them each a glass.

Marla grimaced when she took a sip. Water.

Wedge was nodding appreciatively. "Who's the photographer—?"

"So, you look like you're a busy bee," Marla interrupted, gesturing around her. Deidre's living room was scattered with paper and gift packaging. There were cookies cooling on racks.

"I just got back from a week in Jacob's Point and things have been kind of crazy." Deidre perched on the edge of her couch. She reached for a plate of cookies and held it out to them. "Orange dark chocolate chip. It's probably the fifth version I've come up with for . . ." Her voice trailed off. "Well, never mind. Would you like one?"

Before Marla could say no, Wedge stepped forward eagerly. "These look wonderful, Deidre." He took a bite and a look of delight crossed his face. He stared at the cookie in his hand. "Why, these are absolutely delicious, Deidre! Marla?" He nodded toward her, encouraging her to take one.

She should have followed her instincts and come on her own. She twisted a smile on her face and reluctantly took a cookie in an effort to seem amenable.

"Well, I have to say that you never cease to amaze me. You're just so . . . industrious. With all that you have to do, it must be a relief to have Kevin abroad. No distractions."

"He's the best kind of distraction," Deidre said affectionately, a small smile playing on her lips.

Yuck. Marla was really going to enjoy this.

Wedge reached for another cookie as he read through a Sweet Deidre brochure. Marla leaned in, as if to confide in Deidre. "Well, it *is* a shame that Kevin had to extend his trip by another week."

The startled look on Deidre's face was priceless. Marla could tell that Deidre was struggling to keep her cool. "Oh, I didn't . . . I haven't spoken to him since yesterday. When did this happen?"

"I have no idea." Marla feigned bewilderment. "I just know that he had to go to Paris to take care of some last-minute business for Daddy. Our family has quite a few holdings in France, as you probably know. Wedge, be a dear and get me some more water, will you?" She handed him her full glass and he looked at it, perplexed, but went into the kitchen anyway.

The disappointment on Deidre's face was so palpable that Marla almost felt sorry for her. "Oh. I see."

Marla clucked sympathetically. "I know. It's just *so* exhausting to be on the road, isn't it? Fortunately Paris is like a second home to him." She kept her eyes on Deidre as she added loftily, "And at least we know he'll be in good hands with Sabine."

Deidre stiffened. "Sabine?"

Marla nodded, adding fuel to what was surely a fire in the making. "She flew to Paris the other day. I know they're having dinner tonight at L'Ambroisie in Place des Vosges. I just hope that Sabine isn't making a nuisance of herself. She has that way about her, you know."

"What do you mean? What way?" Deidre asked. She was so transparent; Marla had to keep from grinning.

"Oh, it's old history," Marla said with a wave of her hand. "It's just . . . well, I remember when Sabine first set her sights on Kevin romantically. They'd always been friends, you understand, but she started to see him differently while he was dating a Jennifer something or other. A lovely girl; the two of you would have hit it off, Deidre. Gosh, now that I think of it, the two of you kind of look alike—how funny is that? Anyway, I suppose Sabine can get a little competitive, and when she sets her mind on something, well, look out! I was amazed. Impressed, even. It takes chutzpah to break up a relationship, and trust me, I should know. Five months later, they were engaged." Marla ended her anecdote by holding out her arms in front of her, studying the sleeves of her shirt critically. "I *am* getting tired of the three-quarter cuff. It's just so nineties, don't you think?"

Wedge returned with a fresh glass of water, which Marla waved away. She rose and headed to the door, beckoning

Wedge to follow her. "Well, we must run. Dinner plans. What are you going to be doing with yourself this week, now that Kevin is in Paris?"

"Um . . ." Deidre looked troubled, distracted. She gestured around her. "Just work. I have to drive back down to Jacob's Point to take a friend to a doctor's appointment tomorrow."

"Well, drive carefully!" Marla called, hurrying Wedge out the door. She closed the door behind them with a triumphant exhale. Mission accomplished.

"That was nice," Wedge commented as he took in the hand-painted welcome sign on Deidre's door. "So, where to next?"

Marla was checking her hair in the hallway mirror. "What?"

"You said we have dinner plans. Did you have any place particular in mind?"

Annoyed, she gave him an exasperated look. "Wedge Franklin, are you being dense or just persistent?"

"Is there a difference?" He gave her a knowing smile. "Come on, Marla. I know the owner at Canlis. We'll have a fabulous meal. Drinks, too."

If Marla had arrived in her own car, she would have turned on her heel and left. But she hadn't.

"Fine," she relented. "But it has to be quick. I have to be on the set of *At Home* tomorrow."

"No problem," Wedge said, a pleased look on his face. He offered his arm. "I'll call Mark and make sure we're in and out in no time."

She thought to remind him one more time that this wasn't a date, just dinner, but in the end she let it go. What would be the point? He wouldn't listen to her anyway. She reluctantly accepted his arm and they walked out of the building and into the late-afternoon sun.

CHAPTER ELEVEN

Etiquette enables us to face whatever the future may
bring with strength of character and integrity.
—Peggy Post, *Emily Post's Etiquette*

L eave it to Marla to be the bearer of bad news. God, she wasn't even subtle, not that subtlety was ever Marla's strong point.

Deidre was partially in shock when the doorman had called up to tell her that Marla was in the lobby. She might have bluffed her way out of it if Wedge hadn't been there, too. What choice did Deidre have but to invite them up?

She mulled over the visit, over the news that Kevin was extending his trip. Last-minute changes in his itinerary weren't that unusual, but Deidre just wished she'd heard it from Kevin instead of Marla. Funny that he hadn't told her or even hinted at the possibility when they talked last.

It's just business, she told herself as she washed the water glasses. But it was an odd coincidence that Sabine happened to be there, too. Very odd.

She told herself she wasn't being paranoid when she dialed

Kevin's number. Better to get to the bottom of it now than to suffer for the rest of the day, which she knew she would. If he was in France it was coming up on 3:00 a.m. She hated to wake him, but if she waited until the morning, he'd probably be in meetings. Time zones were quickly becoming her worst enemy.

Kevin answered the phone on the first ring, surprising her. "Hey, there." His voice sounded hollow and far-away. It was a bad connection.

Deidre warmed at the sound of his voice and suddenly felt silly for calling. "You're up late," she said. "Did I wake you?"

"No, but even if you did it wouldn't matter. You know you can call me anytime." There was some static or commotion—Deidre couldn't tell which. "Deidre, I was going to call you later to let you know that I've had to extend my trip by a few more days. I have to check on a few things for my father in Paris, and I figured it would be easier to just get it over with now rather than having to schedule another trip in the future."

That made sense. She definitely preferred that to having him fly off again in the near future. Kevin was practical about these things—she'd been worried about nothing.

"Well, just don't have too much fun without me," she joked.

"Are you kidding? This place is the dumps. Highly overrated."

Deidre doubted that. Paris was probably every bit as wonderful as the guidebooks made it out to be.

There was some fumbling in the background and then a muffled discussion on the other end of the line. She heard him say, "Tabby, just order the Dom Ruinart . . . No, the 1990 Blanc des Blancs . . . Fine, then order that. I really couldn't care less."

What the—? Deidre forced herself to stay calm even though she was on the verge of freaking out. "Oh, is Sabine with you?"

"What? Oh, well, yeah." Kevin sounded slightly annoyed. "Actually, those holdings of my father's that I'm checking up on are joint ventures with Tabby's family. Tabby's here on business, too, and has had a few mishaps, so we're meeting for a nightcap to see if I can help her come up with a solution or two."

Deidre felt the hairs on her neck stand up. This was all entirely too convenient. "It's kind of late, isn't it?"

"Well, you know Paris . . . the city that never sleeps."

No, she didn't know that, and she didn't like the sound of it, either. "Well, tell Sabine I say hi," Deidre said, feigning civility.

"Will do. Oh, wait, she wants to—"

"Deidre!" A laughing Sabine was suddenly on the line. "How *are* you?" she purred.

"Great!" Deidre forced herself to sound exuberant. "How are you?"

"Oh, work, work, and more work. Everything's *always* a crisis. *Thank God* I have Kevin here to keep me on the straight and narrow." Another gay laugh. "I should have never let him slip through my fingers!"

"Tabby . . ." Deidre heard Kevin's voice in the background.

Sabine ignored him. "Oh, she knows it's all in good fun. Right, Deidre? Listen, I'll be on the West Coast again in a month or so. Maybe we can all get together then."

Over my dead body, Deidre thought. Instead she lied and said, "Sure, that sounds great."

"We have to run. It's really a shame you couldn't be here, Deidre. Paris is fabulous. *So* romantic. Right, Kevin?"

Deidre made a noncommittal sound as Kevin came back on the line.

"Sorry," he apologized. "She's a little inebriated. It's how she manages her stress. How are things coming along with Sweet Deidre, by the way?"

Deidre coughed. "Oh. Well . . ." She hedged. She heard Sabine twittering in the background, and knew she couldn't tell him what had happened. "It's coming along great," she lied.

"I'm not worried," Kevin said. "After all, it's got your name on it."

As if she needed reminding.

Deidre tactfully switched the subject, asking about the weather, about Kevin's hotel, then filling him in on Lindsey and the Wishbone.

"She wants to sell?" Kevin asked.

"That's what she says. Sid put a FOR SALE sign up the day I left."

"Well, if Lindsey is serious about selling the Wishbone, I can see if there's potential buyer out there. It won't be easy, but you never know."

"No, Kevin, don't. She might change her mind later. I honestly don't think she wants to sell the Wishbone."

"I think putting up a FOR SALE sign is a pretty good indication that she does."

Deidre knew it didn't make sense. "Just . . . hold off, Kevin. Please?"

"Deidre, why do you assume that keeping the Wishbone is in her best interest? Letting it go may be one of the smartest things for her to do. Running a restaurant is hard work, sweetheart," he pointed out.

"I know, Kevin," she retorted. "I worked there all last week, remember?"

Kevin laughed. "One whole week? Deidre, multiply that fifty-two times, then by however many years you want. You think you're tired? This heart attack may have been a wake-up call for Sid and Lindsey."

"The person I saw up in Jacob's Point was *not* Lindsey," Deidre argued. "That person was moody, mean . . ."

"Deidre, that person *is* Lindsey," Kevin corrected. "It's the same Lindsey that you know, except that she's had a heart attack. Just because she's not back to her old ways may be uncomfortable for you, but she's still Lindsey."

Deidre felt a pang of despair. Maybe Kevin was right. She wished there was some way she could be sure of what Lindsey wanted.

Kevin's tone softened. "You have a good heart, Deidre, but you also have a good head on your shoulders. You need to use both, especially now." She heard Sabine trilling in the background. "I have to go see if I can help Tabby figure some things out. Call you later?"

"Sure," Deidre said, her voice tight. She hung up the phone, her stomach in knots.

She could just see Sabine playing the damsel in distress card, the one Deidre had refused to play. Why hadn't she told him the truth about Sweet Deidre? She could certainly use a drink and a solution or two as well.

Frustrated, she jammed some things into a bag. She had to leave first thing in the morning to pick up Lindsey in Jacob's Point and drive her to her rehabilitation class, then drive her back home before returning to Seattle. It would be a long day, with little if any time to work on Sweet Deidre.

Well, she still had the rest of the afternoon and all night, and she could cover a fair a bit of work if she powered through. Deidre remembered the days of all-nighters: in college, before a test; on the set of *Live Simple*, when they had to hastily improvise at the last minute. The aftermath was ugly, but it got the job done. Besides, she didn't have much choice. She needed to squeeze whatever brain power she had left to get as much done as possible, as quickly as possible.

She needed to be on the road by 7:30 a.m. That would give her a solid chunk of time, almost thirteen hours if she got back to work right now, no sleep, no interruptions. A pot of coffee, loads of chocolate, and she would be set.

Deidre's phone was ringing. Somewhere. Groggy, she lifted her head and looked around.

She was in her living room, having passed out from exhaustion at some point in the early hours of the morning. Her condo smelled of burnt coffee, and her laptop was still on, the power button blinking.

Deidre fumbled for her purse, emptying the contents onto the couch. No phone. She finally found it under a stack of papers and answered it, but she missed the call. She let out a yawn as she checked the display.

KEVIN JOHNSON

Deidre let her head fall back on the couch and gave a big stretch. So maybe she couldn't quite pull off an all-nighter like the old days. She didn't even remember falling asleep. Had she even gotten any work done?

She tapped some keys on her keyboard and the screen came up. Nope, not really. Several false starts, but nothing good. The recipes weren't anything to get excited about, and Deidre's eyes glazed over as she skimmed the possibilities. They fit the budget and tasted fine, but they were far from distinct, at least in Deidre's mind. If the focus groups ended up liking this line better than all the rest, then maybe Deidre wasn't cut out for this business after all.

She was about to hit the RETURN CALL button to ring Kevin back when she saw the time in the upper corner of the display screen. She squinted and the numbers came into focus.

Eight o'clock.

Eight o'clock! She was supposed to be en route to Jacob's Point by 7:30 a.m. Deidre hurriedly began packing up her laptop and shoving things back into her purse. She couldn't be late, not after the big lecture she'd given Lindsey. Lindsey had finally agreed to go, and Deidre had promised to take her.

She dialed Lindsey's number as she climbed into her car and started the engine.

Answering machine.

Deidre waited impatiently for the message to finish. "Lindsey, it's Deidre," she said, maneuvering out of her parking stall and heading out of the parking lot. "I'm on my way to Jacob's Point but I'm running a little late . . ."

Lindsey picked up the phone. "Well, don't hurry on my account. We can always go next time . . ."

"Nice try, Lindsey, but I'll still make it in enough time to get you to your session. Just be ready to go when I pull in."

"Deidre, I can have Sid drive me. You don't need to come all the way down from Seattle."

Deidre wasn't taking any chances, even though she was running on empty herself. "Forget it. I'm on my way, and you know it's a damn long drive, so you'd better be ready to go."

There was a sigh as Lindsey relented. "Fine," she muttered. "Do you know how to get to the hospital?"

"I'll use MapQuest. I have web and Internet access on my phone."

Lindsey snickered. "Of course you do."

Deidre ignored her friend. "Bye, Lindsey. I'll see you in a few hours."

While waiting for the light to change, Deidre picked up her phone and opened up her Internet connection. With one eye on the traffic light, she typed in the address for the hospital from Lindsey's house. With a sigh of relief, she saw that they would still make it in time, though just barely.

Now that she was finally on the road, Deidre took the opportunity to call Kevin back. He picked up right away.

"Hey, I called you earlier," he said.

"I know. I was late getting out the door to take Lindsey to her rehabilitation session. I'm on my way to Jacob's Point now."

"Deidre, don't overdo it," Kevin warned, a touch of concern in his voice.

"Oh, I'm not," she lied.

"Deidre . . ."

Deidre was looking in her rearview mirror, fixing her mascara, which had clumped her lashes together during the night. "I'm just taking it one step at a time," she said.

"Really?"

"Of course. You know me. Queen of Living Simple." Deidre rolled her eyes. She wasn't fooling anyone, least of all herself.

Still, Kevin sounded mollified. "Well, I'm glad to hear it. You know, I told Tabby that she should take a page from your book."

Sabine again. Deidre made a face. "What do you mean?"

"Oh, she's just got a crisis with one of her magazines. Typical Tabby stuff. She could use some live simple philosophy, if you ask me."

Right. Ha ha.

Kevin continued, "She's in line for an ulcer at the rate she's going. In fact, if you have any Deidre-isms handy, I'd be happy to share them with her."

How about "KEEP YOUR HANDS OFF MY BOYFRIEND" *for starters?* "Sorry, nothing comes to mind," Deidre said.

"Too bad. She's actually a little depressed." Kevin sounded sorry for her.

Sabine had seemed anything but depressed when Deidre heard her on the phone the night before. Deidre was suddenly filled with a sense of foreboding.

"Are you going to see her again?" Deidre asked. *Please say no.*

"I'm on my way to her place now, actually," Kevin said. "She invited some old friends of ours over, but she's feeling so low we might stay in and just catch up on old times."

Deidre didn't trust herself to say something kind, so she bit her tongue and said instead, "I should go. Crazy drivers on the road. You know how it is."

"Driving defensively, that's my girl. Call you later?"

"Of course."

She hung up the phone, feeling a shimmer of resentment. He was going to stay in with Sabine, Miss Social Calendar? What about all those times Deidre wanted to stay in, but had faithfully soldiered on to one event or another, wishing they could be at home instead?

Deidre knew this had to be one of Sabine's ploys to get Kevin back. She was certain of it. She trusted Kevin; she did. It was Sabine she didn't trust.

Deidre pulled onto the highway. There wasn't much traffic and Deidre eased into the far left lane.

She turned on the radio, but not finding a station she liked, flipped through her CDs before tossing them aside in disgust. She couldn't get her mind off of Sabine. She wished she knew more about her, had a better idea of what she was up against.

A thought occurred to her. Deidre pulled out her phone, opened up the Internet connection, and put Sabine's name in a Google search. She waited. And then Deidre's jaw dropped.

There were over one million hits for Sabine Durant.

One million hits.

Deidre set her cruise control and tried to think about other things. She was able to drive five minutes before grabbing her cell phone and looking at the Web page again.

It was incredible. There was seemingly endless coverage of Sabine's tabloid-worthy love life, including coverage of her engagement to Kevin. Deidre winced as she scrolled through images of the two of them together, keeping one eye on the road.

But there was more. News reports of Durant Media Group and Durant Magazines International. Of leveraged buyouts and aggressive takeovers. Of a powerful woman who was more than a mere celebutante. Of a woman with extreme sex appeal who wasn't afraid to use it to get what she wanted. Sabine Durant was a force in and of herself, a woman to be reckoned with.

Sabine was a deal maker, a deal breaker. She was fiscally responsible for millions of dollars. Despite her glamorous and oftentimes reckless social behavior, she was a savvy business-woman. She knew how to negotiate; she knew how to get what she wanted.

And Deidre couldn't even get a cookie line off the ground.

In a recent interview with *Fortune* magazine, Sabine was asked about whether she saw marriage in her future. "I almost got married once," she said. "And there are days I regret that I didn't go through with it. But I think I've matured a lot in the past ten years, and all I can say is, I believe in second chances."

Second chances? What did *that* mean?

Deidre felt a rise of panic. Despite what everyone was say-ing, if Sabine had set her sights on getting Kevin back, Deidre didn't stand a chance.

"Well, it's about time," Lindsey grumbled as Deidre burst through the door. She picked up her purse and jacket and then stopped to stare. "What happened to you?"

Deidre's eyes were red from crying. Between feeling like a fail-ure with Sweet Deidre and the thought of Sabine and Kevin together, Deidre had needed to stop several times just to pull herself together. "Bad day. Come on, let's go . . ."

"Whoa, Nelly." Lindsey planted her hands on her hips. "I'm not going anywhere with you in this condition. Come on, spill."

Deidre glanced at the clock on the wall. "Lindsey, we're going to be late."

"Then you'd better spill quickly."

Deidre sniffed and pulled out a wadded-up tissue from her pocket. Lindsey's nose wrinkled as she handed Deidre a fresh box of tissues. Deidre dabbed her eyes. "I'm going to sound petty and insecure, but I definitely think Sabine, Kevin's ex, is after him."

Lindsey wasn't impressed. "Yeah, and?"

"And what? What else do you need?"

Lindsey gave a snort. "You must have rocks in your head, Deidre McIntosh. Kevin Johnson is the catch of the century—of the millennium. Of course he's going to have women after him. Sheesh!" She marched out the door, leaving a stunned Deidre trailing behind her.

"Maybe, but you don't know this woman," Deidre said as they got into her car. "She's gorgeous, sexy, brilliant, and an old friend of the family's . . . Remember, they were once engaged."

Lindsey just sat in the passenger seat and stared out the window.

Deidre continued, "Not only that, but she was recently quoted in the press as saying that she wished she hadn't let him go, and that she believes in second chances. And, right now, *she's* in Paris with Kevin."

"Did he invite her?"

"No. She was supposedly there on business, but I don't believe that. I think she intentionally timed her trip to be there with him. But that's not the point."

"Well, what *is* the point? Surely you have better things to do with your time than worry about this. I know *I* have better things to do than listen to all this hoopla. This is worse than daytime TV." Lindsey crossed her arms and looked at Deidre stoically. "No offense."

"Well, I guess you would know," Deidre said, a little hurt. "Because that's all you do these days. Watch TV and lament about how sorry your life is."

"Well, then I guess I'm in good company, aren't I?"

"Lindsey, don't you think I have better things to do than have you attack me?"

Lindsey's cheeks pinked and her nostrils flared. "Excuse me, but I sure as heck didn't ask you to come down here!"

"Maybe I shouldn't have! I haven't slept in days, I haven't had breakfast, and with the price of gasoline these days, I probably could have bought a first-class ticket to France by now!" Deidre was yelling now.

"Well, don't let me stop you!" Lindsey yelled back.

"It's not you, it's *her*!" Deidre wildly punched a couple of buttons and thrust her cell phone in Lindsey's face. The screen was taken up completely by Sabine's nearly naked image from a *Maxim* photo shoot.

Lindsey squinted for a moment. "Hold on, I need to get my specs." She fumbled in her purse and then pulled out her reading glasses, holding them up for a better look. "Oh. Yeah. Damn, you are in trouble." She let out a low whistle.

Deidre stared at Lindsey, flabbergasted.

"How old is she? Twenty-five?" Lindsey took another close look.

"Thirty-six." Deidre's knuckles were white on the steering wheel.

"Huh." Lindsey frowned as she took a closer look at the

picture. "Well, she sure looks good for thirty-six. What's that she's wearing?"

"She's not wearing anything. That's a $10,000 vintage Hermès scarf that's barely covering her perfect body."

"Well, you'd think she could get a little more fabric for that kind of money." Lindsey removed her glasses and started cleaning the lenses.

Deidre threw her phone down in frustration. "So are we still competing for whose life sucks the most?"

"Oh, no question. Yours."

"What?"

"Yeah. I don't know *what* I was thinking, worried about a little thing like a heart attack, dying and leaving my family behind."

Deidre knew Lindsey was making fun of her now.

Lindsey held up her reading glasses, inspecting them in the light. "If that good man were to break your heart, I'm sure it would hurt like hell. I mean, I was in the hospital for days, pumped up on drugs and connected to monitors. But that's *nothing* compared to what you have going on. I mean, Lindsey Geraldine Miller, pull yourself together!" She gave herself a pretend knock on the head.

"Fine, Lindsey. I get your point. My life is great, yours sucks." She blinked back tears.

"I didn't say your life was great. But you have your youth, your health . . ."

"News flash, Lindsey: You do, too. You're still here, after all."

"Yeah. Big whoop." Lindsey grunted.

"Well, I hate to break it to you, but there is the other option, which is that you could be *dead*. You're the one who said that heart attacks are the number one killer of women, but it didn't manage to kill you. Doesn't that mean anything to you? It's like life gave you a second chance. You should be grateful!"

Deidre stopped mid-tirade, her own words echoing in her head. *A second chance.* Sabine and Kevin.

"I didn't ask for a second chance—*Deidre, watch out!*"

Deidre's eyes refocused on the road just as a semitruck came sharply into view. Deidre swerved to avoid it and the SUV went off the road, spinning once before slamming into a tree.

CHAPTER TWELVE

Grace is to the body, what good manners are to the mind.
—François de la Rochefoucauld

Deidre's lids felt heavy as she struggled to open her eyes. The room slowly came into focus. White walls, beeping monitors, blinds partially drawn.

There was an IV running from her arm, and she was dressed in a hospital gown. Her whole body ached, and she couldn't move her neck. Frantic, Deidre found the call button on the side of the bed and pressed it repeatedly.

A nurse hurried in.

"Oh good, you're awake," she said with a smile. "I'll let the doctor know."

"My neck," Deidre tried to say. Her throat was dry and scratchy.

"That's just the brace holding it in place. It'll come off in a day or so. Now you just relax and I'll have someone in to see you shortly." The nurse scribbled something on a chart at the foot of Deidre's bed before giving her another bright smile and leaving the room.

Deidre felt her eyes well with tears. What had happened? What day was it? Where was Lindsey?

The door to her room opened and a doctor in a white coat entered. "I'm Dr. Carlisle. How are you feeling?"

Tears spilled onto Deidre's cheeks. "The woman I was traveling with . . ."

"Lindsey Miller? We've already released her. Minor cuts, a few bumps and bruises, but otherwise she's doing fine. She's one lucky woman, that's for sure. You took the brunt of it—your car hit a tree on the driver's side. The CT scan came up clean but you did suffer a minor concussion so I want to monitor you overnight. Is there anyone you'd like me to call?"

Kevin . . . William . . . Manuela . . .

Deidre shook her head.

The doctor warmed his stethoscope before checking Deidre's heart and lungs, then flashed his pen light into her pupils. He nodded satisfactorily as he pocketed the pen light. "Do you have any questions for me?"

Deidre managed a hoarse, "No."

"The hoarseness will go away. It's from the oxygen that was administered to you when you were brought in. You'll be fine, Deidre. Just get some rest." He patted her shoulder before updating her chart and leaving.

Deidre watched the door to her room close slowly. Her lids grew heavy again and she drifted back to sleep.

"That's some shiner you've got there."

Deidre's eyes fluttered open. The room was fully lit but she could tell that night had fallen. In a chair sat Lindsey, with a few small cuts on her face and a bandage across her forehead but otherwise looking surprisingly normal. Even the expression on her face seemed somewhat amused.

"What, did you hit me?" Deidre managed to croak.

Lindsey grinned. "No, the steering wheel got you before I did. How are you feeling? Want some water?"

Deidre nodded and Lindsey reached for a ready cup of water with a straw. She helped Deidre take a sip.

"Well, doc's going to release you tomorrow. Sid will take you back to Kevin's place. Heading back to Seattle right now might be a bit ambitious, but it's up to you. Sid doesn't mind driving you there, if that's what you'd like."

"What about my car?"

"Oh, yeah, that. I hate to be the bearer of bad news, but your fancy SUV is totaled."

It was just a car, but Deidre felt her insides collapse. It had been the only possession of value she'd owned until she'd put the mortgage down on the condo. But even that didn't feel totally real yet. She and the Volvo had been through a lot together.

Lindsey took a tissue and helped wipe Deidre's tears. "Come, come. I've got an '83 Durango that I can sell you, cheap."

Deidre managed a smile. She accepted another tissue from her friend. "You certainly seem to be in a good mood, despite the fact that I almost killed us both."

"Well, it was less you and more that semi. But yeah, I was going to thank you for that."

"Ha ha."

"No, actually, I'm serious." Lindsey took Deidre's hand and gave it firm squeeze. "Thank you for caring enough about me to try to run the Wishbone while I was moping at home and making everybody miserable. Thank you for caring enough about me that you'd drive all the way down from Seattle to take me to that damn rehabilitation class."

"Which we obviously missed." Deidre gave a wry smile.

Lindsey snapped her fingers, feigning regret. "Yeah, bummer about that. But I'll go next time. Scout's honor. The point is, I just really want to thank you, Deidre. You're a good friend, and I'm grateful. Sid and I both are."

Deidre felt her eyes well up with tears again.

"Oh, shoot. I didn't want to start up the waterworks again. Are you hungry?"

Deidre shook her head, but then her stomach growled. "Maybe a little."

"I have a bunch of goodies from the Wishbone. I sent Sid on a mission of mercy and the girls outdid themselves this time. How about some cornbread to start? I've never eaten it with a fork before, but I'm pretty sure your doc would be upset if I got crumbs on that nice hospital-issued gown you got on."

Deidre nodded. Lindsey pulled her chair closer and helped her friend start to eat.

The doctor released her the next day. Sid was waiting to drive her to Kevin's place on Lake Wish. For the first time since she'd started coming down to Jacob's Point, Sid looked like he was finally getting a good night's sleep.

"Lindsey wanted to come, but I told her that she needed to get her rest. I hope that's okay." He gave her an apologetic look.

"Of course. I'm glad she's taking it easy, and I'm glad she's listening to you again."

Sid nodded. "Her doctor had diagnosed her with persistent clinical depression when we saw him the other day. He was really concerned. But it looks like that car accident served as some kind of intervention, and she probably won't have to go on the drugs."

"Oh, Sid, I'm so happy to hear that."

"Me, too." He was driving carefully, taking his time in the slow lane. "So, I don't know if Lindsey told you, but we got a buyer for the Wishbone."

"What?" Deidre couldn't believe it.

"Some guy from LA. Used to be in the movie business—maybe he still is, I don't know. Anyway, he was driving through and he stopped at the diner for lunch or dinner, I don't know which, and saw the sign. He talked to the girls and then he called me. Says he wants to get away from it all."

Deidre tried to grin but some for reason it made her teeth hurt. "I can relate to that. Did he make an offer?"

Sid nodded his head. "Yeah. It's a little under asking but it's not bad. He asked a lot of good questions and seems pretty excited about the possibilities. Lindsey wants to go back to the Wishbone next week to start cooking again and get everything together. Make sure it stays profitable."

"Huh." Deidre gazed out the window at the scenery whizzing by.

"Yeah." Sid scratched his chin. "Another good thing is that he wants to keep Lindsey on for a couple of days a week. It'll definitely help with the money situation, and her cardiologist says it'll be good for her so long as she doesn't overdo it."

They drove in silence for a while. Deidre stared glumly at

the cracked vinyl on the door. Her car, her beautiful Volvo SUV, was now a twisted heap of metal sitting behind a locked gate somewhere until the insurance company could send someone to look at it. She'd have to work with them to get a rental, and then, eventually, a new car.

Just add it to the list of things to do, she thought with a sigh.

When they pulled up to Kevin's house, Sid cut the engine and cleared his throat. "You know you can stay with us," he offered.

Deidre shook her head. "Thanks, but all I really want to do is sleep."

"I understand. But you'll let us know if you need anything?"

"Of course," she said. Sid didn't look convinced, so she fastened on a bright smile. "You just go home and take care of that wife of yours."

Sid helped her to the front door and left her with a bag of food from the Wishbone. Deidre watched him as he drove down the driveway, waving good-bye and debating whether or not to call out to him, to tell him to come back and get her.

When his taillights disappeared from her view, Deidre let her shoulders drop as she closed the door heavily behind her. She tossed her purse on the floor and went into the living room.

She caught a glance at herself in the hallway mirror. The black eye was almost comical. No amount of concealer was going to cover this up. Deidre could just picture herself going into the meeting with Manuela and Frank. Yeah, that would be a real confidence booster.

Sweet Deidre.

She gave a heavy sigh. There was no point in stalling

anymore—she might as well get it over with. Sweet Deidre was dying a slow death, and it was time to put everyone out of their misery.

Deidre started the call by apologizing profusely, explaining about the car accident but assuring Manuela that other than a few bumps and bruises, she was fine.

"I knew something had happened!" Manuela exclaimed feverishly. "You're a professional, Deidre. I knew you weren't ignoring my calls without good reason."

"Er . . ."

"I am *so* relieved to hear you're all right! In fact, I'm going to send an e-mail right now"—Deidre heard the furious tapping of a keyboard in the background—"to Paige in our PR department and have her send out a national press release ASAP. What was the name of your doctor?"

"Dr. Carlisle," Deidre stuttered, caught off guard. "Why are you sending out a press release?" *Or, more specifically, about what?*

"Any news is good news," Manuela said firmly. "People across the nation will want to know that you're okay."

"But people across the nation don't even know who I am, much less that I was in a car accident."

"They will now." More furious typing.

"Manuela," Deidre said firmly. *"I'm fine.* Like I said, I just have a few bumps and bruises, a mild concussion—it was hardly a life-or-death situation."

"Oh, that 'life-or-death' line is good. I'm going to have Paige use that. Let me just hit Send . . . and there it goes! With any luck we might get on one of the wire services tonight."

This was going to be harder than Deidre had thought. She'd been planning to bow out gracefully, to let Sweet Deidre just slip out of the limelight, but Manuela was turning it into a potential media circus. "Manuela, I have to tell you honestly that while I had a few ideas . . ."

"Well, send them over!" Manuela said eagerly. "E-mail them or fax them. Frank and I are anxious to see where you are."

Deidre was beginning to regret that she hadn't wimped out and sent Manuela an e-mail instead.

"As I was saying, I had a few ideas, but none of them got me excited. I don't think you'll be bowled over by them either. And I think if JCC is going to invest in the Sweet Deidre line, it should be something that would bowl you over, don't you agree? So I guess what I'm saying is that I can't do it. I'm sorry, Manuela. I thought I could, but it turned out to be so much harder than I expected. I'm sorry."

There was long silence on the other end of the line. Deidre nervously waited for Manuela to say something.

"You know I've gone to bat for you, Deidre," Manuela finally said slowly. "Sold the idea of you to the JCC team. *Convinced* Frank that you were worth taking a risk on. He warned me of exactly this sort of thing, and now I have to tell him that he was right. And now he gets to green light that damn holiday chocolate line."

Deidre felt terrible. "I'm sure the holiday chocolate line will do very well . . ."

"The Sweet Deidre brand was supposed to put us back on the map for gourmet retail," Manuela said, her voice chilly. "*You* were going to be the new face of the JCC family of products! People don't want to see me and Frank or hear our story—the mom-and-pop appeal went out ages ago. People want young, fresh, inspiring. New stories; rousing can-do testimonials.

You were my 'can-do' girl. I had Paige working on a whole backstory for you—'If Deidre can do it, so can you!'" Manuela's voice was shaking. "I'm so disappointed, Deidre," she said again, and then to Deidre's horror, Manuela hung up.

Well, that was fun. Deidre just burned the only bridge she had, and now Sweet Deidre was no more. She knew she should feel or depressed, but what she felt was an odd sense of relief.

She thought of the Sweet Deidre binder with its frumpy logo and unimaginative ideas. There was nothing wrong with it per se, but it definitely wasn't her, would never be her.

It was just past noon, but Deidre was calling it a day. She crawled into bed, her achy body sighing with relief as she sank into the featherbed. She left the curtains open and gazed at Lake Wish, placid and glittering in the midday sun.

How did her simple life get complicated so quickly?

The next day the sun rose calmly over the lake, sending a stream of sunlight into Deidre's bedroom. She had forgotten to close the curtains the day before but didn't mind the early morning wake-up call.

She was sore, but rested. She hadn't realized the toll of the past few weeks, the stress of Sweet Deidre and Sabine, the late nights with Kevin and his family. She'd forgotten what it was like to just slow down and breathe, one of the important lessons she learned the year before. But life in Jacob's Point was different from life in the city, and Deidre needed to find a way to balance the best of both places in her life.

Lindsey called to say she would be bringing by breakfast. Deidre and Kevin always kept the pantry stocked with a few staples, including coffee, so Deidre decided to get up and get a pot started while she waited for Lindsey's arrival.

Her good friend arrived an hour later holding two foil-covered plates.

"Breakfast burritos," she announced. "Egg whites, spinach, peppers, veggie sausage, shredded potatoes. Heaping order of fresh salsa on the side. Doctor's orders—mine, not yours—but I figured you wouldn't want me to eat alone."

"Definitely not." Deidre reached hungrily for a plate. It smelled so good. "I was thinking about going for a walk around Lake Wish after we eat. Is your doctor okay with that?"

"Are you kidding? After what we just went through, a stroll around the lake is the least of his worries. Besides, they've been trying to get me on some kind of 'exercise regimen' for weeks now."

Lindsey was of the old school of thought regarding exercise: it was just something you did as a part of life, like chasing your kids or raking the leaves. It shouldn't require a gym membership or special clothes.

"Of course, there is the secondary issue of you having sustained a minor head injury, but I do recall someone once telling me that life's too short. Not in so many words, because she was too busy yelling at me, but I got the gist." Lindsey gave a good-natured smile as she bit into her burrito.

"Lindsey, I can't tell you how good it is to see you smiling again."

"I know. Everyone thought I'd gone off the deep end."

"Thought? You *had* gone off the deep end."

"Well, could you blame me? I was prepared for cancer, not a heart attack. And I always expected I would have fair warning, you know, enough time to get my affairs in order. I hadn't considered that I could die, just like that."

"And you didn't," Deidre reminded her. She dipped her burrito in the salsa and took a bite. Heaven.

"I didn't. But it was still a shocker. Everything felt so futile. But now things are looking up. Sid told you that there's a guy interested in the Wishbone, right?"

Deidre had hoped that Lindsey's desire to sell the Wishbone would disappear along with the depression. Obviously it hadn't. "He mentioned it."

"Yeah. He's picked out a new name. A Piece of the Point."

"A Piece of the Point?" Deidre didn't like it. "You're going to let him change the name?"

"Well, if he owns it, he can do whatever he wants."

"Lindsey, I really don't think you should rush into selling the Wishbone right now."

Lindsey didn't say anything as she polished off her burrito. Deidre could tell from Lindsey's stance that the topic of the Wishbone was now closed.

"Fine," Deidre sighed. "I won't say anything else about it."

Lindsey scoffed. "I'll give you ten minutes." At Deidre's hurt look, Lindsey pulled her friend into a good-natured hug and gave her a reassuring squeeze. "Come on—let's finish up so we can get out there while we're still young. Some of us have lives to get back to, you know."

Deidre spent the rest of the day sleeping and lounging on the dock. The sun was warm on her face as she watched the ripples on the water, the trees yielding to the gentle breezes. Birds flew overhead, sometimes flying down to the lake, their bodies barely skimming the surface. Deidre sat, her mind quiet, and when the sun dipped below the horizon and the temperature dropped, she went inside and had a simple dinner of chicken noodle soup.

Now for the part she was dreading. She had been putting off checking her voice mail and answering machine, not wanting to be reminded of all the things that still needed to be done. There were sure to be several messages waiting for her.

You have twenty-three messages.

Sighing, Deidre grabbed a pen and paper. This was going to take a while, and that wasn't even counting the messages that might be waiting for her on her home phone.

The first message was from William, his voice urgent: "Deidre, this is William. Call me when you get this message—it's important."

Deidre frowned. That didn't sound good.

The next message was also from William: "Deidre, where are you? We have to talk. It's about the commitment ceremony. I need you to call me, okay? Call me. Call me!"

A third beep. "Deidre, this is really, really important. We have to talk about the commitment ceremony. Something, well, something has come up. Call me or page me. I'll be waiting."

Deidre had a bad feeling about this. She knew that planning a wedding or commitment ceremony was stressful, and that couples often fought more during that time, sometimes calling off the whole thing. William and Alain had been bickering a lot, but over the most trivial of details. Maybe that's all it took. Maybe making too big a deal over the little things was enough to jeopardize what really mattered.

Had she been doing that with Kevin?

The next message was also from William, and bordered on hysterical. "Deidre, I don't know what to do! *You have to call me.* I've been by your place, I've gone to your office—what's going on? Are you okay? Assuming you are if you're listening to this message, then I need you to call me! *Call me call me call me call me.* Don't do *anything* with the commitment ceremony until we talk, okay? Just . . . hold off. AND CALL ME!"

That was it. Deidre exited her voice mail and dialed William's number, her fingers crossed. William and Alain were good for each other; she knew this in her heart. She only hoped they knew it, too.

"Deidre!" She could hear the relief in his voice. "What's going on? I've been trying to reach you for days!"

Where to begin? "I was in a car accident," she said, surprised that her voice was starting to wobble. She wasn't expecting the swell of emotion that came with telling someone she loved what had happened. "The Volvo is totaled."

William was shocked. "Are you all right?"

She took a deep breath, calming herself. "I'm fine. Well, a minor concussion and some bumps and bruises. I have an ugly foam neck brace that I can't bring myself to wear, and I have a killer black eye."

"I'm coming over right now . . ."

"No, no. I'm not in Seattle. I'm back in Jacob's Point, at Kevin's place."

"What happened?"

Deidre recounted the details of the accident, embellishing a bit here and there to keep it interesting.

William whistled. "You're lucky to have walked away from an accident like that," he said.

"Yeah. Word to the wise: Don't Google and drive."

"I tell my patients that *all* of the time," William said fervently.

Deidre wanted to laugh, but knew it would make her tender ribs hurt. "So William, what's with the eight million messages on my machine? Is everything all right? For a second there you really had me worried; I actually thought you might have changed your mind about declaring your love for Alain in front of twenty guests."

"Yes, well," William said a bit reluctantly. "I don't think I want to do that anymore."

Oh no. "William, what do you mean?"

"Deidre, Alain and I had a long talk about it, and we decided that it's not what we want."

"William, are you sure?"

"Sure we're sure. We're going to take your advice instead."

Now she was officially confused. "*My* advice?"

"That this is a once-in-a-lifetime event. That we should have what we want, have it our way. Alain and I are in this for the long haul, and we want our family and friends to know that."

So they hadn't broken up or called the whole thing off, thank goodness. She chided herself for her foolishness, happily relieved. "That's wonderful, William. I'm so happy to hear that."

"I'm glad you think so, Deidre. Because Alain and I want *everyone* who's close to us to be there!"

Deidre paused, wondering if she'd heard right. "What do you mean by 'everyone'?" she asked uncertainly. "Are you increasing the head count?"

"Um, just a little. Like fifty or seventy-five or something. Is that possible?"

Deidre took a deep breath. Okay, that wasn't too bad. It

wasn't unfeasible, at least. It would be a slightly bigger production, but doable. Most of the grunt work would already be done, and . . .

"Although the backyard can actually accommodate up to a hundred people if we wanted to do rounds of ten," William added.

"Rounds of ten? What are you talking about? What's your final head count, William?"

There was a pause. "A hundred and ten people" came the guilty reply.

She suddenly felt dizzy, unsure if it was the medication or the fact that she now had a full-blown event on her hands. "Hold on."

She ran the numbers in her head. They'd need more linens, tables, chairs. A bigger cake. More favors and centerpieces. More invitations, more programs. They would definitely have to bring in portable bathrooms. They'd need a valet to help with parking. They might need a permit. Their simple commitment ceremony was now anything but, and Deidre was guessing they wanted all the bells and whistles. "I assume there's a bigger budget to go along with this bigger guest list?"

There was a concerning pause on the other end of the line. "Um . . ."

"William, there is *no way* you can have a hundred and ten people on your current budget unless we're buying everything from Costco and Ikea!" If that wasn't a wake-up call for William, she didn't know what would be.

"Deidre, you're one of the most creative people I know," he said. "If anyone can pull of an exquisite event for a hundred and twenty people, it's you."

"A hundred and twenty people!" Deidre felt her neck pinch.

"Like I said, the backyard can accommodate up to a hundred and thirty people . . ."

"Just stop there!" Deidre ordered. "You're asking for the impossible, William. I'm good, but I'm not a miracle worker. I'm not going to be responsible for hacking up your big day by trying to pull it off on a shoestring budget. You're both doctors—find the money so I can do it right!"

"Dee, it's been a rough year. You know that. Plus we're flying in Alain's sister and her family from France . . ."

"William!" She could feel her heart racing. Her blood pressure was probably up there as well.

"I know." William sounded genuinely apologetic. "If you can't do it, I understand. It's just gotten to the point where we want everyone who's been important to us to be there. We don't want to leave anybody out. Not on that day of all days. Just like you said."

So now it was her fault. Deidre sighed. "I know. You should have the people there that you want to have. But I need you and Alain to sit down and finalize your guest list. We'll do a probability to figure out how many will RSVP yes. And I didn't say I couldn't do it, I just said I wasn't sure I could do it well. If you're okay with cutting corners, then I guess I can figure something out."

William cleared his throat. "I mean, if there was a way so that we don't *have* to cut corners . . ."

The man was clearly on drugs. "William!"

"Okay, okay!" he said hastily. "I just thought that there was a chance you could pull one of those magic rabbits out of one of your many hats."

"I'm fresh out of miracles and magic rabbits, I'm afraid." Deidre thought regretfully of Sweet Deidre.

"Well, we love you for trying. Call me when you're back in town. We'll bring dinner over."

Deidre was comforted by the thought. "Okay," she said. "See you soon."

She had no idea how they were going to pull it off, but she could probably convince them that the people were more important than the place settings. She knew she could convince Alain, at least. William was more like her. He'd want it to be perfect, from the officiant to the flowers to the napkin rings.

Talking with William had sobered her up. She *was* lucky to have walked away from that car accident—her Volvo bore the brunt of the impact and saved her life. Lindsey's, too. Lying in that hospital bed, Deidre mostly had been in shock, unable to process what had happened, but Deidre knew now that it had been a close call. Really close. She had a lot to be thankful for, and it was time to make the most of what she had.

All of this nonsense about Sabine had made Deidre crazy, but Deidre and Kevin were in love. She loved him, and he loved her. That was all there was to it. Deidre had made a mistake by not being up front with her feelings, by not telling the truth, and now she was paying for it.

Well, not anymore. She was going to call Kevin and tell him everything—about the accident, about Sweet Deidre, about how insane Sabine was making her—and they were going to get back on track. She was going to tell him how she really felt, how she never thought she'd meet anyone who made her feel so treasured and loved, and how much it so meant to her that he thought she was wonderful and adorable even when her mind was all over the place and she was acting like a complete klutz. How his belief in her helped bring out the best of who she was. It was mushy but true. If this were a Disney moment, bluebirds would be singing in the background.

The phone was ringing on the other end and Deidre eagerly waited for him to pick up.

" 'Allo?" came the sleepy, unmistakably feminine, greeting.

Deidre's eyes flew open. Who was answering Kevin's phone at 6:00 a.m.? "Hello?" she said cautiously. "Is Kevin there?"

There was a languid yawn. "He's asleep," came the flippant reply. It was Sabine. "Who's calling?"

Deidre hung up the phone, livid. So much for the bluebirds. She had no idea what was going on, but she as sure as hell was going to find out.

THE SEATTLE SCOOP

THIS JUST IN! DEIDRE'S HARROWING BRUSH WITH DEATH
A *Seattle Scoop* Exclusive! By Rosemary Goodwin

We just received word that Deidre McIntosh was driving on I-90 when her car spun out of control, crashing headfirst into a tree. Deidre and an unidentified female passenger were taken to the hospital.

It was unknown if she was driving to or from Seattle. The weather was purportedly clear.

Hospital workers say EMTs fought vigilantly to save Deidre's life and that there was a sigh of relief when it became clear she was going to make it.

Updates will be posted on our blog as they become available.

Log on to our blog and tell us what you think!

CHAPTER THIRTEEN

Courtesy means understanding that nobody is perfect.
—Peggy Post, *Emily Post's Etiquette*

It could have been worse.

For starters, there may not have been a ticket available. But there was. Just one. And while the price of her last-minute fare made her cringe, she was now on her way to Paris.

Isaac, the driver of the Town Car hired by the insurance company, could have said no when Deidre asked him to stop by her place, wait for fifteen minutes, and *then* drive her on to the airport, but he didn't.

Deidre, who liked to make a list of what to pack to ensure she didn't forget anything, managed to throw a few things into an overnight bag in just under five minutes. And, by some small miracle, remembered to bring her passport, too.

Airport security had VIP'd her through to the gate, thanks in large part to the neck brace and bruises. She would have liked to board with a little more dignity, but the truth was her neck was killing her and she couldn't quite remember where she'd put the orange bottle of painkillers the doctor had pre-scribed. So when she took the neck brace out of her bag and put it on, people literally parted like the Red Sea. A quick glance at her reflection in the window confirmed that she'd seen better days.

Again, it could have been worse.

Deidre repeated this mantra to herself as she sat squeezed in the middle seat between a woman holding a screaming baby on her right and a slightly overweight gentleman on her left. He was in his seventies and had fallen asleep, his head on Deidre's shoulder. He was snoring loudly in her ear and, to top it off, was in desperate need of a breath mint.

Deidre had been in such a rush to leave that she'd barely had enough time to call Lindsey, not wanting her to worry.

"You are *crazy*," Lindsey had told her, agitated. "You can't go running off to France right now! Do I need to come over there and knock some sense into you?"

"Too late," Deidre had informed her. "I'm already in the Town Car heading back to Seattle. I just didn't want you to worry."

Lindsey swore. "Why would I be worried about you travel-ing halfway around the world two days after being in an auto-mobile accident? I have a mind to call your doctor or call the airport."

"Please don't," Deidre begged. "I don't know what's going on over there, but I need to find out. I need to see if he's decided to get back together with her."

"You could always just call him, Deidre. It's a heck of a lot cheaper."

"I *did* call him. And *she* answered."

There was a heavy sigh. "Deidre, listen. Love is a fickle

thing, but Kevin's not that kind of guy." Sid and Lindsey were huge Kevin fans, but they knew him more professionally rather than personally.

"I know, Lindsey, but Sabine's that kind of girl. I think I need to go and get my boyfriend. Think of it as a rescue mission. And if he is with her, well, then I guess I'll finally have a stamp in my passport."

Lindsey had ultimately relented. "You go get him, Deidre. And call me when you get back!"

The airplane dipped and Deidre felt her stomach drop. She was trying to formulate a plan or strategy about what to do once she landed at Charles de Gaulle International Airport. She'd only gotten as far as making her way to Kevin's hotel and confronting him and Sabine. Deidre could get emotional or she could get angry, but neither were really her style. She wasn't going to Paris to throw a hissy fit. What she wanted more than anything was to see for her own eyes what was really going on, to see if Kevin had any feelings for Sabine. If she waited until he came back to Seattle, she'd always be wondering what it would be like if Sabine showed up again.

When Sabine had answered Kevin's phone, Deidre's first reaction had been shock, then anger. She knew they weren't sleeping together—they couldn't be. Kevin wouldn't do that to Deidre, no matter how sexy or slinky Sabine was. He was a man of integrity, and she believed that.

Or did she? As the minutes ticked by, Deidre became increasingly less confident. She had no idea what was going on over there. Maybe seeing Sabine in Paris cast things in a new light for Kevin. Sabine, who didn't mind the dinner parties and the hobnobbing; who had the right attitude and the right wardrobe to go with it. Deidre knew that Kevin was out every night, visiting friends or attending business dinners. She had no doubt that it all involved copious amounts of alcohol, and while she knew that he could hold his own and rarely got drunk, it was easy to get caught up in the moment. Plus there was the old familiarity between Kevin and Sabine. They had a history. They'd kissed and they'd . . . well, they'd done other things, too. But more importantly, they'd been engaged. It wouldn't be completely inconceivable that something might have happened in a moment of weakness. Kevin was only human, after all.

Deidre sighed and shifted uncomfortably, shrugging her shoulder in the hope that her sleeping neighbor would lift his head and turn away. He was in a window seat and could easily sleep against the side of the plane. But he didn't, and instead nuzzled deeper into the crook of Deidre's neck, his head bumping against her neck brace.

"Your father?" the woman next to her asked, bouncing the baby on her lap. The baby had stopped crying and was now hiccupping, her fingers in her mouth. The baby stared at Deidre, her eyes large.

Deidre didn't feel much like talking, but she didn't want to be rude. "No," she said. "I actually have no idea who he is. We didn't have a chance to introduce ourselves before he fell asleep." She gave her shoulder another little wiggle. Nothing.

"Oh. Well, he looks very comfortable. What I wouldn't give for a little sleep."

Inwardly, Deidre groaned. A full-on conversation was obligatory now, and they were only two hours into the flight. "Yes, well, it's hard getting a good night's sleep with such a young baby," she said. That's what she'd heard anyways.

The woman's eyes lit up. "Do you have children?"

"No. I'm not married."

"Oh. Well, neither am I." The woman gave a small smile then turned her head to gaze down at her daughter. She looked back at Deidre and shrugged. "Best-laid plans . . . you know."

Deidre cracked a smile. "I'm quite familiar with that one, yes."

The woman held out her hand. "I'm Sarah Evans. And this is Petra."

The baby gurgled then let out a squeal. The gentleman who was asleep on Deidre's shoulder gave a sleepy snort and, by some small miracle, raised his head and let it drop against the window. Deidre breathed a sigh of relief and smiled gratefully at the little girl, unsnapping the neck brace with a sigh of relief.

She shook Sarah's hand, smiling broadly. "I'm Deidre."

The ten-hour flight from Seattle to Paris seemed to fly by. She found herself chatting with Sarah, even giving the mother a break by walking baby Petra up and down the aisle and letting the stewardesses coo over the baby, who hadn't screamed once since Deidre and Sarah had begun talking.

Sarah was thirty-one, but had the wisdom of someone several years older. She lived in Spokane and was a former copy editor who had been taking random temp jobs for the past year to accommodate her schedule as a new mother. She didn't watch much TV and wasn't familiar with Deidre's old show, *Live Simple*—a detail that Deidre found immensely refreshing. She'd gotten pregnant at her best friend's wedding ("It's so cliché, I'm almost embarrassed," she admitted) by someone who, Sarah discovered later, was both unavailable ("Married with two young kids!") and uninterested in Sarah's new predicament, of which he claimed no responsibility. In a way, it made things easier for Sarah, but harder, too. Someday her daughter would want to know her father, and Sarah hadn't quite figured that part out yet.

"I finally decided that I'll figure it out when we get there," she was telling Deidre now. "I know who he is, so he should be easy enough to find if it's important to Petra."

"I'm just in complete awe," Deidre told the young woman. She wasn't exaggerating. She'd never given it much thought, but watching Sarah in action gave Deidre a new appreciation for mothers, single mothers especially. "It's amazing what you're doing."

"Me? *You* had a TV show. Two! And the cookie line."

Deidre coughed. "Well, that obviously didn't work out."

"I know, but still. Talk about a chance in a lifetime! I'm envious! One of my longest running temp jobs was as a prep chef at Red Robin. I've even done a stint at Chuck E. Cheese's. I can say without reservation that Petra will never be eating the pizza there."

Deidre laughed. "Why didn't you stick to copyediting?"

"I tried. I freelance when I can, but the work comes and goes. I can't work regular office hours because I'm home with Petra. I can only do odd hours, when my mother can babysit for me."

Petra was sitting on Deidre's lap, playing with the table tray. "That must be hard."

"It is. But what's really hard is that I hate leaving Petra either way, even though I do love the break. I just know she's going to grow up fast, and who knows if I'll ever have more children? That's one reason I decided to go through with it. I wasn't sure if I'd have another chance."

"You're still young. You could still meet someone."

Sarah laughed. "Are you kidding? I'm in my early thirties with a kid. I live in Spokane. I rent a two-bedroom apartment a block and a half away from my mom's house. No substantial savings. My wardrobe hails from the Salvation Army—50 percent off Tuesdays—and my hair has seen better days."

"I think you look great," Deidre told her honestly. True, Sarah looked exhausted and hadn't bothered with makeup, but her skin tone was fabulous and her eyes were a vibrant blue. Her sandy blond hair was due for a trim and maybe highlights, but despite all of that, she had a fresh, attractive air about her. "There are lots of great finds at the Salvation Army, and it's clear you have good taste in clothes. You're trim and fit as well. Do you work out?"

"Yeah, with an eighteen-pound baby who wants to be held all of the time."

Deidre looked thoughtful. "Hmm. Maybe I should get one."

"You're welcome to borrow mine anytime. Do you get out to Spokane often?"

"Never," Deidre admitted. "But I do go down to Jacob's Point quite a bit. It's close to Pullman."

"Pullman's about an hour and a half away. I've never heard of Jacob's Point, though."

"Most people haven't. You should come out and visit sometime when I'm there. There's a beautiful lake, and the people are really friendly. It's a small town, but that's what I love about it."

"Sounds dreamy."

"It is." Deidre could almost smell the scent of fresh pine; hear the sizzle of Lindsey's griddle. God, she was going to miss the Wishbone—it made Deidre sad just thinking about it. "There's a great little diner called the Wishbone, if you're

ever out that way. My friend runs it, but it might be changing ownership soon. Hopefully they'll keep the recipes. Her
meatloaf is to die for. I swear it's the best in the entire Pacific
Northwest."

"Ooh, I *love* meatloaf." Sarah rolled her eyes in ecstasy.

"Well, then I'd get to the Wishbone as soon as you get
back," Deidre advised. "How long are you in Paris for?"

Deidre learned that Sarah had been the big vacation sweep-
stakes winner at Fred Meyer, a local superstore. Since Petra
was under the age of one, she was able to fly for free. They
were booked on a tour and would be put up in a hotel for five
days and four nights.

"I've never been out of the country," Sarah confessed. "Not
even to Canada, if you can believe that. I had to get us passports
and everything. I downloaded a French language program"—
she held up an iPod—"but I haven't exactly had time to listen much. I keep hearing about how Americans are such awful
tourists and that we always expect everyone else to know
English, but we never bother to learn other languages. I was
hoping to at least pick up a few words or phrases, but I never
got past *bonjour* and *parlez-vous anglais*." She looked guilty.

"Don't be too hard on yourself," Deidre said. "You have a
baby, for starters, and you're a single mom. Besides, being on
the ground is much more educational than trying to figure
something out from a book. If you keep your ears open, you'll
probably pick up more than you realize."

"I hope so," Sarah said. "And what about you? What are
you going to Paris for?"

Deidre looked out the window beyond Sarah. Fluffy white
clouds, blue skies. They were somewhere over the Atlantic, en
route to London, where they'd catch the connection to Paris.

She'd appear at the hotel, surprising an unsuspecting Kevin and Sabine. What would happen after that was anybody's best guess.

The airplane hit a patch of turbulence and the FASTEN SEAT BELT light came on. Deidre handed Petra back to Sarah and buckled her seat belt.

"I'm not quite sure," she said truthfully.

It was possible that Kevin would be completely put off by Deidre's impromptu visit. It was possible that there was nothing going on between him and Sabine, but Deidre's apparent lack of trust might end the relationship anyway. It was possible that he wasn't even at the hotel anymore, or even in Paris. Anything was possible, and Deidre was starting to wonder if maybe this trip had been a bit foolhardy. She'd just been in a car accident and was sporting a black eye *and* a neck brace. She was too impulsive at times, this time clearly being one of those times.

Paris! What was she thinking? When would she ever learn?

She obviously couldn't turn back now. The pilot came on over the PA, reminding people to return to their seats as they would be experiencing moderate turbulence. Deidre pulled the belt strap snug across her lap and watched as Sarah attached Petra to a lap harness. There was nothing else they could do until the flight attendant told them it would be safe to move about the cabin again.

Once they landed and cleared customs, Deidre bade farewell to Sarah and Petra, who were greeted immediately by a chipper young Parisian woman holding up a sign with their names in bold letters.

"*Bonjour!*" the woman said cheerily. "*Vous êtes Sarah Evans? Je suis votre guide. Je m'appelle Paulette.*"

Sarah looked at Deidre, slightly terrified. Deidre gave her an encouraging nod and Sarah turned back to the woman.

"*Bonjour,*" Sarah said. "*Parlez-vous anglais?* Please say yes!"

"*Oui, bien sûr.*" The woman laughed at Sarah's puzzled expression. She said in English, "That means 'yes.'" Sarah smiled in relief.

Deidre and Sarah quickly exchanged numbers and promised to stay in touch, but Deidre knew how these things went. Airplane friendships rarely ever stuck, but that was okay. She had enjoyed Sarah's company and their conversations had put her at ease, taking her mind off of what was to come.

Deidre had never been to Europe, and while she boasted a smattering of high school French, it dawned on her quickly that nothing had prepared her for actually being in France. Her senses were immediately bombarded with new sights, smells, and sounds, and Deidre found herself both giddy and slightly overwhelmed. She had a strong desire to see everything and go everywhere.

And she hadn't even left the airport yet.

Given the throngs of people rushing past her, it was apparent that Deidre was visiting during the peak travel season. While waiting to board her flight in Seattle, Deidre had stopped in at Hudson Booksellers and picked up a travel guide for Paris. She referred to it now as people pushed past her, trying to decide the best mode of transportation into the city. She had assumed that catching a taxi would be the easiest, but it looked like a shuttle or train might be a better option.

The airport was circular and a bit confusing, even though there were plenty of signs and markers in English. It took

Deidre a while before she was able to find her way to the street. Once there, she remembered she would need to change her dollars into euros. She has no idea what the exchange rate was. Again, she consulted her guidebook. It advised ATMs over money changers. Good to know.

It was quickly occurring to Deidre that she could spend the next few days in the airport alone at the rate she was going. If she wanted to find Kevin and Sabine, she'd need to get moving, and soon.

Kevin was staying at Hôtel Meurice on rue de Rivoli, in between Place de la Concorde and the Louvre in the heart of Paris. It would be easy enough to get to there from the airport, and after checking the guidebook and exchanging some money, she found herself on a shuttle bus that would take her to an RER train station, Paris's rapid transit system. She'd be able to catch a connection that would drop her off within walking distance to Kevin's hotel.

Deidre was tempted to call him and tell him she was there, but she didn't have a new cell phone yet, and figuring out the payphone was too intimidating. Besides, the whole point of her coming was to catch him off guard. She didn't want to trap him, but she didn't want to give Sabine a chance to prepare for Deidre's arrival. If Sabine was still hanging around Kevin, as Deidre expected she was, it would be better if Deidre just showed up and saw for herself what was really going on.

As the train sped toward the city, Deidre couldn't believe she was actually in Paris. Cafés, *boulangeries*, the Louvre, the Mona Lisa, the Eiffel Tower, to start. Boat cruises along the Seine. The Sacré-Coeur. Notre-Dame. Arc de Triomphe. Deidre wanted nothing more than to start exploring. She couldn't wait to choose a restaurant and have her first French meal. That would be the first order of business once she was reunited with Kevin.

If she was reunited with Kevin. Deidre shook her head, dismissing the thought. There was no reason to worry.

So what was she doing here, then?

Less than an hour later Deidre was walking into the Meurice. She tried to keep her amazement in check but the ornate furnishings and gilded paneling blew her away. It was eighteenth-century French elegance coupled with the more modern upgrades of Philippe Starck, a well-known French designer. Deidre took in the lobby's green and white marbled floor, along with an exquisite collection of antiques and art. Eight-foot-high white and gold china lamps and chandeliers lit up the reception area, and Deidre had to force herself to stop gawking and move toward the elevators before she attracted too much attention.

She knew Kevin was staying in the Marco Polo Suite, room 628. It didn't take her long to find it.

Now that she was finally here, she wasn't quite sure what to do. It was just before noon, and she doubted he would be in his room. It was worth a try, and if that didn't work, she could stake out the lobby, hoping to catch him when he entered the hotel. If she got really desperate, she'd throw in the towel and give him a call on his cell phone and track him down.

As she approached the suite she saw a housekeeping cart in front of the door. The door to the suite was propped open and Deidre heard the unmistakable sound of someone moving about the room.

She took a deep breath and stepped past the cart and into the suite.

Deidre had never seen anything like it. The Marco Polo

suite had a triangular shape and was draped in soft blue fabrics that hung from the peaked ceiling to the wooden parquet floor. There was a romantic, almost luscious energy to the room that evoked a sense of embarking on a journey. But that wasn't what had Deidre stunned.

The suite was basically trashed. Skimpy lingerie, glasses half-filled with champagne, rose petals strewn everywhere. Somewhere a maid was muttering in French, no doubt lamenting the clean-up job in front of her. The sheets and duvet on the generous king bed had yet to be made and were rumpled and tossed about, the pillows having fallen to the floor. Deidre recognized Kevin's luggage on the valet in the closet, his suits hanging on the bar. She had the right room, no doubt.

Deidre walked into the bathroom. Under any other circumstances she would have loved it, the big, open space with an antique-style claw-foot tub and stone floor. Kevin's razor was next to the sink, the one she gave him for Valentine's Day. It was barely noticeable amid an ungodly amount of makeup taking up every inch of available counter space.

A maid emerged from around the corner, her arms filled with fresh towels. She stared at Deidre, uncertain as to whom she was or if she should be there.

Deidre didn't need to see any more. She just wanted to get out of there, make her way back to the airport, and fly home. Her eyes filled with tears and she turned her head to look out the door.

"Deidre?"

Deidre glanced up and saw Kevin and Sabine standing in front of her, an expression of surprise on both their faces. Kevin was the first to recover, striding quickly toward her. He gathered Deidre in his arms and then held her at arm's length, looking her up and down as if to make sure that she was in one piece, before pulling her back to him.

"God, I have been worried sick about you." He frowned as he gently touched the bruise around her eye and brushed away a tear. "I've been trying to reach you for days."

"I was in an accident."

"I know. I saw a release on the AP wire this morning, something about you being in a car accident near Jacob's Point."

It took Deidre a moment to realize what he was talking about. "Oh, that must have been a press release sent out by JCC. Manuela was supposed to cancel it, but I guess she forgot to tell her PR person. I'm fine, though. More banged up than anything."

"William told me. I called him when I couldn't get through to you and he told me everything. Why aren't you answering your cell phone?"

"It was totaled along with my car. I haven't had a chance to get a new one yet."

Kevin checked his watch. "Well, I have a flight taking me back to Seattle in about three hours to check on someone who I thought needed checking up on, but it seems I was too slow."

"Really?" she asked. Her eyes grew wet, but she didn't care.

"Really. I've had enough of this town, anyway." He leaned over and gave her a kiss, then took a loose strand of hair and hooked it gently behind her ear.

Sabine was staring at Deidre, a look of quiet concentration on her face. Her arms were gracefully folded across her chest and in one hand she held a clipboard. She wore a fitted top with a stretch skirt and designer stilettos that showed off her long, bare legs. Her hair was styled away from her face and she looked every bit as competent and successful as Deidre expected her to be. She still hadn't acknowledged Deidre or said anything to her, obviously put out by her arrival. Deidre was about to say something when there was a commotion in the hallway.

A man dressed in a solid black shirt and slacks walked in, carrying a huge camera around his neck. He looked frustrated and impatient. A younger man came in behind him, lugging what appeared to be photography equipment and an umbrella flash kit. There was the sound of women speaking rapidly in French, and then two young and somewhat anorexic women suddenly appeared in the doorway, wearing little more than lacy bras, panties, and high heels.

Deidre looked at everybody, confused. Sabine still wasn't saying anything. Suddenly, a look of intense displeasure crossed Sabine's face.

"Lucien, I *already* told you that this just isn't working for me . . ."

Sabine was using a Bluetooth earpiece that looked like a small jeweled barrette to make a call. Sabine shook her head in irritation before looking at the photographer and making a slashing motion across her throat. The photographer gave a frustrated kick, sending a cascade of rose petals through the air, swearing under his breath.

"How hard is it for you to come up with a decent idea for a photo shoot?" she demanded before pressing a button on the cell phone clipped to the waistband of her skirt. She threw up her hands in disgust and muttered something in French or Danish or one of the other languages she spoke in addition to English, ending with ". . . that's it. I give up."

The maid had emerged from the bathroom and started arguing with Sabine.

"What's going on?" Deidre asked, thoroughly confused.

"Oh, Sabine and her art director planned a photo shoot for a spread in one of her magazines, *Adoré*, but Sabine didn't like the setup. She's partial to this room, so I offered to let them shoot in here," Kevin explained. Then he lowered his voice and confided, "It's not working out, though. They just can't seem to get the right shot."

"I can hear you, Kevin," Sabine said irritably. Gone was the flirtatious sex kitten Deidre remembered. Instead the woman standing before her, while still exuding sensuality, was all business. She came over and arched an eyebrow, taking in Deidre's black eye. "Hello, Deidre. You look like you've seen better days."

"Given the past week, today is actually one of them."

"Well, lucky you. Me, not so much. *Adoré* has been going through an identity crisis." Sabine had a sour, pissed-off look on her face. "We're trying to revamp the magazine, but nothing seems to be working."

Deidre surveyed the room and the models as she recalled past issues of the magazine. It had gone the celebrity route, the interview/strong editorial route, the travel/lifestyle route, the fashion/beauty route. It was all excellent content, but completely all over the place. Sabine was right—the magazine was suffering from an identity crisis, more like a multiple-personality disorder.

"I think *Adoré* is a fabulous magazine," Deidre said truthfully. "But to be honest the hotel room with the lingerie and the skinny models has been done a million times. There's nothing distinct or even interesting about it."

The look on Sabine's face was venomous. Obviously she didn't take too well to criticism.

"Never mind," Deidre said, quickly backing off. It wasn't her any of her business and all that really mattered was that Kevin was standing here beside her.

Sabine waved her hand impatiently. "No, go on."

Deidre glanced at Kevin who shrugged. "She asked for it," he said.

Deidre began to walk around the room, picking things up off the floor. "If you're going to do a photo shoot in a gorgeous room like this, then it just makes sense to work with what you've got. It's naturally set up to be intimate and romantic. It's cozy and sensual without being sleazy. *Adoré* means beloved, right? So why not focus more on love, or being in love, or people who love being in love . . . The whole magazine could revolve around that theme. I don't think there's anyone else who's doing that. It would appeal to people who are in love as well as people who want to be in love, who want to find that Mr. Right. Go for images that evoke tenderness and sensuality. Connection. Intimacy. Things that help people fall in love all over again." Deidre sighed, suddenly self-conscious that all eyes were on her. "Oh, I don't know what I'm talking about. I haven't had anything to eat for a few hours and I'm just babbling."

"Let's get you some food and then some rest." Kevin put his hand on the small of Deidre's back and led her toward the door.

Sabine stepped in front of them. "One minute," she implored. "Tell me more."

Kevin had a stern look on his face. "You know I love you like the sister I already have, Tabby, but I'm taking Deidre to get something to eat. You need to move. *Now.*"

Deidre touched his arm. "No, it's okay." She looked around the suite again. "It's a shame to let such a fabulous room go to waste. Since you're here and you have the photographer and the models, maybe let housekeeping clean everything up and you can tone down the makeup on the girls. Thoughtful shots, maybe wearing a man's white dress shirt while staring out the window. She's missing someone, or dreaming of that perfect guy. Or a tousled hair shot, first thing in the morning. Give the impression that she's not alone. Happy. Content."

Sabine said something in French to the maid and the two models disappeared into the bathroom. "Go on."

"Maybe you could do a spread on romantic hotels, or have a theme like romance-on-the-go, emphasizing that romance can be found anywhere. It's the little things that can make a big difference. A single flower on a pillow, two glasses side by side, French-milled heart-shaped soaps in the bathroom. Poetry, maybe, or snuggle shots in the big plush bed. A couple reading together. Close shots of a hand entwined in her lover's hair. A smile."

Sabine was nodding now, and even her photographer had perked up and appeared to be listening. Deidre didn't know if he spoke English or not, but he looked intrigued.

"Or use food," Deidre said. "Food is one of best ways to a person's heart. Couples feeding each other, maybe. Or recipes for two. Cooking together. Experimenting." She gave Sabine a sheepish grin and blushed, embarrassed. What was she thinking, giving advice to someone like Sabine? "This is all probably too hokey for a high-gloss magazine like *Adoré*."

"Deidre, your ideas are fabulous," Sabine said briskly. She said something in French to the photographer, who in turn began barking orders at his assistant. "What may sound 'hokey' to you can be made glamorous by me. Just wait and see."

Kevin firmly steered Deidre out the door. "You can send her the next issue in the mail."

In the hallway, he pulled her close to him as they headed toward the elevator, his strong arm circling her waist. It was such a comfort after all she'd been through, and Deidre didn't want it to ever end.

"This trip was entirely way too long," he said as he pressed the call button for the elevator. "I never thought I'd say that, but it's true. I didn't realize how hard it would be to be away from you."

"So, no more trips?" Deidre grinned, knowing that would never be the case.

"Shorter trips," he amended. "Unless I can convince you to go with me, that is."

Now that Sweet Deidre was no more, her time was her own again. Anything was possible. "I like the sound of that."

"Me, too."

Deidre felt a sudden rush of adrenaline. Now that she was with him, she couldn't wait to start experiencing Paris. "So where are we going for lunch?" she asked. "I saw so many wonderful cafés and restaurants along the street . . ."

"I'm going to get us a fresh room," Kevin said, interrupting her. "And then we are going to order room service and rest. It's what you're always asking me to do, right? Stay in?"

Deidre gave him a crestfallen look, then punched his arm when she realized he was teasing her. "That's not funny. We're in *Paris*. I want to see everything."

"Later," he said, pulling Deidre into his arms for one more kiss. "And then I promise to show you everything."

Chapter Fourteen

Good manners have much to do with the emotions. To make
them ring true, one must feel them, not merely exhibit them.
—Amy Vanderbilt, *The Amy Vanderbilt*
Complete Book of Etiquette

It's often said that make-up sex is the best kind there is. Deidre, however, would disagree. There was nothing better than a homecoming, be it physical or emotional, to reestablish intimacy with someone you loved.

Their reunion was tender and heartfelt, passionate and intense. They took their time exploring one another, remembering what it was like to be together again. Afterward, Deidre rested her head against Kevin's chest, lacing her fingers through his.

"I missed you," she said.

Kevin kissed the top of her head. "Enough that you came all the way to Paris to tell me that?" His fingers walked up her back and then settled on the nape of her neck, stroking her.

Deidre snuggled closer to him. "Not exactly. I may have been a little insecure about Sabine. Okay, maybe a lot. I was certain she was trying to get you back. But that's not what was bothering me."

Kevin waited, his eyes intent.

"I was afraid that maybe you wanted to get back with her, too," Deidre admitted. "You're so familiar with each other, and then when I called the other morning and she answered . . ."

"Her cell phone was dead so she borrowed mine and conveniently forgot to return it," he said, remembering. "I should have known better. If it's any consolation, I'm pretty sure Sabine is remembering why we were never really a good match for each other. We have completely different priorities, and it didn't work back then for a reason. And now, it's even more apparent." He lifted her hand and brought it to his lips. "I'm sorry. The last thing I want is for you to doubt my feelings for you."

"I don't," Deidre said honestly. "It's just that, well, it's *Sabine*. I mean, she's so completely beautiful and accomplished. I'm trying to figure out whether or not to add coconut crème to a recipe and she's making multimillion-dollar business deals. I'm Little Debbie and she's, I don't know, Dom Pérignon. Vintage. How can I possibly compete with that?"

"Deidre, you don't have to compete with that." Kevin propped himself up on his elbows. "You're the one I want to be with. And don't underestimate yourself. Sabine is a very successful and savvy businessperson, but she inherited her success. So did Marla and I, to a certain extent. You, on the other hand, built yours from scratch. Literally."

Deidre had never thought of it that way.

"Look at what you've achieved, Deidre. You have a lot to be proud of. I think the JCC press release said something about you being an inspiration to thousands of young entrepreneurs and women across the country. They're right."

Deidre squirmed, not feeling deserving of the praise. "Kevin, there's something you should know."

"What?"

She avoided his eyes. "JCC pulled the plug on Sweet Deidre. It's not going to happen."

"Why?"

She told him how her original vision for Sweet Deidre didn't match up with the reality of the marketplace. How Manuela had given her one last shot and she had blown it. She told him about the damn binder with the frumpy logo and the value-based recipes. Even without Lindsey's heart attack, Deidre would have been at a loss for how to save Sweet Deidre. As much as she wanted to come up with a solution on her own, she couldn't. And now she had damaged a valuable relationship with Manuela and JCC in the process.

"I'll probably lose all credibility after this," Deidre said. Her only consolation had been an update from Amber, who told her that the rest of the Sweet Deidre team thought the direction JCC wanted to take with Sweet Deidre "sucked, too."

Manuela wasn't talking to Deidre yet, communicating only once by e-mail. She was giving them two weeks to wrap up the line and to tie up any loose ends. She offered to keep the entire Sweet Deidre team on payroll, instructing them to visit the HR department so they could be assigned to a new JCC division. Many of her staff members had been borrowed from other JCC divisions to begin with, but Deidre was grateful for Manuela's generosity.

"I feel terrible that everybody took a risk with me," she told Kevin now. "I feel like I let everyone down."

Kevin gave a little shrug of his shoulders. "Start-ups are risky," he said. "And even though you had JCC behind you, the Sweet Deidre line was just like a start-up. People know that it can go either way. There's a huge upside if you're successful, but you've got to go out on that limb. There are never any guarantees."

"That's still no excuse. I was completely unprofessional."

Kevin shook his head. "No," he said. "You just lost your passion."

Deidre frowned. "What do you mean?"

"You're driven by your instincts, Deidre. You're a smart woman, but you let your emotions dictate the experience. You couldn't come up with a solution to Sweet Deidre because the watered-down approach they wanted you to take wasn't in line with your original vision. When you lost your vision, you lost your passion. Lose your passion, and, well, that's pretty much all she wrote."

Deidre didn't like the sound of that. "But that's not a good way to run a business," she said. "Sometimes you have to just do it."

"You will always be able to 'just do it' and do it well if you're passionate about it," Kevin said. "Passion is a big part of any successful business. Sucking it up and struggling through is no way to run a business, especially not in the very beginning."

"Well, that's all fine and good, but what now?"

Kevin stretched languidly on the bed. "Well, since I had planned to return to Seattle to check on you, I cancelled the rest of my meetings. And since you no longer have a business to return to, it doesn't look like we're in a rush to go anywhere. I suggest we take the next few days to kick back and enjoy Paris."

Deidre looked out the window, excited. It was nighttime. "Is it too late to get started now?"

Kevin got out of bed and reached for a robe. "There's a reason they call Paris 'The City of Lights,'" he said. "We can be out all night if you want, and the streetlamps and Eiffel Tower will light our way. But it's Paris's other nickname that I prefer. Do you know what it is?"

Deidre waited, a smile on her face.

He offered her his hand and pulled her up, wrapping his arms around her.

"The City of Love."

They spent the next several days taking in all that Paris had to offer. It was ambitious, but Kevin knew the city like the back of his hand and easily navigated them through the busy streets, the perfectly manicured gardens, and the impressive art collections at famous museums that could keep Deidre occupied for hours. They stopped in a few couture houses and high-fashion shops for Kevin to pick up some last-minute things for Beverly, but Deidre preferred the trendier shops and smaller boutiques that had their own distinct personality and flair. She picked up a few pieces that she knew would go well with her clothes at home.

They had a car but Deidre wanted to walk or take the Metro whenever possible, not wanting to miss a thing. They ate breakfast and lunches in bistros and *brasseries*, ducked into cafés and *boulangeries* for *pain au chocolat* and hits of caffeine. There was the most amazing hot chocolate and *mont blanc* pastries at Angelina's, a tea salon right next to the Meurice. They had dinner at Taillevent, an haute cuisine restaurant in a grand nineteenth-century town house off the Champs-Elysées. One evening they strolled along the Seine, jumping onto a *bateau mouche*. They stood on the deck of the boat as it glided along the river, listening to the sounds of the city along the riverbanks and taking in the sweeping views.

The icing on the cake was a late-night sojourn up the Eiffel Tower. The breathtaking views made Deidre long for more time in Paris, especially with Kevin by her side. They were scheduled to leave the next day, and even though Deidre would have loved to spend what time they had left wandering through the neighborhoods and *arrrondissements*, Kevin was insisting on a couple of surprise stops before heading to the airport.

"Tell me," Deidre begged the next morning as they left the hotel.

"Nope." Kevin grinned mischievously. "I've got it all mapped out. We only have a few hours before we leave, so it's important that we stay on task."

"Don't you think it would be easier for me to stay on task if I knew what the task was?"

"For other people, yes. For you? Definitely not. I want it to be a surprise."

The surprise turned out to be Ladurée, a luxury pastry shop and tea salon. There were four in the city, and Deidre knew they were legendary for their delicate double-stacked *macarons*—small, round almond meringue cakes that were crisp on the outside, yet smooth and soft in the middle. They were baked fresh every morning and Deidre sniffed the air appreciatively the minute they entered the shop in the Saint-Germain-des-Prés district.

It was heaven. Not just the pastries and the food, but the atmosphere and Ladurée's exquisite packaging. It was everything: the colors, the smells, the textures. *This* was the kind of treat worth spending money on, regardless of what was happening in the economy. It was such a multisensory experience that Deidre couldn't even remember what was happening with the economy. As she looked around at the people standing in line or waiting for a table, she didn't see celebrities or the rich and famous—she saw *everyone*. Locals, tourists, mothers, grandmothers, students, workers, businessmen, clergymen. Some selected a single *macaron* while others filled boxes with an assortment of delectable pastries. Everyone left with their purchase in beautiful Ladurée bags and boxes.

Deidre still hadn't had a bite to eat, yet she felt fully sated just by being there. Kevin beckoned her to join him at a table and she did so, eagerly. Then the parade of food and pastries began. Deidre was beside herself as she and Kevin picked up their forks and began to eat.

Crème mousseuse de feuilles—delicate cream pastry with smooth artichoke leaves, poached egg, and Parmesan cheese; *saumon fumé*—Scottish smoked salmon served with citron; *salade Nabucco*—fresh salad with scallops, corn, kidney beans, citron, filo pastry, almond cream, olive oil, and lemon juice; *millefeuille aux pétales de rose*—rose petal and taramasalata millefeuille with boutargue chips; *religieuse au fromage blanc*—puff pastry buns with cottage cheese and wild mushrooms; *foie gras rôti*—roasted duck foie gras with Morello cherry juice, quince stew, and Kugelhopf leaf. It was delicious and absolutely lovely.

But it was the sweet pastries and tea cakes that captured Deidre's heart. Deidre had never received any formal culinary training, but she could see now how years of training under the best chefs and pastry chefs yielded the most stunning and delectable creations.

Tarte tout chocolat—smooth chocolate biscuit with a dark chocolate cream filling and cocoa nougat; *tarte tatin*—puff pastry with crystallized caramel apples and cream; *savarin Chantilly*—pastry soaked in old dark rum with Chantilly cream and apricot jelly; *Saint-Honoré rose-framboise*—flaky puff pastry with a light rose petal confectioner's custard, raspberry stew, Chantilly cream, rose syrup fondant, and fresh raspberries. Then, finally, *les macarons Ladurée*—delicate domes of almond meringue sandwiching a range of delicious flavors: orange blossom, chocolate, vanilla, praline, raspberry, pistachio, dark chocolate, coffee, caramel with salt, lemon, chestnut, red fruits, liquorice, violet-blackcurrant. Kevin ordered a pot of oolong tea that had a hint of violets, and it was the appropriate end to one of the best culinary experiences Deidre had ever had.

"Oh, that was so worth it," she said an hour and a half later as they stepped out onto the street.

"I think you've taken the term 'savoring your food' to a whole new level," Kevin said with admiration as he looked at Deidre's bulging Ladurée carrier bag.

"I know. I couldn't help myself." She licked her lips.

"That good, huh?"

"Better."

"Well, we're not finished yet," Kevin said.

He took her to the shops of Pierre Hermé, Gérard Mulot, and Jean-Paul Hévin. More exceptional *pâtisseries* that featured the extraordinary. Deidre sampled more pastries and chocolates, then took her time to choose well-appointed gift boxes to bring back home.

It was the perfect ending to a perfect trip, Deidre thought as they got back into the car. They had just enough time to drive around the city for a bit, and Deidre was leaning back in her seat, content, when something caught her eye.

"What's that over there?"

Kevin looked over to where Deidre was pointing. "It looks

like a *marché*," he said. "One of the many farmers markets. Why?"

Deidre was already fumbling for her purse. "We have to stop. *Excusez-moi!* Kevin, how do I get the driver to stop? *Attendez, s'il vous plaît!*"

Kevin frowned. "Deidre, we're late as it is . . ."

"It will just take a minute, Kevin. I promise."

Kevin nodded to the driver and the car pulled over. Deidre jumped out with Kevin following behind her.

The farmers market was a bustle of people and produce stands tightly packed together on the cobbled street. There was a vibrant energy here, a chaotic but organic busyness. Deidre saw stall after stall of an abundant harvest of the freshest produce, fruits and vegetables, as well as cheese, fish, meats, and bread. Vendors were laughing and talking, offering samples to customers as they walked by: marinated olives, slices of sausages, chunks of fresh fruit, homemade jam spread on a crust of bread.

She chose a cheese stall first, her eyes roaming over the many choices. The vendor looked at her expectantly, and Deidre turned to Kevin.

"I have no idea where to start," she said. "There are ten different versions of goat cheese alone!"

Kevin nodded. "We'll let him recommend something," he said. "*Un chèvre bien frais, s'il vous plaît.*"

As Deidre tasted her sample, she could only nod and gesture for the vendor to wrap up a round of the goat cheese for her to purchase. "I can pack it into my suitcase somehow, right?" she asked Kevin, but before he could answer she was already at another stall, this one laden with fresh summer vegetables.

"Deidre," Kevin said, glancing at his watch. "We have to go, honey."

She was clutching a handful of fragrant herbs and inhaling deeply. "I just . . . Hold on . . ."

Kevin watched her, a bemused look on his face. "We have farmers markets in Seattle, you know," he reminded her.

"Kevin, come on. Just look at these squash blossoms. And these chanterelles! And, over there, look at those berries!" Basket after basket of beautiful raspberries, blueberries, blackberries, and gooseberries, all different varieties and colors. Deidre was in heaven.

"Deidre . . ."

As Kevin waited patiently, Deidre scanned the market longingly one last time, taking in everything she could. On more than one occasion she'd wished she had brought a camera, though that was the last thing on her mind when she boarded the plane in Seattle. This time was no exception.

She spotted a crêpe vendor and watched him as he poured the batter and spread it evenly over the hot griddle. After a moment, he used a crêpe spatula to expertly flip it over. He cracked an egg and spread it to the edges before adding handfuls of shredded cheese. Some salt, fresh cracked pepper, and then he folded the crêpe in half and then into quarters before sliding it into a paper sleeve and handing it a customer.

Voilá.

And just like that, Deidre had her answer.

She turned to face Kevin, a look of incredulity on her face.

"You can't possibly be hungry already," he said, astonished.

She looked down at the bags in her hands from their visit to the *pâtisseries*, and then took another look around the farmers market. Her eyes were bright.

"I'm ready to go home," she declared excitedly. "And I think I know how to save Sweet Deidre."

This time she was the one leading the way to the car.

Kevin was right behind her. "Really?" he asked, intrigued.

Deidre nodded as she took out a pen and piece of paper and began to write, ideas pouring out onto the page. "And that's not all."

CHAPTER FIFTEEN

Anyone can replicate the tabletop from Tiffany's,
but the host who can mirror his style onto the
table will enhance any guest's experience.
—Charlotte Ford, *21st-Century Etiquette*

No," Manuela said flatly. She was looking out the window of her office, her back to Deidre.

Deidre had expected this, but she still flinched. "Manuela, I know you're still very disappointed. But I wouldn't be standing here before you if I didn't have something good. *Really* good. I honestly think this is something you're going to be excited about. I know I am."

Manuela shook her head. "I'm sorry, Deidre, but you had that chance, *several times*, and it's time we all moved on."

This was going to be harder than she thought. Deidre wasn't below begging, but she hoped it wouldn't come to that.

"Manuela, when you brought me in, you knew I didn't have a history of corporate jobs or traditional training as a cook or pastry chef. *I do what I do because I love it.* My success has been built on seeing things a bit differently, on doing things a bit differently. That's not an excuse, just a matter of fact. When I told you I couldn't make Sweet Deidre work, I honestly didn't think I could. But some things have happened, and now I'm telling you that I can. Not only that, but this is better than anything I had originally dreamed of."

Manuela turned, and Deidre could see her profile, could tell that Manuela's curiosity was getting the better of her.

"Now I know it's not statistically significant," Deidre said, "but yesterday we brought in fifteen people from a temp agency and had them taste the new cookies and look at the packaging. We showed them the pricing. They filled out forms and wrote down their initial impressions." Deidre was amazed by how quickly and efficiently Amber was able to pull it together. She and the Sweet Deidre team had even baked the cookies from the first two passes and included them as well, just so they could compare the new impressions with the old.

Manuela finally turned around and faced Deidre, her lips twitching. "And?"

"And their response about the first two batches of cookies was fairly consistent with the focus groups. So we knew that whatever they said about this third batch would probably give us an indication of whether or not they'd like it in Bakersfield."

Manuela gave her a keen look. "So what are you saying, Deidre?"

Deidre smiled. "I'm saying that you might really want to give me a chance to make this presentation to you and Frank."

Manuela studied her for a moment before dropping into her chair. "Fine," she said, tapping something into her computer. She didn't look up. "I'll give you fifteen minutes. Tomorrow morning in the conference room, nine a.m. sharp."

* * *

The next day, all the faces in the conference room at Jamison Cookies and Confections were staring expectantly at Deidre. Manuela; her husband, Frank; Keith Duggan from sales and marketing; Gary Little from production; Paige Farley from public relations; Amber; and the Sweet Deidre team.

Deidre stood at the front of the room, nervous but eager to begin the presentation. The table on her right was filled with the gorgeous packaging from her trip to Paris and pictures of their contents. The table to her left held a mock-up of the new Sweet Deidre packaging and the proposed new line, hidden under a white sheet.

She had been working furiously since returning from Paris five days ago. The ideas tumbled in, one after another, still fresh and organic. She'd organized her thoughts and then began designing the line.

She'd pulled in William to help with the recipes as she tweaked and experimented, and accepted Kevin's offer to borrow one of his employees, a graphic designer named Rudy Velez, to come up with some packaging options based on her rough sketches.

She'd had Gary help her with sourcing ingredients and ran the numbers herself, wanting to see if her ideas were even viable. They were. The question now was whether or not Manuela and Frank were on board.

"When we received the feedback from the first focus group," Deidre was saying now, "it was clear we had missed the mark. So we came up with another line, thinking that a new set of recipes might be the answer. But, again, it wasn't.

"I found Manuela's final charge to be the most difficult: To come up with a cookie and pastry line that would reflect value and quality, something familiar, but with a Deidre McIntosh twist. I tried, but something just wasn't working. The product line was too mainstream, almost typical. A chief concern was pricing, especially given the current state of the economy. People are buckling down, conserving their cash, reluctant to make big purchases. I had no idea how to make this work. And then I went to France."

Behind her was a video screen. She nodded for Amber to start her PowerPoint presentation. Seconds later, stunning images of exquisite pastries and cookies scrolled before their eyes.

"They're works of edible art," Deidre said, looking at the images appreciatively. She could still remember how they tasted, and that was exactly the point she was trying to make. "They affect you on a profound sensorial level—feel, taste, smell, even sound. They create a lasting memory. And memories are what bring customers back for more. The better the memory, the better the consumer loyalty.

"I realized that in order for Sweet Deidre to be successful, we'd need to create emotional and psychological touchstones with our product. People would need to feel comforted—the emotional aspect—and also feel that they were being rewarded—the psychological aspect. I didn't want Sweet Deidre to be trendy, driven by outside influences: the 'what's hot, what's not' experience. I knew it had to be about the emotional and psychological touchstones that spring from internalized experiences."

Deidre walked over to the table that held her mementos from Paris. "But it's not just the cookie or pastry. The packaging and product have to complement each other."

She held up a pale green Ladurée box tied with a matching ribbon. "What do you think is inside of this box?" She held up another box, a red and white petal box from Pierre Hermé. "Or this one? These are pastry boxes from some of the top *pâtisseries* in Paris. The designs alone make you dream of what could be inside. People save these boxes, collect them—they're treasured as much as the delicacies themselves. They are, quite simply, containers of dreams."

Frank spoke up. "This is a tough economy in which to launch a luxury line," he said.

Deidre nodded in agreement. "Absolutely. High prices everywhere have made luxury elusive. People aren't making big-ticket purchases. They cannot afford a fancy new car or an expensive new dress, and because of that people aren't going to deny themselves the comparatively small expense of something like this."

Deidre walked over to the table containing the Sweet Deidre products and lifted the sheet with a flourish. "Beautiful cookies and pastries that taste as good as they look."

There was a murmur of anticipation as everyone strained to get a look. Deidre had decided on four core products to start, but with enough multiple flavor choices to help them manage costs while giving consumers more options.

It was an eclectic range, starting with the familiar: classic chocolate chip cookies with large dark chocolate chunks, available plain or with rolled oats, coconut flakes or toasted walnuts; buttery shortbread, plain or dipped in white chocolate, dark chocolate, or caramel; delicate madeleines, available plain, in honey and orange, or with a lemony glaze; and finally the signature Sweet Deidre mini petit fours, iced and topped with an SD monogram in raspberry, apricot, lemon, vanilla-orange, mocha bean, green tea, and triple chocolate. When considered individually, the Sweet Deidre line now boasted eighteen products in all.

Deidre brought tasting platters to the table as everyone leaned forward eagerly. "Even in a tight economy, the need for people to reward themselves with food favorites or special treats is more important than ever," she continued. "It's an escape from their economic woes. A taste of decadence that won't break the bank or, because of its small size, ruin your diet."

She held up two of the Sweet Deidre gift boxes that she had printed on heavy oversized stock. She used an X-Acto knife to cut it to size, then used her glue gun to seal the sides. The design was simple: rectangular boxes with a pale pink chrysanthemum print on a white background and a mossy green belly band around the center with the elegant SD monogram on a translucent frosted square. Deidre knew the people might throw the belly band away, so she had Rudy sketch in the words SWEET DEIDRE in matching pink script and weave it along the chrysanthemum petals.

"When you put the cookies in beautiful gift boxes that they'll be inclined to save, you're essentially making the brand a part of their daily life. Each time they see the box, they see the brand. The memory of the cookie or pastry comes back to them. A small purchase like this goes a long way, for both the customer and for us. We all know that it's easier and less expensive in the long run to invest in customer loyalty and repeat business rather than chasing after individual sales."

Frank was eating a triple chocolate petit four. Deidre could tell from the look on his face that he was struggling not to enjoy it, but at the same time failing. He reached for another one, nodding to the plate in front of him. "So how do you propose to price the line? If we go with the packaging you're suggesting, it's going to raise the price point considerably. It'll be hard to stay competitive."

Deidre picked up a stack of papers and passed them out. She had come up with a pricing strategy and pro forma for the next three years. Deidre's cousin, Caroline, had a boutique brokerage firm, Open Investments. She'd spent a whole day working with Deidre and her team on the numbers, not once complaining. While Deidre never brought it up, she was fairly sure that Caroline still felt bad about her former employee disclosing Deidre's personal information to *The Seattle Scoop*.

"Customers expect to pay a higher price for specialty foods. If we value price it, it won't be considered a product of unusually high quality. The pricing I'm proposing is consistent with other high-value brands, but I want us to be thinking creatively instead of competitively. You become so engrossed in what everyone else is doing that you lose your own focus. We need to present what works for us first, not the other way around."

"But you're always supposed to put the customer first," Keith pointed out. "It sounds like you want us to put ourselves first."

"By acting on our passion, we *will* be putting the customer first. When we offer products that we're excited about, that we've carefully considered and tested, we're giving them the best we have to offer. It tells them that we think they're worth it. They're *worth* our time and effort to get it right. When they spend their money on a Sweet Deidre product, we're reinforcing the message that they're worth it, because they are. They don't deserve any less."

There was a moment of silence.

"Well, they certainly are delicious," Gary finally said, brushing away some stray crumbs. "And not difficult to produce. We could easily make this work. It's also very adaptable for seasonal specials at Easter and Christmas."

Deidre gave him a grateful smile and waited anxiously for the others to share their thoughts.

Paige shrugged. "I've been working on Deidre's backstory and it'll dovetail nicely into this. The story of her car accident hit the major wires, so we're on everyone's radar now. We could say the car accident prompted her to rethink the line and that she came up with products that reflected her passion for life. If we use the 'life is too short' idea coupled with small, 'you're worth it' indulgences, I think it will be pretty appealing."

Keith was nodding. "I like the more sophisticated packaging. It reads more authentic, more discriminating, higher quality."

Deidre appreciated their support, and even caught Frank's slight nod to his wife. But even with his approval, Manuela could still nix the whole idea. Her confidence in Deidre had wavered, and Deidre didn't know if she'd be able to win it back.

Manuela had only taken single bites of the cookies and pastries, and was now tapping her pen on the table.

"I don't know . . ." she murmured.

Deidre turned to look at her earnestly. "Manuela, you told me that what you wanted was the genuine Deidre McIntosh product. I'm telling you, this is it. This line is classy without being pretentious, down-to-earth without being homey. It's a line that knows its worth. It has just enough sweetness to make you smile, and not so much that it feels like overkill. This is a line that, unlike so many other gourmet brands, has a widespread appeal. There's nothing stand-offish about it—it doesn't exclude anyone. There's a familiarity about it, and yet there's a longing for more, too. It's the promise for the future you were looking for, Manuela." She reached for a madeleine and held it up. "All wrapped up in a cookie."

Manuela's gaze slid down to the plate of cookies in front of her, considering this. Her shoulders seemed to relax as she reached out for a petit four and took a bite.

Everyone held their breath, Deidre included.

Manuela swallowed, took a sip of water. "We'd have to reinvest in the start-up costs since we're essentially talking about a brand-new line," she said. "It'll make our overall investment in the brand much higher than we anticipated. We're looking at a new marketing campaign, and we've already spent a considerable amount of money. Now that we're looking at launching a more sophisticated, elegant cookie line, we'll need a strong media push to get it off the ground. I'm not sure we'll be able to accomplish that." It was clear she wasn't going to let Deidre off the hook that easily, but Deidre had expected that.

"I thought of that, too," Deidre said with a confident smile. She picked up the pro forma and opened it up. "Now if you'll turn to page thirteen . . ."

Chapter Sixteen

The responsibility of the gracious guest
is to keep an open stomach.
—Charlotte Ford, *21st-Century Etiquette*

Deidre was humming happily as she finished straightening her desk. After Manuela had given the green light on the new Sweet Deidre line two weeks ago, Deidre made a decision to come in an hour earlier each day to clean and organize her office. Papers were now filed in their proper place, samples placed in boxes and appropriately labeled. Trade magazines and newsletters were in chronological order and lined up on the shelves. Dusty surfaces were wiped down, drawers emptied and then refilled, the clutter slowly disappearing until what was left was clean and orderly, even inspiring.

William was the feng shui expert and had helped her rearrange her furniture. They moved her desk to the far corner in the "command position" facing the door and added a tabletop water fountain plus the requisite number of plants. William placed a few tasteful figurines around the office: a bronze frog, a pair of fish, even a Maneki Neko or good-luck cat. Deidre didn't consider herself superstitious, but she had to admit the timing was uncanny: an hour after William had left, Manuela appeared with the good news that the feedback from the focus groups was in. The verdict? They loved the new Sweet Deidre cookies, and the line was now officially in production.

All that remained on her desk was her computer, the picture of her and Kevin, and the Sweet Deidre binder—the new one, not the old one. The old binder had been permanently filed away in the back of Deidre's closet at home, a gentle reminder of what could have been. The new binder, with the fresh Sweet Deidre logo and the enticing lineup of recipes, had now become her bible. She was smiling and running her hand along the smooth cover when her phone rang.

"I need some of that Deidre McIntosh expertise." The voice on the phone was clipped and a little snarky, refreshingly familiar.

Deidre grinned. "Lindsey Miller. Feeling better, are we?"

"If I am, I'll never admit it. Have you got a minute?"

"Of course. What's up?"

"I'm trying to redo the menu at the Wishbone. I got to looking at it and realized that the food wasn't very heart-healthy. I can't have the Wishbone feeding the people in this town food that's going to clog their arteries and send them to an early grave. I just don't want that on my conscience."

Deidre thought of Doc Hensen and Bobby Carson at the general store. She couldn't picture them eating salads or tabouleh or tofu anything, no matter how well it was cooked or disguised. "But don't some of your customers actually prefer the artery-clogging items on your menu?"

"I don't give a damn what they prefer," Lindsey said haughtily. "If they want that stuff, they can go somewhere else, but I'm not serving it."

"What about the buyer from LA? Does he care?"

"Why should be care? He's buying the Wishbone from me. I've always set the menu and I know what this town will eat. It's gonna be a better menu, and a healthier one, too. Besides, he's spending all his time figuring out some improvements. New tables and chairs, some equipment in the kitchen, that sort of thing."

Deidre tried to hide her disappointment. "So the sale is final?"

"Almost. He's got some fancy lawyers and they're doing something called due diligence, asking me for every scrap of paper since who knows when. So what do you think, can I go across the street and have Bobby fax this new menu to you?"

"Of course." Deidre gave her the fax number for the Sweet Deidre offices. "So how are you feeling, Lindsey? Are those rehabilitation sessions coming along all right?"

"Yeah, I guess. It's strange to think about what happened now. It seems so long ago, but it wasn't really. Sometimes I think it was a dream, and then all I have to do is look at all that medication lined up in my medicine cabinet and it comes back to me."

"How are Sid and the kids?"

"Good. Things are getting back to normal, if you don't count all this business with the Wishbone." Lindsey cleared her throat.

Deidre expected Lindsey to say she had to go, but Lindsey didn't. Instead, she kept talking.

"So," Lindsey said. "Have you ever cooked with something called stevia before? It's some kind of healthy substitute for sugar. Bobby doesn't carry it."

"You can get it from the health food stores. I'll pick some

up and send it to you to try. I have a few recipes, too." Deidre made a note to herself so she couldn't forget.

"Got any for pie? I want to be able to try it in a pie."

"I'm sure I can find one. I think I saw one for a pecan pie somewhere."

"That'd be great." There was a long, uneasy pause. "So . . . what are you doing right now?"

It wasn't like Lindsey to linger on a telephone conversation—she usually kept things short and sweet, or short at least. Deidre swiveled in her chair, enjoying the chance to chat with her friend. "Working. Looking at paperwork, trying to figure out how to drum up buzz for Sweet Deidre with a nonexistent sales and marketing budget." She had a few ideas that she presented at the meeting to Manuela and Frank, but she still needed more.

"How's Kevin?"

"Lindsey, come on. Is there anything in particular that you'd like to talk about?"

"What? No. I'm just being friendly and saying hi." Lindsey sounded offended. "Excuse me if you're too busy to talk to me. I'll just hang up now."

"Lindsey, stop it. Do you want to talk about the Wishbone?"

"No," Lindsey said curtly. "Why would I want to do that? There's nothing to talk about."

"Are you sure you want to sell it?"

"Selling it would be in everybody's best interest." Lindsey's voice was resolute.

Deidre wasn't convinced. "Even yours?" she pressed.

Lindsey gave a chuckle. "Boy, you never give up, do you?"

"I just don't want you to do anything you're going to regret."

"Deidre, I've done a lot of things in my life that I regret. It's just how things go. I love the Wishbone, but it's getting to be too much for me to handle on my own."

"Well, what about getting some help? Not just with the waitressing and cooking, but with actually running the place; someone to help you with the day-to-day operations."

"What kind of payroll do you think I've got going here?" Lindsey demanded. "We can't all have some big company backing us, you know."

Lindsey always lashed out when she was backed into a corner. Still, Deidre persisted, "But maybe there's some creative way you can . . ."

"Well, I think this conversation's pretty much finished," Lindsey said briskly. "I know you mean well, Deidre, but I've already made up my mind. So be a friend and just be happy for me, okay?"

"Okay, but . . ."

"Be happy me for me, Deidre."

Deidre took a deep breath. "I want you to be happy, Lindsey."

"Me, too. I'm gonna fax this menu over to you in a little bit, okay? Call me later after you've had a chance to take a look."

"I will. Bye, Lindsey."

A few minutes later, Amber entered her office with Lindsey's fax. "This just came in for you."

"Great, thanks."

"And I also thought you should see this." She held out a paper that Deidre instantly recognized as *The Seattle Scoop*.

"Let me guess: Rosemary is on the rampage again?"

Amber nodded.

Deidre was intentionally avoiding the tabloids, knowing that she would just get worked up with whatever she read.

Kevin had coached her not to take it too personally, but she found it impossible not to.

"I know it seems like an invasion of privacy—" he'd tried to explain to her.

Deidre hadn't been swayed. "That's because it *is* an invasion of privacy, Kevin."

He'd sighed, knowing she wasn't going to be easily persuaded otherwise. "In their mind, and the minds of their readers, celebrities and public figures are public domain. The dailies are better about this—they have their fact checkers and tend to be more cautious about what they print. With the *Scoop* and other tabloids, it's no-holds-barred."

"It's just so frustrating that everyone simply laps it up," she'd complained.

"That's the power of the written word," Kevin had said. "The Internet has changed the way we process and receive information, but there's something about seeing it in black and white that's undeniably compelling."

Now, as Deidre unfolded the paper, she knew exactly what Kevin had been talking about.

THE SEATTLE SCOOP

THE COOKIE CRUMBLES FOR DEIDRE MCINTOSH
A *Seattle Scoop* Exclusive! By Rosemary Goodwin

Cookie girl Deidre McIntosh was devastated by the images of millionaire boyfriend Kevin Johnson wrapped up in the arms of his former lover and fiancée, Sabine Durant (visit the photo gallery at our blog). The two were reportedly seen roaming the streets of Paris together while Deidre McIntosh was home in

Seattle, recuperating from a car accident that nearly claimed her life.

Sources close to the couple say they were on a much-needed break, while others say that Deidre had no idea that Johnson had reunited with Durant. Johnson was staying in a romantic suite at the prestigious Hôtel Meurice, where a member of the housekeeping staff said she was shocked when she opened the room one morning and saw the remains of what was clearly an all-night orgy. *Vive la France!*

There are also continued rumors that Deidre's cookie line, Sweet Deidre, may be in jeopardy. Industry experts are expressing their skepticism of Deidre's ability to successfully kick off a new line of cookies amidst so much personal turmoil.

"That's the problem with being on top of the world," an insider explained. "There's no place to go but down."

Deidre remains heavily sedated under doctor's orders. Was living the high life too much for her? Log on to our blog and tell us what you think!

"Well, so much for truth in journalism," Deidre said, shaking her head in disgust.

"It's just that . . ." Amber chewed nervously on her lip. "Well, the word around the office is that Manuela is concerned that Sweet Deidre is getting too much negative press."

"The word around the office, huh?" Deidre didn't know why they even bothered with an interoffice intranet—Elliot and Amber seemed to be doing an excellent job of spreading the word on their own. "I admit that it's not great, but it's not exactly in the same category as 'Food Reviewer Keels over from Tainted Cookies.' Now *that* would be negative press."

"I know, but I think Manuela is worried that this will have an impact on the sales of the Sweet Deidre line."

"I hope not. But it's not like we can control what they print." Deidre frowned as she thought about it. "Rosemary's just looking for anything that will help her sell more papers."

"Well, it's working. Everyone I know reads *The Seattle Scoop*, especially now, since they know I work for Sweet Deidre. I've told them it's not true, but who knows if they believe me."

"I know. It looks pretty convincing when it's splashed across the page like that." Deidre took one more look before folding the paper and handing it back to Amber.

"I went to their blog, too. Just to look," Amber added quickly, her cheeks pink with color. "Anyway, there were a ton of comments after the posts about you."

"Good or bad?"

"A little of everything. Mostly good, though. It was just weird to see how many people have an opinion about whether you spent too much on your dress, or if Sweet Deidre is going to fail."

Deidre couldn't help but be a little intrigued. "Really? And I'm happy to put the question to bed. Yes, I did spend too much on my dress. *Way* too much."

Amber grinned. "That's what the polls said. There was even a place where people were posting their ideas on what you should have worn."

Deidre knew she'd regret it if she looked, but she couldn't help herself. She took the paper from Amber and typed in the address for the *The Seattle Scoop* blog.

"Wow" was all she could say. Hundreds of comments followed every post on Deidre. It seemed that Rosemary knew every fact and figure about Deidre, even if a lot of it was wrong or flawed. "She seems slightly obsessed."

"She was like this last year with Clara Michaels, that local actress who adopted twelve kids," Amber informed her. "It got so much attention that the regular papers picked it up."

"Oh, that's right." Deidre remembered seeing the headlines in the newspaper display bins on the street corners. "Wasn't there some hype about her adoptions being expedited over those of non-celebrity couples?"

"Rosemary was the one behind that hype. It didn't stop Clara from adopting her last baby though. Some say it even helped her. Anyway, all the reporters get assigned people, and then they compete for 'The Scoop of the Month,' kind of a play off the ice cream . . ."

"I get it, Amber."

"Yeah, so whoever's story gets the most hits gets the 'Scoop of the Month' award and a bunch of free stuff. I'm pretty sure that's what Rosemary is going for."

"Do I want to know how you know all this?"

"I did some research after Rosemary tricked her way into the office. And Elliot kind of knows all about this . . ." Amber trailed off, blushing.

Deidre hoped for his sake that he wasn't one of the "industry insiders," which she was fairly sure was completely fabricated anyway. She continued to click through site, her mind thoughtful.

"Will there be anything else, Deidre?"

"One last thing, Amber. Did we ever reschedule that reporter from *Taste* magazine?"

"I tried to, but I haven't heard back."

"Let's try again. I have a short list of magazines that we should probably contact again, see if they would be willing to write something on the line. Oh, and this one, too." Deidre flipped open a box with business cards neatly organized in alphabetical order. Her fingers ran along the top of the tabs until she came to the one marked S. She pulled out the card she was looking for and handed it to Amber. "Give Rosemary Goodwin a call—here's her direct line. Tell her I'm willing to do an interview."

Amber stared at her. "Are you sure?"

Deidre gave a shrug as she closed the box and put it back in its place. "No, but it can't be any worse than what they've already printed. Tell her I'll do a Q and A on her blog, too."

"Okay," Amber said uncertainly. "You're the boss."

The next day Rosemary Goodwin sat in Deidre's office looking fidgety and a little nervous. At Deidre's request, Amber and Elliot had joined them.

"You don't mind if I tape this, do you?" Deidre asked sweetly. She pulled out her own digital recorder and set it next to Rosemary's on the desk between them.

Rosemary frowned. "What is this?"

"My naïve insurance policy. I'll give you this interview, Rosemary, and I know you'll sensationalize things, but I don't want you riding roughshod over me or anybody else in the article."

Rosemary sniffed. "I'm a professional. That's not my style."

Deidre tried not to roll her eyes. "Yeah, I've seen your style." She made introductions. "So, you've had the pleasure of meeting my assistant, Amber Olson, and Elliot Dudley is here from the JCC executive office." Deidre stifled a laugh as Elliot gave a grave nod. He was taking this whole business very seriously, and had even dressed up in a suit for the occasion, which made him look even more lanky than usual.

Deidre figured it would be easier to include Elliot from the very beginning and save him the trouble of having to hunt for the right information. He and Amber were probably the two youngest employees at JCC, but they were typical of Generation Y—plugged in and ready to go.

"So I can ask you anything?" Rosemary was still wary.

"Anything. No guarantee that I'll answer, but I didn't invite you here to hold back information either. I'd rather you have the whole story from me than try to piece together bits of information the way you've been doing it. Plus, it's my intention to help you win the 'Scoop of the Month.'"

Rosemary was surprised, and Deidre saw a greedy gleam in the reporter's eyes. "Why?"

"Because you're going to try to win it anyway; no doubt at my expense. You said you wanted my side of the story, so now I'm willing to give it. At least this way I know you can't screw up the facts." *Even though you probably will,* Deidre thought ruefully. It was a risk, but at this point Deidre figured they didn't have much to lose.

Rosemary was getting excited now. "And everything's fair game?"

"As long as you stick to your end of the bargain. Even coverage over my personal *and* professional life, and my two colleagues here get to review the copy before it goes to press."

"What about the live blog Q and A?" Rosemary asked. "I want an hour."

"I'll give you that, too—" Deidre started to say when Elliot interrupted her.

"That'll be moderated with a time delay, right?" he said. "So Deidre will have the option to delete any question that's inappropriate or inflammatory before it goes up on the board, right?"

Wow, Deidre hadn't even thought of that. She remembered Amber showing her the transcripts of other Q&A chats at *The Seattle Scoop*, and there were a few where the guests were definitely put in the hot seat, even attacked.

"Well, I don't think we should withhold the people's right to the First Amendment," Rosemary said. "It protects free speech."

"I know the First Amendment," Elliot said testily. "In that case, I can only recommend to Deidre that she not agree to a live Q and A on your blog."

Rosemary glared at him. "Our readers aren't like that."

"I'm a reader, and I'm like that," Elliot told her.

Rosemary gave a dismissive laugh. "Well, you'd be the exception."

"I don't think so." Elliot straightened in his chair. "I'm ScooperDuper206."

Rosemary's mouth opened and closed, then opened again. "*You're* ScooperDuper206?"

At Deidre's confusion, Amber leaned over and whispered, "Elliot is one of the top posters on *The Seattle Scoop* message boards and blogs. He's actually a bit of a legend."

"So Deidre will have a chance to exclude any question she doesn't feel comfortable answering, right?" Elliot repeated.

"Fine. I'll make sure our tech guy sets it up." Rosemary gave Elliot a quick once-over before turning to Deidre. "Can we please get started now? I'm on a deadline here."

Deidre took a deep breath. "Fire away."

Chapter Seventeen

The modern rule is that every woman
must be her own chaperone.
—*Amy Vanderbilt's Complete Book of Etiquette*

The fax machine was out of paper. Deidre knew this because the incessant beeping had been going on for well over half an hour, but she couldn't drag herself out of bed to restock the paper tray. Even though her home office was down the hall from her bedroom, the annoying sound seemed to fill Deidre's apartment.

Deidre cast a glance at her alarm clock: 9:15 a.m. She had fallen asleep well before midnight, happily exhausted. Everything for Sweet Deidre was coming together nicely, so much better than she could have ever hoped for. After much discussion, it was agreed that the launch date would be pushed back a month to October, giving Deidre just enough time to implement her marketing plan for Sweet Deidre.

Deidre burrowed deep under her covers. Another hour or two of sleep wouldn't hurt. She certainly deserved it.

Deidre awoke at noon, the fax machine still beeping and

her cell phone ringing. Outside the day was sunny, the bright noon sun slipping its way into Deidre's bedroom through the patterned cotton voile drapes. While she still felt out of sorts, it was obviously time to get up. Groggy, Deidre reached over and answered her phone. "Hello?"

It was William. "Deidre, what are you doing?"

She gave a yawn. "Sleeping, but I'm up now. Why?"

"Why? Because Alain and I are sitting at Le Pichet, wondering where you are!"

Oops. Deidre slowly sat up. "Were we meeting for lunch today?"

"You mean since I talked to you yesterday and you said, 'See you for lunch tomorrow, 11:30, Le Pichet'?"

That would be a yes. "Sorry, William. I'm still jet-lagged and my schedule is completely off." Deidre stretched. "I can be there in half an hour. Better make that forty-five minutes, to be safe."

"No can do. Alain has to get back to the hospital and anyway, our food's here."

"Oh, so you ordered without me?"

"We were famished, Deidre. And I ordered you that goat cheese and asparagus salad, thank you very much."

Deidre was suddenly hungry herself. "Could you bring it by? And get some of that sausage with garlic and chilies. And half a baguette?"

"I'm not Meals on Wheels," William complained.

"Please?" she pleaded. "I didn't have breakfast and I can smell the food from here. And let's not forget that it was French food that inspired your . . ."

A good-natured sigh. "Fine. I'll be by when we're finished."

"You're a peach, William."

"I know. I should get that in writing, just in case you or Alain conveniently forget."

Deidre laughed. "As if that were possible. *You'd* never let us forget, William."

"True. Alain and I are going to finish our lunch, and then I'll come over."

"See you soon."

Deidre made her way to the shower, taking her time under the hot water and steam. She had a nagging suspicion that she was forgetting something. She'd already missed lunch with William and Alain—was there something else?

Deidre shampooed her hair and tried to think. Since their return from Paris a month ago, Kevin and Deidre had continued to be together almost daily, although yesterday he'd had meetings and dinner with a business partner in from Belgium. Were they supposed to see each other today? Not for breakfast, obviously, and she'd made (and missed) her lunch plans with William and Alain. Dinner, maybe . . .

Suddenly she remembered. They were having dinner tonight with Kevin's parents and Marla, in Edward and Beverly's home. It was just a family dinner, and since it had been a few weeks since his mother had seen Deidre, Beverly had kindly invited her as well.

Even with the soothing stream of water hitting her back, Deidre felt herself tense. Marla. She had told Kevin on the plane ride home that she doubted that she and Marla would ever be friends—even amenable acquaintances would be a stretch. Kevin had agreed, saying that he was content with Deidre and Marla coexisting peacefully in the same room. Deidre didn't argue the point, but "peacefully" was a bit of a stretch. Marla exuded enough hostility to fuel a rocket to Mars.

Deidre stepped out of the shower and toweled off. At least tonight would be casual, and she genuinely liked Beverly and Edward. If Deidre had made any other plans for the day, she couldn't think of them. It was just as well—all she could think about was the food William would be bringing over. She had a sudden hankering for ham. Maybe she should call William and ask him to add some *assiette de jambon cru* to her order.

William's arms were full of takeout bags and containers when Deidre opened the door. "Yum," she said.

He handed her the bags. "If I hadn't taken preemptive measures, you'd probably still be calling me. I thought I'd never get out of there."

"Sorry," Deidre said, feeling guilty. She'd called him two more times, adding on an order of olives marinated with pastis, orange, and garlic, and a red potato salad with dandelion greens. By the time she had dialed his number a third time in hopes of scoring some dessert, William had turned his phone off.

"I can't stay," he said, following her to the dining room. "I was on-call this morning, so I'm pretty wiped."

"Well, you're in good company. I'm completely exhausted and out of sorts."

He eyed her terry cloth bathrobe. "Too tired to get dressed?"

Deidre shook her head, popping open the container of olives. "I have dinner plans tonight with Kevin's family. Can't be bothered to change twice." She gave a heavy sigh. "I just can't seem to shake this jet lag. I'm such a novice traveler."

"Even the well-traveled get jet lag," William said. "Whenever I fly to Asia, it takes me at least a couple of days to recover."

"A couple of days? This has been going on for almost three weeks, and it seems to be getting worse, not better. I could sleep forever if given the chance."

"Maybe you picked up a bug in Paris. Bacterial infections are more common these days than jet lag for international travelers. Are you throwing up?"

Deidre opened one of the containers. "No."

"Diarrhea?"

"No." Deidre gazed at the chicken liver terrine and pâté, her appetite diminishing.

"Loss of appetite?"

"No, Dr. Sen, but I'm getting there. Do you mind if we change the subject? I'd like to eat my lunch." Deidre wrinkled her nose. "Damn. Too late." She closed the container with a frown.

"Sorry. Just trying to help. Maybe you should see your doctor."

Deidre shook her head. "That would require making an appointment and then getting into my car and going to the appointment." She found the ham and took a bite. "Ah. That hits the spot."

William watched her devour her lunch. "You don't normally eat ham, Deidre," he said.

"I know. I've just been a complete carnivore lately. I polished off an entire steak yesterday." She let out a dainty burp. "Excuse me."

William arched an eyebrow. "Did you eat a lot of meat in Paris?"

Deidre shrugged. "I don't know. Maybe. I had a thing for goat cheese, too." Deidre rummaged through the bags. "Shoot. I should have asked you to pick up something to drink."

"Don't you have water?"

"Yes, but I don't want water. I need, I don't know, some coffee."

"Can't you make coffee?"

"Yes, but I want a café mocha." She looked at William with pleading eyes.

He gave a start. "What, are you kidding me?"

"There's a coffee shop right around the corner."

"Did I mention I was on-call this morning? And yesterday? I basically just finished a forty-eight-hour shift!"

"I know, and you look great. Please?"

"Since when did you become so needy?" William headed for the door.

"I'm not needy, just thirsty in true Seattleite style. Pick up something for yourself, too. I'm buying."

The door slamming closed was his response.

Deidre continued to eat, savoring the food. She wondered what the Johnsons would be serving for dinner—or, rather, what their chef was serving. She thought about making a dessert to bring, but then she shook her head. Too much work.

William returned fifteen minutes later, just as Deidre was finishing her lunch.

"I can't believe you ate all that," he said, handing her a steaming cup in a corrugated paper sleeve.

"I was hungry. No breakfast, remember?"

"I remember." He held out a small brown paper bag. "Here, this is for you, too."

"You didn't get any coffee for yourself?"

"The last thing I need is caffeine. I'm going to go home and sleep." William settled onto the couch. "I can stay another ten minutes."

"I'm dying for something sweet. Is this a chocolate muffin?"

"Nope."

"Danish?"

"Just look, Deidre."

Deidre peered into the bag. William was right—it definitely wasn't a chocolate muffin. She pulled out a cardboard box. "Is this what I think it is?"

"It is. As I said, I have ten minutes. The test should only take five, provided you have good aim."

She gave a laugh. "William, I do not need a pregnancy test. I am *not* pregnant."

"Really? When was the last time you had your period?"

"A month ago." Deidre frowned. Or was it two months ago? "What month is this?" She felt a chill go up her spine.

Uh-oh.

"I knew it. I didn't live with you all those years not to get a sense of your cycle. Just go take the test, Deidre. It can't hurt."

She put the test back in the bag. "No way. I'm just late because of all the stress. The K Ball, Lindsey's diagnosis, the car accident, the trip to Paris and all that business with Sabine . . ."

"Now I only have eight minutes. You can either do it now while I'm here, or do it when you're alone. I'd prefer you do it now, just so that you don't call and wake me later, all hysterical, and I'll have to come back here." He gave a yawn.

"What makes you think I'm pregnant, anyway?" Deidre asked William. Her eyes darted to the paper bag.

"I don't know. Call it a hunch. That, and it looks like you could sub for a Playboy Bunny. Or a waitress at Hooters." He made a vague gesture toward her chest.

Deidre reddened as she looked down at her chest. She was definitely sporting some serious cleavage. She had noticed that her breasts seemed swollen and her bras were snug, but she'd assumed it was water retention from her travels.

"Kevin did look at me kind of strange the other night when I was putting on my PJs," she said. "But why wouldn't he have said anything?"

"Because he's a wise man. I don't think any heterosexual man would question his girlfriend's breast size, especially if it was increasing. At least, not out loud."

Deidre grabbed the bag and headed for the bathroom. "Don't leave until I'm done," she called to William. She didn't want to be alone, just in case.

"Of course not." His voice, while sleepy, was reassuring.

In the bathroom, Deidre opened the box and read the instructions. It was easy enough. One line, she wasn't pregnant; two lines, she was. Okay, no big deal.

A few seconds later, Deidre was waiting for the results. The box said it had a 98.4 percent accuracy rate. *That's pretty damn accurate*, she thought. Not a whole lot of room for error.

She couldn't be pregnant. She and Kevin were always careful, and they'd never had a mishap with their method of birth control, the ever reliable condom. Deidre had nothing to worry about.

But then she remembered Paris. He hadn't had anything in his bag and neither had Deidre. They had eventually found a *pharmacie* with a flashing green cross and picked up what they needed, but that was the day after . . .

Oh boy.

"Are you all right in there?" called William from the living room.

"Yes. I'm just waiting."

It would take three minutes for the results to show. It had only been about a minute. Curious, Deidre took a peek at the window on the test stick to see what was happening.

There were two pink lines, one fainter than the other, but there were definitely two lines.

Two lines.

Deidre grabbed the instructions and read them again. Maybe one of the lines would disappear since the full three minutes hadn't passed. Deidre watched, but if anything, the second line got darker. She leaned against the bathroom counter.

There was a knock on the door. "Well?"

Deidre opened the door and silently handed the stick to William.

"Oh," he said, his face registering surprise. "Well, at least I didn't waste eight bucks."

"William!" Deidre slumped against the door frame. "I can't believe it. What am I going to do?"

"You should probably schedule that appointment with your doctor now," he said. "They'll pretty much do the same test to confirm your pregnancy, but then he'll order some blood work and get you on prenatals . . ."

"Wait!" Deidre's head was spinning. "I can't be pregnant, I'm not ready to be pregnant. Not yet."

William led a dazed Deidre to the living room. "Dee, if you were ever going to get pregnant, now is probably a good time. Unless you're absolutely sure that you don't want to have kids."

"I don't . . . I mean, I haven't . . ." Deidre shook her head.

William sat next to her on the couch, holding her hand as she processed her thoughts. What would Kevin say?

Pregnant.

Pregnant.

She was pregnant.

"You should probably talk to Kevin," William offered quietly.

Deidre had no idea how that would go over. She knew he liked kids and he absolutely doted on his nine-year-old god-daughter, Claire, who cared about as much for Deidre as Marla did. But Deidre was quite sure he wouldn't be expecting this. And now, after all they had been through . . .

Deidre blinked back tears.

"Hey, hey," William said, putting an arm around her. "Don't cry. It'll be fine." He reached for a box of tissues and handed her one. "When are you going to see Kevin next?"

"Tonight. We have dinner with his parents and Marla."

"Well, it's not exactly dinner conversation. What are you going to do?"

"I don't know." Deidre sniffed into a tissue. Her tears were drying up and it was starting to dawn on her that she was, in fact, pregnant. "Should I confirm it with a doctor first? I mean, before I say anything?"

"You could, but these tests are pretty accurate." William picked up the stick and looked at it, giving a firm nod. "There you go. I'm a doctor and I just confirmed it. You're pregnant, girlfriend. Do you need some alone time?"

Deidre nodded, her face buried in the tissues once again. She needed time to think things through.

Deidre spent a good part of the afternoon curled up in the overstuffed loveseat by her window, gazing quietly at the skyline with a pillow clutched to her stomach. Her phone didn't ring, or if it did, she didn't hear it.

She had already called her doctor and made an appointment for the following week, then went to the drugstore to buy one more test, just in case. She bought a different test this time—instead of indicator lines, it clearly stated PREGNANT or NOT PREGNANT. She didn't feel that she could trust her mind right now, and double lines or crosses could easily be misread. She held her breath when she took the test, and realized that unlike a few hours earlier, she was desperately hoping the test would read positive.

It did.

Deidre knew that it was still too early, that myriad things could still happen, but it came down to one thing, that at this moment she had a baby growing inside of her. It was the last thing she'd expected, and not at all how she expected it. But it didn't make it any less wonderful.

Everything looked different now. Even her condo. Her vision seemed brighter, sharper. She'd replace the loveseat with a rocking chair. Whether it was a boy or girl didn't matter, but she saw a girl. Soft tufts of hair, wrapped in a crocheted blanket. She remembered an old *Live Simple* show where her guest had showcased an impressive collection of baby blankets, caps, purses, headbands, scarves, sweaters, and more. Deidre didn't crochet or knit, but she suddenly felt tempted to try.

Her home office could be easily converted into a nursery. The insurance company was covering the loss of her Volvo and would buy her a new car. Instead of buying another SUV, maybe she'd consider a more baby-friendly vehicle, like a minivan.

But she had no idea how Kevin would react to the news, and she was nervous, *very* nervous, about telling him at all.

She didn't want the conversation to veer for a second into any "alternatives"— that decision had come quickly, almost immediately. The other alternatives weren't alternatives because she wasn't interested in them. She didn't think he would be either, but it wasn't as if they'd ever had this conversation before.

Deidre knew Kevin well enough to know that he would want to do the right thing, but that's not what she wanted. She wanted . . . well, it was overwhelming to even go there at all. It was one of those things you didn't let yourself even think about, in case the very thought ruined the possibility forever.

She'd have to tell him, of course. And soon. Give him the chance to do the noble thing, and then say thank you, no, don't worry about it.

Kevin would be picking her up in an hour to take her to his parents' house. She'd have to wait until after dinner to say anything, which was probably a good thing, because right now she had no idea what to say.

CHAPTER EIGHTEEN

*The best venue to bring family members together
without interruptions is to lure them through
food, notably at the dinner table.*
—Charlotte Ford, *21st-Century Etiquette*

Marla hung up the phone, indignant. She'd just had a brief conversation with Sabine, who bluntly informed Marla that she was no longer interested in trying to win Kevin back. First, he was clearly enamored with Deidre, and second, she'd forgotten what a pain in the ass he could be.

"Don't get me wrong, I love him," Sabine said shortly. "But he's got a mind of his own, and trying to change it is harder than getting one of my models to lose five pounds before a photo shoot."

So that was the end of that.

"God," Marla complained as she pulled on a heeled boot. She should have known that Sabine would wimp out in the end. No gratitude for everything Marla had done to help her out, either. Of course, the last thing Marla had expected was that Deidre would get on a plane to Paris. She had to admit that even she hadn't seen that one coming.

Marla carefully applied her makeup. She was expected for dinner at her parents' house in an hour, and of course Kevin and Deidre would be there, too. Marla had no interest in making it any more of a family event than it needed to be, so she had invited Wedge to join them, turning it into more of a dinner party. He would be picking her up in fifteen minutes.

She had reminded him *again* last week that she wasn't interested in anything serious, and he'd nodded solemnly, hanging on to her every word. But the very next day another generous bouquet of wildflowers had arrived, this time along with an exquisite diamond bracelet. The note simply read, "To one of the most generous women I know," and signed with his scrawl of a signature. That was the other thing—he always signed his own cards and letters, something Marla just didn't understand. That's what assistants and calligraphists were for. Who had the time these days?

And while Marla was fine receiving compliments whether they were due or not, she had to admit that this one left her a bit perplexed. *Generous* was not a term most people would use with Marla. Even she didn't use it with herself. She'd tossed the card to the side, only to pick it up a few minutes later and read it again. Really, what was he talking about now? It wasn't worth asking him about it—if he thought she was generous, so be it.

She selected a pair of large diamond stud earrings and put them on. She needed to keep her wits about her. Her mother had been acting strange these past couple of weeks and Marla was convinced something was going to happen at dinner tonight. She knew Kevin had picked up Beverly's ring from the jewelers and yet she still didn't know what was going on. This whole business was making her so agitated that a small rash had broken out on her neck. She had extremely sensitive skin and didn't need this kind of stress. This was clearly all Deidre's fault.

Stanton announced Wedge's arrival, and Marla took her time finishing her toilette before heading downstairs to meet him.

"There she is," Wedge said proudly as she descended the marble staircase. He was handsomely dressed and Marla grudgingly gave him credit for being a respectable dresser. His clothes were well made but nondescript, not flashy or slick. Marla's last husband had been a clotheshorse, constantly competing with Marla for attention. With Wedge, it was clear that all eyes would remain on her.

Wedge was beaming. In one hand he held a nosegay of wildflowers. Sheesh. But what caught Marla's eye was what was in his other hand. A narrow black rectangular gift box, tied with a white ribbon. Another diamond bracelet, no doubt.

"Marla, you would make Forbes Watson a very happy man. *Any* man, for that matter."

"What are you talking about?" Marla asked testily. Stanton met her at the base of the stairs with her coat. "And who the hell is Forbes Watson?"

"An artist and naturalist who lived in the eighteen hundreds," Wedge said as he approached her. He held out the box, which Marla readily accepted. "I just think you're wonderful, that's all."

She cocked an eyebrow, uncertain if he was serious or having fun with her. "Me?"

"Yes, you. You can fool a lot of people, Marla, but you can't fool me. I know that inside that tough exterior is a heart of gold." He thumped his chest for emphasis.

Marla wanted to roll her eyes. Instead she pulled the ribbon off the box and opened it. She didn't say anything for a moment as she contemplated his gift. "You're giving me a *pen?*"

Wedge reached inside and gently pulled out a Montblanc fountain pen. The barrel was a violet calf leather. The cap and rings were platinum, and the clip set had a marquise-cut purple amethyst. "It's platinum-plated with an eighteen-karat gold nib," he said eagerly. "It's for you to write your memoirs."

"My memoirs?" Marla stared at him.

"I'm sure I'm not the only one who wants to know more about you." He reached out to take her hand.

Marla wasn't into hand holding and quickly pulled away, handing the gift to Stanton and heading for the door. Her face was hot. What was he doing? It wasn't like her to be easily unnerved by a man, and certainly not someone like Wedge. He was so unassuming, so earnest, and he treated her with respect but also like . . . well, like a normal person. She wasn't sure if that was a good thing or not.

"We should go," she said, keeping her eyes averted. "I don't want to be late."

In the car he handed her the flowers. "You forgot your flowers," he said pleasantly.

She hadn't, but she accepted them reluctantly now. Large and small blossoms in bursts of color; weedy looking stalks and stems. It just seemed so . . . pedestrian. She hoped for his sake that he hadn't spent too much on them—they scarcely seemed worth it.

And what was the deal with that pen? It was a handsome pen, and certainly not cheap, but also not the kind of gift she was used to receiving. Wedge had proven that he wasn't a frivolous man, and Marla knew that he put a lot of thought into his gifts, this one in particular.

Oh, what did it matter? Marla had had enough of men and relationships, and certainly enough of marriage. If life had taught her anything it was that things were much easier when you only had to worry about yourself. She hadn't misled Wedge at all. In fact, she'd been so bluntly clear about her lack of interest in anything beyond a mere acquaintanceship that she was surprised he still bothered to show up. And bearing gifts, no less.

They drove in silence. Wedge didn't seem perturbed and kept his eyes on the road, humming as they made their way to her parents' house.

Marla thrust the wildflower bouquet to the maid as soon as she entered the house. "Put these in water." The maid nodded, then scurried away.

Deidre and Kevin were already there, deep in conversation with her mother. They were all laughing gaily over something or other, and Beverly had her hand resting affectionately on Deidre's arm. Marla noticed that Deidre seemed to be glowing—she had the look of a woman who knew something was up. Marla was definitely going to need some alcohol to get through the evening.

She left them to chat amicably with Wedge while she sought out her father in the great room. He was behind the bar, pouring himself a drink.

"What'll it be?" he boomed, holding up a bottle of bourbon. "I've got everything. We just restocked the bar."

"Vodka martini," Marla said, tossing her things to one side. "Listen, Daddy, is something going on tonight with mother's ring?"

Marla wasn't sure, but she thought she saw her father pause as he reached for an empty martini glass. "Which ring?" he asked. He placed the glass on the bar.

"Her diamond ring. The Johnson family heirloom. *The one you gave her when you got engaged?*"

Edward turned around and considered the vodka selection. "Nope, sorry. Don't know anything about it."

Kevin, Deidre, and Wedge entered the room and Edward was quick to take their orders. A bit too quick, in Marla's opinion. She tried to catch her father's eye but he seemed to be avoiding her.

"Scotch for me," Kevin told Edward. "And a glass of white wine for Deidre. Chardonnay or pinot blanc, Deidre?"

Deidre's cheeks pinked. "Oh, I'll just have some sparkling water, thanks," she said. She added quickly, "My stomach's been a bit unsettled since we came back from Paris."

Marla made a face. Did they really need to know that?

The maid reappeared with Wedge's wildflowers in a small crystal vase, setting them on one of the antique sideboards. Marla was hoping no one would notice, but of course Deidre had to give a gasp that turned everyone's attention to the flowers.

"Oh, how lovely," she exclaimed. "Snapdragons, forget-me-nots, violets, Indian blankets, poppies . . . they're all so beautiful! I love roses just as much as anyone else, but there's something about wildflowers that are just wonderful."

"You can't be serious," Marla said, looking at her family in disbelief. "They're practically weeds!"

Deidre was now standing by the vase, gazing at the arrangement it as if it were a work of art. "Wildflowers are resilient flowers that grow even under difficult conditions. The flowers are beautiful but also have a fragility to them as well." She continued to stare at the flowers, lost in thought.

"I couldn't agree more," Wedge said. He looked at Marla intently. "'None can have a healthy love of flowers unless he loves the wild ones.'"

"Why Wedge, I didn't know you were a poet!" Beverly looked impressed.

Wedge stared at Marla for a moment longer before turning to Beverly with an embarrassed smile. "Oh, I'm not. That's a quote from Forbes Watson."

"Who's Forbes Watson?" Beverly asked.

Marla recalled the conversation at her house. "He's a naturalist," she said impatiently, wanting to get this conversation over with. "Can we eat now?"

"Hear, hear," Edward agreed. "All this talk is giving me an appetite."

Beverly crossed the room to loop her arm through her daughter's as they headed for the dining room. "That blouse really brings out the color in your eyes. Wouldn't you agree, Edward?"

"Absolutely," said her father.

Marla regarded her parents suspiciously. They were buttering her up for something, no doubt.

"Something smells wonderful," Deidre commented as they sat down.

"Duck," Edward informed her, dropping the cloth napkin in his lap. "My favorite." He smacked his lips.

Beverly looked at Deidre and Kevin. "Now I want to hear all about Paris. Tell me everything."

"Oh, God," Marla snorted. That was the last thing she wanted to hear. "Kevin flies to Europe all of the time. We don't need the details."

Beverly gave her a stern look. "This trip is different, Marla, because Deidre was able to join him."

Well, Marla obviously knew that, which was precisely the reason why she had no interest in hearing anything about it.

Wedge had to make it worse by leaning forward and asking, "So how was it? Not all work, I hope?"

"No, no." Kevin gave Deidre a smile. "It was Deidre's first time, so I got to discover everything all over again. She has a knack for making everything seem fresh and new."

"I was a bit like a child in a candy store," Deidre admitted, embarrassed. "Kevin had to drag me out of some of the shops, especially the *pâtisseries*. But if we hadn't gone there, I probably wouldn't have been able to save Sweet Deidre. We've redesigned the entire line—the recipes, the packaging, the marketing—and have decided to upmarket the products. It's what I had originally envisioned, but this is so much better."

"It's pretty incredible," Kevin confirmed. "Though I expected no less."

"Now he tells me," Deidre said, giving him a playful shove. Marla winced. They were at the dinner table, for God's sake. Where were her table manners?

Kevin placed his hand on top of Deidre's. "Then Deidre made a last-minute stop at a farmers market. We barely made our flight."

Deidre laughed. "I couldn't help it. It was inspiring—I got so many good ideas, it was all I could do not to stuff suitcases full of fresh flowers and cheese. The caterer is completely stressed out since I redid the theme and upped the head count. We now have a hundred and thirty guests, if you can believe that." She looked at Kevin and they both chuckled, as if sharing a private joke.

Beverly was nodding with great interest. "It's just so wonderful how everything works out, isn't it?"

Marla felt the hair stand up on the back of her neck. "What are you talking about?" she demanded.

Deidre sipped her water. "Oh, it's nothing," she said. "Just a little ceremony to say 'I do' over Labor Day weekend. Well, not so little anymore, but luckily everything has fallen in place." She gave a relieved smile and pretended to wipe her brow. Kevin grinned and took her hand in his.

Marla was indignant. Nothing she needed to worry about? Why hadn't Kevin said anything? He was probably worried that she'd say something negative, and he'd be right. But even so, it wasn't like him not to tell her, much less not invite her to his wedding. His own sister! This had to be Deidre's doing.

"Labor Day weekend?" Marla asked coolly, looking pointedly at Deidre. "That's in about a month. It's a bit soon, isn't it?"

Deidre acquiesced. "I thought that at first, too, but I guess when you know you want to spend the rest of you life with someone, you don't want to wait any longer than you have to. As it is, the invitations were barely sent out in time. But they're gorgeous, definitely worth the wait."

That was it. Marla was livid. "Did you know about this?" she demanded of her parents.

"Marla," Beverly said, surprised. "Deidre just told me about it earlier in the kitchen . . ."

"This has gone on long enough." Marla threw down her napkin and stood up. Somebody had to say something. "She may have you all fooled, but she doesn't fool *me*."

"Marla, what are you talking about?" Kevin asked, genuinely surprised.

Marla turned to face her brother. "*Deidre*. Don't you see? She's been trying to get you to marry her ever since she met you!"

"What?" Kevin looked incredulous. Was he really so naïve? "What are you talking about?"

"Marla, you're being ridiculous," Beverly admonished, a shocked look on her face. "Please sit down." She turned to Deidre. "I'm so sorry . . ."

"Why are you apologizing to her? You should be apologizing to *me*. I'm the one who's had to watch her finagle her way into this family!"

"That's enough," Edward said quietly.

Marla shook her head. This was exactly what she didn't want to have happen—her parents choosing Deidre over her, their own flesh and blood. "No. No, it's not. Why is it that nobody in this family listens to me? I know what you all think. You think that I'm this frivolous person who cares only about herself. Well, I'm not. I care about this family. I want what's best for this family. What I don't understand is why you constantly seem to prefer her. You treat her more like a daughter than you do me. I'm a part of this family, too!" Her voice trembled, and she hated that.

Everyone seemed at a loss for what to say.

"Marla," Beverly said quietly. She looked at Kevin and gave him a nod.

Kevin reached into his coat pocket and brought out a ring box. Marla knew it held Beverly's ring inside.

"Oh, fabulous," Marla said vehemently. "Let me guess. You're giving the ring to Kevin so he can propose to Deidre. That's just great."

"No, Marla," Beverly said gently. "We're not passing the ring on to Kevin. We're passing it on to you." She motioned for Kevin to hand her the box, which she then pressed into her daughter's hand.

"Your father and I talked about it, and while I know it's been a Johnson family tradition to pass the diamond down to the oldest son, we want you to have it instead."

It took Marla a moment to find her voice. "But how can I pass the ring down?"

Edward was taking a long drink. "Screw tradition," he said.

Beverly frowned at her husband's language, then turned back to her daughter. "You don't have to, Marla. Your father and I want *you* to have it. We know you'll take good care of it."

Marla looked at Kevin, who gave her a kind smile.

"I had Leroy size it for you," he said. "He cleaned it up, put it back in its original setting. Mother thought you might want to add some other stones, make it less like a wedding ring, but that's up to you. You can wear it or just keep it. I'm sure you'll do the right thing with it."

"Perhaps it would be best to keep it in that setting," Wedge said in a low voice. "Just in case." The look on his face was so revealing that Marla suddenly felt nervous. She turned away, blushing furiously.

"What about . . . ?" She cleared her throat and gestured imperceptibly toward Deidre.

"I never had any intention of giving Deidre that ring," Kevin assured her as Deidre turned several shades of red. "And the wedding she was referring to is for her best friend, William. *He's* having a commitment ceremony with his partner over Labor Day weekend."

Marla bit her lip as she reached in and gently tugged the ring out of the box. She slipped it on the ring finger of her right hand.

"Like a glove," Edward said. "It looks lovely on you, Marla."

Marla sat back down, still staring at the ring on her finger.

"Very nice," Wedge agreed. He reached over and patted her hand and, for once, Marla didn't pull away. He whispered, "It's certainly better than anything I could ever choose." At Marla's sharp glance, he said no more, just smiled enigmatically.

There was an awkward silence as everyone sat around the table, avoiding one another's eyes, unaccustomed to Marla's rare show of emotion.

"Well," Edward finally said, clearing his throat. "I'm starving. What say we get some food on the table?"

"An excellent idea," Beverly said. She nodded to the waitstaff.

Wedge cleared his throat and held up his glass. "May I propose a toast?" He was looking directly at Marla.

Oh God. What now?

Everyone held up their drinks obligingly.

"I can't think of anyone more deserving of happiness," Wedge started, "than the woman sitting next to me. I know now where Marla gets her kind and thoughtful heart." Wedge was caught up in his toast, oblivious to the gaping faces around him, Marla's included. "I'd like to toast her generosity— her gift to the local Dress for Success chapter has already prompted others to give generously. She is truly an asset to our community—"

"Wedge," Marla interrupted impatiently. "What are you talking about?"

"Yes," Edward said. "What the hell are you talking about?"

Wedge looked at the faces around the table, surprised. "A friend of mine who is on the board of directors said that Marla's donation of several couture gowns raised over $50,000 at their auction a couple of weeks ago. Not only that, but apparently she's started some sort of trend. It seems that other prominent women in Seattle heard about Marla's donation and have done the same. Since the fund-raiser won't be for another year, one of the members has been selling the clothes on eBay on behalf of the organization. Apparently they're going to raise upward of $100,000 just from these donations alone."

"Really?" Beverly looked proud and impressed. "Marla, that's wonderful!"

Marla frowned. "I didn't make any donation to Dress for Success," she said. She didn't even know what that was.

It was Deidre who spoke next, glancing between Marla and a perplexed Wedge. "Um, yes, you did," she said quickly. "I'm sure it slipped your mind with everything you have going on. The dresses you lent me for the K Ball?" She gave Marla a knowing look, waiting for her to catch on. "You told me to donate them, so I did. Remember?"

Marla remembered now. Well, good for Deidre . . .

Deidre's eyes darted to Wedge. "And, er, I thought it was brilliant when you suggested the donation to Dress for Success, too, Marla."

Marla was about to deny it when Deidre started coughing. Kevin handed her a glass of water and she took a sip, then smiled at him in thanks.

"I think you told me that it's a great nonprofit organization that helps disadvantaged women by providing professional and career attire so they can go on job interviews," Deidre recalled. "They also offer job training and employment retention programs. They don't take evening wear, but since it was couture and in practically new condition, I thought you were brilliant to suggest they auction it at their fund-raiser, Marla."

"Well done," Beverly said, raising her glass to her daughter. "I'm so proud of you, Marla."

"I'll drink to that." Edward and the men followed suit, raising their glasses in salute before taking a long drink.

Deidre continued talking, her eyes radiant with mirth. "I was just *so* inspired, Marla, that I decided to take a page from your book. We're setting up a donor-advised fund through the Seattle Foundation to make charitable contributions on behalf of Sweet Deidre. I thought it would be a good way for us to not only give back to the community, but also make decisions as a group. The entire Sweet Deidre team will decide how to disburse available funds each year. Thank you, Marla. Really." She held up her glass and smiled sweetly, and everyone around the table toasted Marla again.

Marla narrowed her eyes over her glass. She didn't know what Deidre was doing, but she was up to something.

"I also thought you were onto something when you came to my condo a few weeks ago. Remember?"

"No," Marla said tightly, hoping Deidre would shut up.

Deidre continued, clearly enjoying herself. "About doing a charitable segment for *At Home with Marla Banks*? Something about how the rich and famous give? Profiling Wedge? I thought about it and I couldn't agree more—there's so much new money in this town that it might be really helpful to show different ways the wealthy can give back. Like with your dresses. That it's not just about large monetary donations, but about getting people into the spirit of giving." Deidre was shaking her head, feigning admiration. "It *really* is an inspired thought, Marla. You have so many good ideas!"

If Deidre thought she was going to influence Marla's programming, well, she was sorely mistaken. Marla was on the verge of telling her off when Wedge grasped her hand and brought it to his lips, giving it a kiss.

"I think that's a wonderful idea," he said, beaming at Marla.

Even Edward was nodding slightly. "Could be interesting," he said.

Beverly had such a look of intense pride and pleasure that Marla couldn't bring herself to contradict Deidre. And, as much as she hated to admit it, it wasn't a bad idea.

She thought of Wedge's do-gooder friends, especially Lana Risdale Parks, who sat on a dozen prominent boards and always acted as if Marla wasn't deserving of Wedge. Well, she'd show her. After all, she *had* told Deidre she could donate those dresses, hadn't she? Marla could be just as generous as the rest of them.

Maybe that Dress for Success program was on to something. She'd talk it over with her producer tomorrow and test the waters. But Marla had a pretty good intuition when it came to matters like this. She could tell when a segment would work and when it wouldn't. That was one reason why *At Home* was still on the air.

Wedge and her parents were still grinning at her, looking proud. Marla squirmed, not having been the object of such intense focus from her family in some time. She may be her own woman on the verge of turning fifty-four (fifty-six, according to her birth certificate, but no matter), but she had to admit that it was kind of nice.

Marla regarded Deidre, who was nibbling her food like a bird. On a diet, no doubt. Deidre wasn't in bad shape, and by some standards—not Marla's—she might be considered attractive, but losing a couple of pounds would definitely give Deidre a more toned look. Marla didn't want to be the bearer of bad news, but they weren't getting any younger and time had a way of walking across your face and body. Marla could recommend her personal trainer to give Deidre a few pointers.

Marla stopped herself. What was going on? Was she actually going to start being nice to Deidre?

She almost started laughing. Of course not, the world hadn't turned upside down, after all. Deidre still didn't deserve Kevin, but really, who did? Marla watched her brother smile tenderly at Deidre and instead of feeling her normal revulsion, she felt, well, nothing. Okay, maybe a little annoyance over the fact that Deidre had forgotten to touch up her lip color before coming to the table and her lipstick was now feathering, but other than that Marla didn't feel a thing.

Wedge was now offering to replenish Marla's martini, which she graciously accepted. Generous, gracious Marla. That's what they'd start calling her in the papers. She'd have to talk to her publicist about that. And maybe she'd invite Deidre on the show to talk about her Sweet Deidre charity thing—Juliette had been right; their ratings had gone through the roof with that special wedding episode. It certainly wouldn't hurt to try it again.

Maybe.

Everyone was ready to go when Deidre lifted the crystal vase holding Wedge's flowers. "Wedge, would you mind if I borrowed this?" she asked. "The arrangement is so simple and beautifully put together. It's giving me ideas for William's commitment ceremony."

Wedge nodded. "Sure, Deidre. They're Marla's but I don't think she really cares for—"

To everyone's surprise Marla marched across the room and plucked the vase from Deidre's hands. "Sorry," she said. "We'll have the name of the florist sent to you." She turned on her heel and prepared to leave, then hesitated, dropping her voice to a fierce whisper. "And don't think I don't know what you just did, because I do."

Deidre gave Marla a pat on the arm. "Consider it an early wedding present," she whispered back, then went to give Wedge a kiss good-bye.

As Wedge escorted a speechless Marla out the door, a feeling of contentment settled over Deidre. Marla would never forgive her, she knew, but she didn't care. It had been totally worth it to see the dumbstruck look on Marla's face when she realized that Deidre was speaking the truth. Marla and Deidre might never be friends, but there was no reason Marla couldn't find her own patch of happiness somewhere.

"Can you believe Marla?" Kevin was saying as they bade good-bye to his parents and stepped out into the warm summer night. "Just when you think you've seen it all." He chuckled.

"I'll agree to that." It was the perfect ending to the evening, and the ideal segue for the big talk Deidre was preparing to have with him once they reached his apartment.

"I mean, I can't believe she honestly thought I was going to propose to you with that ring!" Kevin was shaking his head in amused disbelief.

Deidre felt her serenity fade. "What do you mean?"

He gave an offhanded shrug. "It's just not my style. I mean, you know that, right, Deidre?"

Deidre felt a wave of anguish, her serenity gone. What was he saying, that proposing wasn't his style? Or that getting married wasn't his style?

Kevin slipped his arm over her shoulders. "I don't think I could be any happier than I am right now." He kissed the top of her head. "I don't want this to ever end, Deidre. You and me . . . we're good like this, don't you think?"

Deidre felt numb. She was grateful for the darkness, which gave her a chance to collect herself, to give her a moment to blink back tears. Kevin was whistling now, and Deidre knew in her heart that she couldn't do it. She couldn't tell him that his life was about to change drastically, whether he liked it or not.

CHAPTER NINETEEN

Good manners will open doors that the best education cannot.
—Clarence Thomas

On Monday morning, Lindsey Miller was the first to arrive at the Wishbone as usual. She unlocked the doors and turned on the lights. She put her purse and keys away, checked for phone messages, then propped open the back kitchen door for the delivery of fresh fish and vegetables she was expecting at any minute.

She preheated the oven and took out two sheets of premade cranberry walnut scones from the refrigerator. When the oven was ready, she slid in the cookie sheets and set the timer. Then she turned to warm the griddle and set about prepping a couple batches of pancake batter.

She was going to do a silver dollar pancake special using two kinds of batter—a multigrain and the kind she'd been serving over the past few years. It was taking her customers longer to warm up to the new menu, so she figured she needed to ease them into it. It didn't help that her prices had to go up a bit to accommodate the increase in fresh vegetables and fruits in the dishes. Bobby Carson, one of her oldest customers and neighbors, was the most outspoken about these changes.

"Dammit, Lindsey, since when did a slice of cherry pie almost double in price? And the slices are skinnier, too. Don't think you can fool me, 'cause you can't!"

She'd placed her hands on her hips, a dish towel tucked in her apron. "Bobby, there's a big difference between fresh and canned. I'm giving you fresh cherries here. No high fructose corn syrup, no shortening, no unidentifiable ingredients. It's better for you, and each slice is a correct serving portion. You could probably stand to lose a pound or two anyway." She gave a nod to his protruding stomach.

He'd huffed indignantly, but bought a couple slices anyway, complaining the whole time.

She knew it was going to take a while for everybody to come around, but Lindsey wasn't worried. It was a good town, filled with good people, and they trusted her to serve them good food. She took that responsibility seriously, especially now.

Lindsey knew there were some grumblings about her selling the Wishbone, but no one had said anything to her outright. No one other than Deidre, that is, but that girl always spoke her mind. She appreciated Deidre's candor, but her friend really had no idea what it was like to live, breathe, eat, and sleep the diner 24/7. Holidays, too.

The prospective buyer was from Los Angeles, a Mr. J. D. Peterson. Lindsey didn't know much about him, just that he was some big-shot movie producer who was thinking about an early retirement. He was a slight man in his fifties, and in Lindsey's opinion didn't seem like the sort of person capable of getting away from it all. If anything, it looked like he was bringing it with him. Lawyers, accountants, real estate agents, the whole works. He was looking to buy some property and build a house right outside of Jacob's Point, and he was anxious for the sale of the Wishbone to go through.

Well, so was she, and she didn't take kindly to his insinuations that she was dragging her feet in getting the necessary paperwork and financials to his team of advisors. She was just one woman, for pete's sake. And she still had to take care of the Wishbone, didn't she?

Lindsey brought out a flat of eggs. She was giving people the option of egg whites or egg replacement, but she was okay serving regular eggs, too. Everything in moderation, she was learning. Hannah would be walking through the door in a few minutes and she could finish chopping up the tomatoes, mushrooms, bell peppers, and spinach that Lindsey had started prepping the night before.

Lindsey flicked on her new CD player, and the melodious strains of Patsy Cline and "Walkin' After Midnight" filled the kitchen. She hummed as she worked, dicing potatoes and soaking greens for her lunch special.

"Good morning, Lindsey." Hannah Boyle came in and unbuttoned her jacket, then reached for an apron. "Janet Everett and César are outside, waiting for their morning coffee. She wants to know if you have any cinnamon rolls."

"Not today, but I have some scones that are just about to come out. Can you take over here?"

"Sure, Lindsey."

Lindsey wiped her hands then went outside. Sure enough, there was elderly Janet Everett with her parrot, César, reading the morning paper.

"Good morning, Janet," Lindsey greeted her. "I forgot to put the coffee on, but I'll get right to it."

"*Squawk!* No decaf! *Squawk!*"

Lindsey shot the bird an annoyed look. Janet was under doctors' orders to limit her caffeine intake. For a long time Lindsey and the girls had made a special effort to brew a pot of decaf in a regular coffeepot, but Janet's new pet was a retired service animal who had a knack for sniffing out decaffeinated coffee. "Janet, now you know I'm not supposed to serve you regular coffee. Bobby'll get on me like nobody's business."

"*Squawk!* No decaf! *Squawk!*"

Janet didn't bother looking up from her paper. "You heard the bird."

Lord, it was the same routine every morning. "Half a cup, Janet," Lindsey said sternly, giving in as she always did. "That's all. Then it's decaf or tea, your choice."

Mary Martin arrived and quickly began taking breakfast orders as customers started to fill in. Lindsey alternated between being in the front and working in the back, going wherever she was needed the most.

It was approaching lunchtime when J. D. Peterson walked through the door, a bulging redrope file tucked under his arm. "Hello, Lindsey. Can we talk?"

Lindsey glanced at the clock. "Sure, I have a quick sec."

"Well, this will take more than one second. I want to go through the list of furniture and fixtures, as well as the value of the current inventory and stock. My lawyers say you haven't gotten back to them with any details."

"Mr. Peterson, in about ten minutes we're going to have our lunch crowd in here. Can we do this later?"

He shook his head. Then he frowned when he noticed the CD player on the counter. Lindsey had purchased one for the front cashier area, too. "Is that new?"

"What? Oh, yeah, do you like it? I was getting sick and tired of the garbage they were playing on the radio. I picked up a couple of CD players from the Walmart in Pullman last week. There's one in the kitchen, too."

His nose flared. "I thought we agreed that there wouldn't be any more purchases other than food and supplies until the sale was complete," he said. He sounded petulant. "You should have at least checked with me for approval."

For approval? Lindsey crossed her arms. "Well, with all due respect, Mr. Peterson, I don't work for you yet. Last I heard, we were still negotiating here."

"We already agreed on the sale price!"

"Well, sure, but there's all these other details we have to go over. I haven't talked to you about the girls yet, but I was fixing on giving them a raise . . ."

Mr. Peterson spied Janet Everett, who was still parked in the corner with César perched on her shoulder. "What the . . . ? Excuse me, miss!" he called. He marched forward, with Lindsey quick on his heels. "I'm sorry, but there are no animals allowed in A Piece of the Point."

Janet cocked an eyebrow, shooting both Mr. Peterson and Lindsey a menacing look.

"Uh, Mr. Peterson, Mrs. Everett is a long-time customer of the Wishbone, I mean, A Piece of the Point," Lindsey tried to explain.

"And I certainly hope she'll continue to be," Mr. Peterson said, importantly. "But it's the FDA, not me. Animals— *including birds*—are not permitted in establishments where food is being served. Now if you'd like your animal to wait outside . . ."

"César here is a service animal," Lindsey said quickly, shooting Janet a hard look. "Mrs. Everett suffers from . . . psychotic tendencies. César helps keep her in check."

Janet still hadn't said anything and Lindsey prayed she wouldn't start lecturing them or getting indignant. Janet was stubborn and unpredictable, and now that Lindsey thought about it, she might not have been too far off the mark with Janet's fake diagnosis.

Janet suddenly made a scary face and pretended to claw at Mr. Peterson, making him jump. "I feel on the verge of snapping," she declared, and made a growling sound.

"Let's leave her be," Lindsey suggested, grabbing a startled Mr. Peterson and dragging him back toward the cash register.

The diner was starting to fill up and Lindsey could see Hannah through the double doors, frenzied as she tried to fill orders. "I need to go back in the kitchen and help Hannah," she said. "She looks like she's about to tear her hair out."

"In a minute," Mr. Peterson said. He dropped the file on the counter with a heavy thump. "Now, I've been looking at the daily receipts for the past couple of weeks and there's a very apparent drop in revenues. I think it's due to the new menu. You'll need to go back to the old one."

The old one? Over her dead body. "Mr. Peterson, this is a much better menu, and it'll just take some time for folks to get used to it. But they'll come around."

He shook his head. "I can't afford to wait for people to come around. Let's face it, Lindsey. The diner isn't exactly a cash cow, now is it? Which brings me to your last point. No raises for the girls, at least not until we start making some real money."

Some real money? Where did he think he was?

The bell above the door chimed as another customer walked in. Lindsey didn't recognize this one, a young woman in her early thirties. She had sandy blond hair and she was holding a baby. When she spotted Lindsey she instantly brightened.

"Are you Lindsey Miller?"

"That's me."

"My name is Sarah Evans and this is my daughter, Petra." Petra was fussing, her face red and unhappy. She was clearly not in the mood for introductions. Sarah hefted the baby on her hip, talking a mile a minute. "Anyway, I met a friend of yours, Deidre McIntosh, on a plane ride to France and she told me that you had the best meat loaf in the entire Pacific Northwest and I haven't been able to stop thinking about it for weeks so I packed up our things and me and Petra drove down from Spokane which I know is absolutely crazy . . ."

"You drove down here from Spokane?" It was at least a three-hour drive, and while the woman looked elated, she also looked exhausted. "Go sit yourself in a booth and we'll talk later. I'll bring around a high chair. Mr. Peterson, do you want to grab one? They're over by the bathrooms."

Mr. Peterson didn't budge. "Lindsey, I'm getting a sense that you don't want to sell."

Lindsey hesitated, her mind suddenly filling with possibilities. "Mr. Peterson . . ."

"I can assure you that you won't get a better offer anywhere else. In fact, maybe I should just rescind my offer altogether. What do you think about that?"

And at that moment, Petra's face turned bright red and she threw up all over Mr. Peterson.

CHAPTER TWENTY

People can get married any way they please.
—Letitia Baldridge, *New Manners for New Times*

L abor Day weekend heralded the unofficial last day of summer.

On the day of William and Alain's commitment ceremony, the skies were clear and blue. The weather was comfortably warm, but a gentle breeze carried the hint of fall, of the inevitable change of seasons that was soon to come.

"You look wonderful, William." Deidre pushed a jasmine boutonniere through the buttonhole on William's suit. "Very debonair and ready to do this."

William quietly regarded himself in the tall mirror of the guest room. Alain was getting ready in their bedroom, his sister by his side. They had decided not to see each other before the ceremony, but would enter the garden from opposite directions, meeting in the middle and then walking together along a walkway of crushed lavender sprigs, up to a simple platform made of smooth bamboo flooring where an officiant would be waiting.

William fussed with his tie. "I'm nervous," he confessed to Deidre.

Deidre smiled reassuringly as she shooed his hands away from his tie and checked the knot to make sure it was perfect. "I know. That's okay. It's your big day, you're supposed to be a little nervous."

"I'm not a little nervous; I'm a *lot* nervous. I knew we should have kept it simple." He peeked through the curtains into the backyard where the guests were gathered, drinks in hand. With the exception of a few elderly people, William's parents included, everyone would be standing for the brief ceremony. "Hey, what say you and I take that trip to Fiji that we've always talked about? We can sneak out the front door—no one will ever notice."

"I'm pretty sure at least one person would notice. Besides, I'm not about to run off with one of the grooms. What kind of woman would that make me?"

William was pacing anxiously. "I told Alain we should have eloped. This is too much. I think I'm getting an ulcer."

"William, cut it out," Deidre scolded him. "There are brides that would have knocked you out for a reception like this. It's turning out better than anything I could have hoped for, even for myself."

"In that case, why don't *you* get out there instead?"

She ran a lint brush over his suit. William and Alain had decided to forgo the traditional tuxedo for something more contemporary and fashionable. William's suit was a stylish dark brown, the perfect late summer attire, but unfortunately seemed to be a magnet for dust. "I would, but Alain doesn't want me, he wants you."

"I can think of one person who'd want you." William gave

her a look, which she ignored as she continued to brush his suit. "When are you going to tell him, Deidre? You're almost nine weeks pregnant."

As if she needed him to remind her. Deidre hadn't meant for things to go on this long, but once it was clear that Kevin wouldn't be amenable to the news, she hadn't found the right opportunity to break it to him. She didn't want things to end between them any earlier than was necessary, and the truth was she was just plain chicken.

"There just hasn't been a good time. He's got a hectic travel schedule, plus it's been nuts with Sweet Deidre and getting everything pulled together for your commitment ceremony . . ."

"Don't even try to stick this on me!" William scolded her. "Deidre, you *have* to tell him."

"I will, I will. By the time you're back from your honey-moon, I'll have told him." William and Alain were going to France and Italy for two weeks.

"Promise?"

"William, you are exchanging vows in five minutes. I don't want to discuss my out-of-wedlock situation on today of all days." She looked at the clock. "Okay, do you have the ring?"

William felt his breast pocket and nodded. "Check."

"Remember your vows?"

He closed his eyes and took a deep breath, running through them in his mind. "Check."

"Did you go to the bathroom?"

"Check."

She placed her hand on his spine. "Good. Now, keep your back straight and give me a kiss good-bye. This officially ends any hopes I had of having you being my fallback guy." Until she'd met Kevin and William had met Alain, Deidre had always expected that they would continue to be the closest of friends, always living together. He'd been her safety net for years, but that was all ending today. "Are you ready?"

He nodded. "I'm ready."

The ceremony was simple and heartfelt. There wasn't a dry eye after William and Alain exchanged the vows they had written themselves. Alain upped the ante by speaking in both English and French. William's French was conversational at best, but it was clear he'd heard those words before as he blinked back tears.

When the officiant concluded the ceremony, there was a round of applause with loud whoops and catcalls followed by a showering of rice that Deidre had specifically forbidden, but obviously no one had listened. Even she found herself with a small handful of the contraband (who had snuck it in?), and flung it joyfully at the new couple.

They'd done it. And it was time for the party to begin.

William and Alain's backyard had been transformed. On any other day it boasted a spacious but modest yard with simple landscaping and enough shade for a lazy afternoon barbecue and touch football with friends. Today, however, it was a hallmark of sophistication and provincial whimsy.

Crisp white tents dotted the lawn, softened with flowing silk tulle that billowed in the breeze. The buffet was laid out like a farmers market, a cross between Seattle's Pike Place Market and the *marché fermier* Deidre had visited on the streets of Paris. In lieu of tailored flower arrangements there were baskets and wooden crates overflowing with fresh produce and tall rustic containers filled with vibrant wild flowers.

Smaller bunches of wildflowers were tucked into tin pails

and served as the centerpieces on each table, along with a petite wooden chalkboard with the table number scrawled in chalk.

Servers were dressed as Parisian street vendors, donning clean white aprons over charming work shirts and pants. More wooden chalkboards identified the various dishes on the buffet in both French and English. The food had a distinct Asian-Franco-Pacific Northwest flair—*panisses*, crispy fried wedges made from chickpea flour and generously coated with coarse sea salt and fresh ground pepper; vinegar-roasted shallots with a sweet-and-sour tang; warm petite fig and mozzarella sandwiches with fresh basil; a selection of savory tarts and creamy gratins. The summer fare continued with a selection of fish, beef, and lamb, all cooked to perfection.

Deidre found a chef who had set up a station and was preparing crêpes to order. There was also a cheese station, a *boulangerie* with a mobile oven, and a well-stocked bar.

But the *pâtisserie*, with its makeshift pale blue awning, was by far the crowd favorite. Neatly lined up in tight rows were chocolate truffles, cheesecake triangles, miniature green tea tarts with lychees and raspberries, *macarons* in every color and flavor and, of course, the petit fours, dipped shortbread, and other delicacies from the new Sweet Deidre line.

At the center of attention was William and Alain's magnificent cake. Sugar Templeton, Deidre's friend and pastry chef, had created a masterpiece unlike anything Deidre had seen before. It stood almost four feet tall, built of a selection of individual cakes, each a work of art, spiraling all the way to the top to a dramatic peak.

"Sugar, you've outdone yourself," Deidre said admiringly. Sugar had volunteered to make William and Alain's cake as a thank-you for Deidre's help at Edward's party.

"Are you kidding? It's my pleasure. You're doing *me* a favor, Deidre." Sugar patted her head nervously. "I just wished I had gotten my hair done or something."

"You look great, Sugar," Deidre assured her.

Weaving their way through the crowd were Sabine and a small crew of photographers and stylists from *Adoré*.

"Deidre!" Sabine called out. "I want to get a shot of you and the cake designer by the cake. And where's Kevin? He looks absolutely delicious. I want to make sure we get him in a few of the shots with you as well."

It had been Deidre's idea that *Adoré* feature romantic occasions in the inaugural issue of the redesign. Sabine had jumped on it, especially when Deidre shared her ideas about the theme for William and Alain's commitment ceremony. Deidre had been struggling with their small budget but it was Sabine who sailed in with an answer.

"Advertisers," she said confidently. "Being covered in an article has much more selling power than running a full page ad. It's a vouch of confidence. Beautiful photos and strong editorial can do a lot for a brand."

Sabine had her assistant contact select advertisers and sponsors whom she knew would want to be a part of the upcoming *Adoré* spread. They donated products and services, even manpower. The result was an $80,000 event that didn't cost William and Alain a dime.

Sugar and Deidre followed the photographer's instructions, posing in one shot and busying themselves around the *pâtisserie* in another. Sugar was delighted to have her cake showcased in the magazine, which would enable her to reach a new level of exclusivity. She could be more discriminating, accepting fewer projects while making more money and finally getting a chance to relax a little more.

Sabine appeared with Kevin by her side. She positioned him exactly where she wanted him, in front of the pastries and desserts. "Deidre, feed him a petit four. The pink one; no, the pale green one."

Kevin opened his mouth obligingly, causing Sabine to smack his arm. "Ow," he said, frowning. "What was that for?"

"Look natural, dammit!"

Kevin looked exasperated. "Sabine, I'm not a model. I . . ."

Sabine turned to Deidre. "Grab him by the front of his lapel and pull him toward you. Tease him with the petit four."

Deidre did as she was told, planting a kiss on his lips afterwards as a reward.

"Sweet," he said, then kissed her back.

Meanwhile, the photographer was snapping away. Sabine murmured her approval. "Jean Paul, did you get that?"

"*Oui.* It's our money shot."

"Perfect." Sabine looked satisfied. Jean Paul was talking to his team, who had been taking pictures of William and Alain. Deidre had no doubt they'd have one of the best wedding photo albums ever seen. He gave Sabine a wave before working his way back into the crowd, snapping shots as he went.

"See? You're a natural," Deidre told Kevin.

"Well, I definitely need a drink. Do you want to try the lychee martini?"

Deidre was getting good at dodging the alcohol question. "I'm a bit dehydrated—I'll try the lemongrass green tea first. Thanks."

"You're welcome, sweetheart. What about you, Tabby?"

"Do you really have to ask?" She turned to Deidre as Kevin walked away. "Frustratingly adorable."

Deidre blushed. "Sabine, I owe you an apology."

"You do? For what?"

"For a couple months ago. I thought that you were trying to steal Kevin back. Marla said you hardly ever came to Seattle, then all of the sudden you were here all of the time. Then when I heard you were in Paris the same time as Kevin . . . talk about coincidence. I completely lost it." Deidre laughed, relieved that it was behind them. "It was completely childish and immature. I'm so embarrassed."

Sabine chose a madeleine and took a delicate bite. "Deidre, you're so sweet, but you're a bit naïve. I *was* trying to win him back. Kevin had no idea, of course, but you were right to be worried." Sabine gave the stunned Deidre a composed smile.

"So . . . what . . ."

"Oh, don't worry." Sabine turned to look at Kevin, who was at the bar and laughing with some of the other guests. "Fortunately for you, I care more about having a successful business than having a successful relationship, which has always been a problem for Kevin and me. I also forgot how much work it was just to be with him. God!"

Deidre couldn't understand this. Being with Kevin felt effortless—she couldn't imagine how it could ever feel like work.

Sabine was serious now. "Besides, it was really becoming quite pointless for me to keep throwing myself at Kevin's feet. For one thing, it's completely demeaning. I mean, I don't have a problem getting men, Deidre."

Deidre had no doubt.

"But Kevin is one of the most stubborn men I've ever

known, and the one thing he's made clear is that he's in love. With you."

Deidre blushed. "Thank you, Sabine."

"I'm just stating the facts, Deidre. And I owe you a debt of gratitude for helping me save the magazine. I'd much rather have you as a friend than as an enemy. I hope we can become that."

"Me, too, Sabine."

Sabine picked up another madeleine. "Exquisite," she told Deidre, then headed toward Jean Paul, crossing paths with Kevin in time to pluck her martini from him and continue on her way.

"Do I even want to ask what that was about?" Kevin asked.

Deidre accepted her drink gratefully and took a sip. "Sabine just said she wanted to be friends. We're going to have slee-povers and do each other's hair. That sort of thing."

"Really?" Kevin looked at his ex-fiancée, who was now trying to stage a shot with the crêpe vendor and two of the younger guests, the son and daughter of Alain's sister, who were holding the oversized crêpes in their hands and taking a big bite. "I'm sure she figured out pretty quickly that being friends with you would be a lot cheaper than paying you for your good ideas."

Deidre laughed. "That's fine by me." She loved to brainstorm, but if being friends with Sabine meant that it would make Kevin permanently off-limits to her, then it would definitely be worth it. No sense in taking any chances if she didn't need to.

"You saved Tabby from what could have been a very expensive attempt to try and revive the magazine. She was getting advice from business consultants and media experts, people with business degrees and a long history in the industry."

Deidre had a liberal arts degree and that was it. "Well, there's always more than one way to learn something." She finished her drink and handed the empty glass to a server who was passing by.

Kevin was studying her. "Maybe you should write a business book someday," he said. "Women-owned businesses account for thirty percent of all businesses and more than fifty percent of start-up businesses. There's probably a lot of people out there who would benefit from hearing about your experiences and getting some advice from you. You're never short of good ideas."

Deidre couldn't tell if he was joking or not, but the idea certainly appealed to her. Funny she'd never thought of it before. "Maybe I will."

There was the sound of a scuffle and Deidre heard Alain protesting loudly over the din of the party.

"It is not a real bicycle," he was saying, "It will break in half if I try to sit on the handlebars!" He gestured to William, who was trying to keep his balance on the frayed leather seat.

"It will just take one minute," came Manuela's familiar but firm trill. The boys and Manuela had finally met. From the moment Deidre had made the introductions, the squabbling had started up, as if they were old friends.

Manuela had agreed to supply the favors from Sweet Deidre for free in exchange for an invitation for her and two guests. Each generously-portioned gift box was tastefully letterpressed with the Sweet Deidre logo and tied with a silk ribbon, filled with the new line of Sweet Deidre products. They considered this the soft launch, hoping to generate a word-of-mouth buzz among the gourmet food community who were clamoring for a taste of the new line, which JCC was intentionally holding back. By letting the product "slip out" every now and then for special events such as William and Alain's commitment ceremony and mysteriously sending out boxes to select reviewers, industry insiders were becoming almost competitive in the race for who had tasted a Sweet Deidre cookie or pastry. There was even a rumor that a coveted Sweet Deidre box had been sold at auction on eBay, fetching around $100. *For a box*, which was empty at that.

Rosemary's extensive article on Deidre came out in *The Seattle Scoop*. It started a frenzy of online speculation, kicked off by the outspoken but anonymous ScooperDuper206. There was even a small bunch of devoted groupies who dubbed themselves the "Sweet-Ds," making it their business to compile any and all news about Deidre and the line.

Bloggers posted their best guess on which item was Deidre's favorite. They reported Sweet Deidre sightings at different events and parties, even putting a countdown clock for Sweet Deidre's official launch date in October. Photo galleries had picture after picture of the pastries and decorative boxes, all taken by those lucky enough to get their hands on a Sweet Deidre product (though Deidre suspected that Paige occasionally slipped in a photo or two). The live Q&A had gone well, with Elliot coaching her every step of the way, and soon after Rosemary won the Scoop of the Month. Deidre didn't hear much from her after that, but the online buzz continued. Deidre knew this boded well for them, bringing them right up to the official launch date in less than a month.

Sweet Deidre seemed destined to be a hit. Already they were generating more attention than Manuela or Deidre could have hoped for, more than they could have ever paid for.

Manuela's two guests turned out to be a food reviewer and

his photographer, both of whom complimented Deidre on the menu. When the guest list had swelled to one hundred thirty, Deidre knew the event had grown beyond her and had brought in a caterer with a full staff. They used her original menu and recipes, which included several dishes she had created in honor of William and Alain. Deidre was putting the recipes into a keepsake cookbook for her real gift to them. Now, as she watched Manuela insist that the boys pose on the bicycle Deidre had leaned against the fence as a prop, she hoped the photographer was able to get the shot so she could include it on the cover of the cookbook.

"It won't hold!" Alain was still complaining.

William looked at Deidre pleadingly, but she just gave him a wave before ducking away with Kevin. Manuela had done her part in making their perfect day a reality, and surely suffering through a few photographs wouldn't hurt them. Besides, Deidre had a sneaking suspicion that despite their protests, they enjoyed having Manuela cluck over them like a mother hen.

Kevin led her out onto the small dance floor. He pulled her close to him, and she could feel his heartbeat when she put her cheek against his chest.

"You know what I'm thinking?" he asked.

"What?"

"I'm thinking that I've had enough excitement for a while. The business traveling, the parties. Now that the commitment ceremony's over and Sweet Deidre's on its way, what do you say that we take our own little vacation and grab some R and R?"

"Where to?" she asked, her mind thinking back to France. She couldn't wait to go back.

He twirled her on the dance floor before pulling her back in, his arms around her once again. "Someplace special that you'll love," he promised.

Deidre wanted to press him for more details, but decided she'd let him surprise her instead. She just hoped he was up for a surprise as well.

CHAPTER TWENTY-ONE

Etiquette is the science of living. It embraces everything.
—Emily Post, *Etiquette in Society, in Business, in Politics and At Home*

Jacob's Point was quiet when Deidre and Kevin arrived, the brief tourist season having ended as children went back to school and adults went back to work.

"Now I remember why I love coming down here," Kevin said.

They had the car windows down. Deidre felt the wind on her face and took a deep breath. As much as she would have loved to travel someplace new and exotic, there was something soothing about coming to a place that was familiar and welcoming. When Kevin told her that they would be staying the next few days at his place on Lake Wish, she had been thrilled.

She knew she couldn't put off telling him about the baby any longer. It was William who pointed out that she was no longer talking about "the pregnancy," but talking about "the baby." She knew then that it was time for Kevin to know.

Deidre ran through several scenarios in her head, considering every possible response. He could be happy, hesitant, apprehensive. It was possible he might shut down entirely. She didn't think he would, but they'd never been in a situation like this before. No matter how crazy things could sometimes get with her, it never really affected the quality of his life. This bit of news certainly would. In less than seven months, his life would be changed forever.

The hardest part was accepting that this wasn't quite how Deidre saw her future, and certainly not how she'd expected to start a family. But time and time again she was learning that life was never that neat. And, as she rubbed her stomach, which was just starting to gently protrude, she gave thanks for small accidents.

Deidre had a life that she was proud of, that she had built for herself. It would take some adjusting with a new baby, but she knew she could do it. She had William and Alain for backup, and she knew Lindsey would be over the moon when she found out. Deidre also knew in her heart that Kevin would want to be involved. How involved, though, she wasn't sure.

Deidre would be lying if she said she hadn't considered marrying him. Of course she'd thought about it, maybe even dreamed about what it would be like to see him each and every morning for the rest of her life. But now, under these circumstances, there would always be the question of whether or not they married for love or for obligation. She didn't want the latter. In a way, she regretted that it had happened this way, because she knew Kevin was a man of conscience. She only wanted to be with him if he was choosing to be with her for no other reason than that he loved her. She didn't want him to make the same mistake with her as he did with Sabine.

"Should we drive straight to the Wishbone?" Kevin was asking now. "We could grab some lunch before heading to the house. If you're hungry, that is." They'd had a huge breakfast in Seattle before getting on the road.

"Let's go to the Wishbone," Deidre said. She was already quite hungry. When she had first learned that she was pregnant, her appetite seemed to have diminished. Now, however, it was back with a vengeance, and she was even starting to feel a pinch in her jeans. "I could really go for her chicken fried steak. Oh, rats. I forgot she replaced it with an eggplant scallopini." Deidre gave a big sigh.

They pulled up to the Wishbone. Across the street was the hardware/general store, where they would go after lunch to pick up a few things and say hi to Bobby Carson, the owner. Deidre was planning on cooking a huge dinner and then proposing a walk around Lake Wish. She was going to bite the bullet and tell Kevin about the baby then.

She got out of the car and walked eagerly up to the Wishbone, then slowed when she saw that the FOR SALE sign was no longer in the window.

"What is it?" Kevin asked.

"The FOR SALE sign. It's gone. The sale must have gone through." Deidre looked at him dejectedly. For all her talk about wanting the best for Lindsey and her family, Deidre had secretly hoped that Lindsey would opt to keep it.

"The Wishbone is a big job for somebody who's just had a heart attack," Kevin said. He opened the door for Deidre. "Just smile and be happy for her."

Though she didn't want to, Deidre put on a smile and walked through the door.

Lindsey was wiping off some tables and straightened up in

surprise. "Well, looky looky," she said, a broad smile on her face. Then she turned to Kevin and whispered, "I hope to God you didn't let her drive you down here."

Kevin held up the car keys and gave them a jangle, then bent over and gave Lindsey a kiss. "I'm doing what I can to keep the roads safe," he said conspiratorially.

Deidre pretended to look offended. "May I remind you both that it wasn't my fault?" She stepped forward and gave her friend a hug. Other than a few extra gray hairs, Lindsey looked wonderful.

"Yes, the semi got into our lane, but if you hadn't been so intent on arguing with me, a sick woman, and Oogling or whatever you call it on your cell phone"—Lindsey held Deidre in her arms a moment longer before releasing her—"I probably wouldn't be standing here today. I'd be in bed at home, feeling sorry for myself and making my family miserable. So thanks again to you and your lousy driving."

"I think that's as close to a compliment as I'm going to get, so I'll take it," Deidre said.

The double doors to the kitchen swung open and Sarah Evans emerged holding a platter of food. "Deidre! You're here! Let me serve this and then I'll be right over."

Deidre turned to Lindsey, surprised. "What's she doing here? Is she waitressing for you now?"

"Waitressing, cleaning, bookkeeping, managing inventory, pretty much doing everything I used to do. And more."

"I don't understand. Didn't you sell the Wishbone?"

"Nah. Turned out that guy didn't care for the new menu, or me, for that matter. We were arguing, and that's when Sarah came in. Walked right in on the middle of our conversation, holding her sweet little baby. She had just started going on about how she met you and how you said I had the best meat loaf, and meanwhile this gentleman was getting himself all worked up in a lather." Lindsey looked at Sarah and the two women giggled.

"So then what happened?" Deidre demanded.

"Well, he asked me if I was going to sell the Wishbone to him or not and threatened to cancel the sale altogether. To be honest, I didn't know what to say, because I started thinking that maybe you were right. If I had help, not just in the kitchen or with serving, but someone who could take over some of the managerial responsibilities of running this place, then I'd want to hold on to the Wishbone a little while longer. So while I'm thinking this, he's getting into a steam, and then the baby up and spits up all over him. It was like that scene in *The Exorcist*."

"Stewed prunes," Sarah remembered with a laugh. She came over, wiping her hands on her apron. "It had been a long ride from Spokane and Petra's tummy wasn't feeling so good. She cried for a lot of the way, but once she got it out of her system, she was happy as could be."

"So I told that guy from LA, 'I guess that's your answer,' and the deal was off." Lindsey gave an appreciative nod toward Sarah. "Sarah stayed for lunch and we got to talking and now you're looking at my new manager."

Sarah's eyes were bright with excitement as she gave Deidre a big hug. "Can you believe it? And you were right—her meat loaf *is* to die for. I told her it's the one thing we are definitely keeping on the menu."

"Though I've altered the recipe to use one less egg, more veggies, and less sugar and salt," Lindsey was quick to amend.

Deidre introduced the young woman to Kevin and explained how they had met on the plane.

"So where is Petra?" Deidre asked.

Sarah nodded to a playpen that was set up in the corner. "Over there." Petra was inside gurgling and laughing. Lindsey's daughter, Daisy, and her middle son, Brandon, were sitting at the table next to the playpen, their studies laid out in front of them, taking turns entertaining Petra. They gave Deidre an excited wave.

"Turns out this job includes on-site day care," Sarah said with a sparkle in her eye. "She's still with me, which I love, though the kids do take her out in her stroller for a walk twice a day. I know a good thing when I see one. I'd be a fool to pass it up!"

"It's good for the kids, too," Lindsey said. "Caleb is taking an advanced physics program with some other homeschoolers and Sid is switching to the day shift at the plant. Brandon and Daisy are old enough that they can be at the diner and do some of their work here, even help out a little bit. Then we all get to go home and have dinner. *Together.*" Lindsey shook her head, as if she still couldn't believe it. "After years of being like two ships passing in the night, Sid and I actually get to sleep in the same bed. At the same time. Will wonders never cease?"

"Sit down," Sarah said, leading Deidre and Kevin to a booth. "We have a couple of lunch specials up on the board that you might like. I highly recommend the corn chowder or the chicken and spinach calzone."

"I'll take the meat loaf," Deidre said immediately. "And a tall glass of water. Double the mashed potatoes, if that's okay."

"I'll try the calzone with the green salad on the side," Kevin said.

"Good choice." Sarah gave them a broad smile as she collected their menus.

"So where are you staying?" Deidre asked. Jacob's Point was a small town. There weren't any hotels or apartment buildings.

"Oh, that's the funny thing. Lindsey put me up the first couple of nights . . ."

Lindsey shrugged. "Had to show her some small-town hospitality," she said. She slid in the booth next to Deidre. "Oh, it sure does feel good to get off my feet. Go on, Sarah."

"But obviously that wasn't going to work in the long run. I couldn't really afford to rent a house, and I just figured if I couldn't find a place, maybe that was a sign it wasn't supposed to work out. But then this man came into the Wishbone the day before I was planning to head back to Spokane."

Here, Lindsey covered her mouth with one hand to stifle a laugh and motioned for Sarah to finish with the other.

"Anyway, the other girls didn't want to serve him—he's kind of a difficult customer, I guess, but I didn't mind. So I took his order and we got to chatting. Well, he wasn't really chatting so it was mostly me, but I was telling him about living in Spokane, and about Petra, and about Lindsey offering me this job, and how I was looking for a place to stay. He came back in for dinner and we chatted again. Well, the next day when he showed up for breakfast he offered to rent me his place. Fully furnished!"

"You're kidding." Deidre looked to Lindsey for verification, and Lindsey nodded. "Where?"

"Not even ten minutes away! You should come and see it, Deidre. It's a small cabin, just perfect for Petra and me. Two bedrooms, completely quaint and nestled in the woods. It's in walking distance to Lake Wish, if you can believe that. Petra and I go for a walk every morning before I come to work. I couldn't believe that he didn't want to be there all the time, but apparently he lives in Seattle and owns a lot of rental buildings or something . . ."

Kevin and Deidre were both grinning, and Lindsey barked out a laugh. "Can you believe it?" she guffawed, looking at Kevin. "Ol' Harry Johnson is renting his place to Sarah!" The three of them broke out in laughter.

Sarah watched them, perplexed. "I don't get it. I thought you told me it was a good deal, Lindsey."

"Oh, it's a good deal all right," Lindsey said, wiping her eyes. "I didn't want to say anything because I wanted Deidre to be here when I told you. But if you had seen that place last year, I guarantee you would have hightailed it back to Spokane."

"What do you mean? It's lovely!"

"Lovely because Miss Deidre here got it into shape. Uncle Harry—*Kevin's* Uncle Harry—kept it like a pigsty. Even the spiders were afraid to be in there."

"But not the mice," Deidre remembered. At the look of alarm on Sarah's face, Deidre assured her that they were all gone.

"You'd never know to look at him, but Uncle Harry has a good heart," Kevin said. "I'm glad things worked out for you, Sarah. Welcome to Jacob's Point." He checked his watch. "I have to make a quick call to a real estate broker in Hawaii. I won't be a minute." He excused himself from the table and went outside.

Sarah watched him leave. "Is he who you went to Paris for?" she whispered even though Kevin was out of earshot. "Wow, he's really nice. And really cute!"

Deidre couldn't agree more.

"I wanted to call you and tell you the good news, but Lindsey told me to wait. She said she knew you'd be back soon. I'm glad she was right." Sarah gave Deidre another hug before scribbling their order on her notepad and heading back to the kitchen.

"I'm going to get back in the kitchen to help prep the new evening cook. His name's Jimmy Gusman. Sarah just hired him and I'm training this week. I don't know why I couldn't get my act together and hire someone earlier. The numbers never seemed to add up, but with Sarah's help, it's working."

"Sometimes you just need another perspective," Deidre said. "And it helps to have help. It's just too hard to go at it alone, sometimes. Doable, but hard."

"Ain't that the truth." Lindsey was regarding Deidre intently, and then seemed to dismiss whatever thought was in her head. She stood up. "Well, I'm going to go check on your meat loaf. And Deidre?"

"Yes?"

"You might want to do a couple laps around the lake later. It looks like you're starting to put on some weight."

That evening, Deidre cooked a hearty meal of linguine with turkey sausage and yellow bell peppers, along with a spicy arugula salad. She preempted the wine question by pouring them both tall glasses of herbal iced tea and leaving a full pitcher on the table.

Afterward, Kevin was helping her clean up and Deidre found herself stalling, washing the pasta pot twice and debating whether or not to bleach the sink. What if Kevin wasn't happy about the baby? What if it changed everything?

"So," Kevin said, leaning against the counter. He hung a dish towel back on its rung. "Are you up for a walk?"

Shoot, he beat her to it. Deidre didn't know if she was

grateful or relieved. She still needed time to organize her thoughts.

Kevin, I have some exciting news!

Kevin, you know how they say everything happens for a reason?

Kevin, I'm so glad you want to stay in more, because in about seven months we'll be staying in a lot . . .

She was at a complete loss. Deidre looked at Kevin who was waiting expectantly. "I, uh, should finish the dishes . . ." she started.

"Leave the dishes. Come on, let's go. The moon's rising; I don't want to miss it." Despite Deidre's protests, Kevin grabbed their jackets and dragged her outside.

Once outside, Deidre felt herself calm down in the cool autumn air. They quietly made their way around the lake, hand in hand, and Deidre considered telling him the news tomorrow. Or the next day. It appeared that she wasn't as ready as she thought.

Suddenly Kevin stopped and turned to face her, taking both of his hands in hers.

"I have something to ask you," he said.

Deidre was seized with the realization that perhaps he already knew. "What?" she asked. She began to shiver, but it wasn't from the chill in the air.

Kevin reached into his jacket pocket and pulled out a square ring box, then got down on one knee. Deidre was speechless as he opened it, revealing a stunning diamond ring.

"Deidre, I can't imagine my life without you, without your ingenuity and creativity, without your understated business savvy and kind heart. Life with you is exciting and full of the unexpected, and I wouldn't have it any other way. Deidre McIntosh, will you marry me?"

Deidre was fanning her eyes, blinking back tears. "Wait," she said, choking up. "I need to ask you something first."

Kevin looked alarmed. "You're not saying no, are you?"

"That night at your parents . . . when you said you wouldn't propose to me . . ."

"With *that* ring," Kevin said. "It just wasn't my style. I worked with a jeweler for weeks to find the right stone and setting that I thought reflected me. Us. Is that . . . is that okay?"

She laughed and then shook her head, dabbing the corners of her eyes. "It's more than okay. But do you really mean what you just said? About life with me being full of the unexpected and you wouldn't have it any other way?" She knew the answer but wanted to ask anyway. Wanted to hear his answer for herself.

"Of course. I love you, Deidre, and I love not knowing what's going to happen next." He reached up and took her hand, holding it tight. A promise.

Deidre felt her heart soar as she turned to face him. "Then we might need to forgo the champagne and pick up a bottle of sparking apple cider instead, because I have something to ask you, too." She took a deep breath. "Kevin Johnson, will you be the father of my child?"

The look on his face was one of astonishment, and then pure elation. "Yes," he said, picking her up and lifting her off the ground as he covered her face with kisses.

"Yes, I will."

THE RECIPES

A good dinner menu is a balance of richness and simplicity.
—Peggy Post, *Emily Post's Etiquette*

William & Alain's Buffet

Panisses

Sticky Rice Siu Mai

Vinegar-Roasted Shallots

Fig and Mozzarella Warm Sandwich

Washington Apple Salad with Cougar Gold and
Holmquist Hazelnuts

Bacon and Kale Gratin

Leek and Prosciutto Tart

Summer Beef Bourguignonne Skewers

Pan-Seared Rainbow Trout with Warm Summer
Tomato-Olive-Caper Salad

Hunan-Style Marinated Lamb Lollipops with
Niçoise Vegetable Ragout

Ricotta Cheesecake with Fresh Seasonal Fruit

Green Tea Tart with Lychees and Raspberries

Macarons Chocolat

Cassis Truffles and Dark Chocolate Truffles

Pomegranate Lemonade

Lemongrass Green Tea

William and Alain's Summertime Sake

Lychee Martini with Crystallized Ginger

Panisses

SERVES 40

Recipe courtesy of food blogger David Lebovitz, Living the Sweet Life in Paris *(Broadway Books), davidlebovitz.com*

1 quart water
2 teaspoons olive oil
¾ teaspoon coarse salt
2¼ cups chickpea flour
olive oil, for frying
coarse sea salt and freshly cracked pepper, for serving

1. Lightly oil a 9-inch square cake pan, or similar sized vessel.

2. Heat the water with the oil and salt in a saucepan. Once hot, but not boiling, whisk in the chickpea flour.

3. Whisk over medium heat until the mixture thickens, about three minutes.

4. Switch to a wooden spoon or heatproof spatula. Continue to cook for 10 minutes, stirring constantly, until very thick and the batter holds its shape.

5. Scrape into the oiled pan and let cool.

6. To form the *panisses*, unmold the solidified mixture on a cutting board and slice into batons about as wide as your fourth finger and as long as your middle one.

7. In a heavy-duty skillet, heat ¼–½ inch of olive oil. When shimmering hot, fry the *panisses* in batches; avoid crowding them in the pan. Once the bottom is nicely browned and

crisp, turn with tongs, frying the panisses until they are a deep golden brown on each side.

8. Remove *panisses* from pan and drain on paper towels, sprinkling generously with salt and pepper. Continue frying the rest, heating more oil in the pan as needed.

9. Serve warm.

FROM THE KITCHEN: *Panisses* are the perfect snack food, excellent when served with rosé or alongside meat dishes, like they do in Provence. Dust them with sugar for the kids or sprinkle coarse salt and cracked black pepper for adults (serve with a cool glass of wine).

Sticky Rice Siu Mai
YIELDS 30

Recipe courtesy of Seattle food blogger Amy Chen, nookandpantry.blogspot.com

4 dried shiitake mushrooms
1 tablespoon dried shrimp
1 cup glutinous rice (also called sweet rice)
1 cup water
2 Chinese sausages (can substitute with ¾ cup crisped bacon or cubed ham)
1 green onion
1 clove of garlic, minced
1 tablespoon oyster sauce
⅛ teaspoon white pepper
30 *siu mai* wrappers

1. Rehydrate dried shrimp and dried mushrooms in hot water for 5 minutes.

2. Rinse and drain glutinous rice, add water, and steam for 30 minutes.

3. Meanwhile, finely dice Chinese sausages, mushrooms, shrimp, and green onion.

4. Heat 2 teaspoons of oil in a skillet or wok and stir fry the sausage, mushroom, shrimp, and green onion for about 2 minutes, until the mixture is fragrant and some pieces are lightly browned. Add garlic, oyster sauce, and white pepper, and stir fry another few seconds.

5. Remove from heat and stir in steamed rice and 2 tablespoons of water to help loosen the mixture. Let the filling cool until it is warm or room temperature before making the *siu mai*.

6. To make the *siu mai*, form a *C* shape with your fingers and thumb, much like if you were to hold a cup. Place the wrapper on top of your index finger and thumb.

7. Add less than a tablespoon of filling in the middle of the wrapper. Cup the *siu mai* with your index and thumb, forming a collar around the top of the *siu mai*, and squeeze lightly. While holding the *siu mai*, use the back of a spoon to push the filling in and flatten the bottom with the heel of your palm.

8. Place finished *siu mai* in a steaming basket or steamer and steam for 7 to 10 minutes. Serve immediately.

FROM THE KITCHEN: *Siu mai* (also spelled *shu mai*) wrappers or skins are paper-thin circles of dough made from flour and water. If you can't find *siu mai* wrappers, look for round dumpling/gyoza wrappers or trim the edges off of square wrappers.

Vinegar–Roasted Shallots
SERVES 4

Recipe courtesy of Seattle food blogger Molly Wizenberg,
A Homemade Life: Stories and Recipes from My
Kitchen Table *(Simon & Schuster), orangette.blogspot.com*

2 pounds shallots, trimmed and peeled
2 tablespoons olive oil
2 tablespoons sherry vinegar
sea salt, for serving

1. Preheat the oven to 400° F.
2. Put the shallots in a baking dish large enough to hold them in a single layer.
3. Add the oil and vinegar, and toss well with your hands to coat. Cover the pan tightly with a sheet of aluminum foil.
4. Bake for 45 minutes, then remove the pan from the oven and gently flip the shallots with a spatula. They should be beginning to soften nicely and starting to brown.
5. Cover the pan again and return it to the oven for another 15 to 45 minutes, checking occasionally, until the shallots are very soft and well caramelized. Don't be afraid to let them brown in spots. They should bake for 1 to 1½ hours in total.
6. Serve warm or at room temperature.

FROM THE KITCHEN: You could use any number of vinegars here, such as balsamic or *vinaigre de Banyuls*; sherry vinegar isn't essential.

Fig and Mozzarella Warm Sandwich

SERVES 4

Recipes courtesy of Parisian food blogger Clotilde Dusoulier,
Chocolate & Zucchini: Daily Adventures in a Parisian
Kitchen *(Broadway Books), chocolateandzucchini.com*

4 small loaves of bread (about 2 ounces each)
1 ball buffalo mozzarella, sliced
3 ripe figs, washed and quartered
12 leaves basil, rinsed and dried
4 teaspoons Pesto de Roquette (see recipe below)
salt and pepper to taste

1. Preheat the oven to 430° F.
2. Slice the loaves open. Spread the top half of each loaf with a teaspoon of pesto. On the bottom half of each loaf, lay a fourth of the mozzarella.
3. Sprinkle with salt and pepper. Add three fig quarters and three basil leaves. Put the tops of the loaves back on.
4. Transfer the sandwiches into a baking dish, and put it into the oven for about ten minutes, until they are heated through and the bread starts to get crispy. Let rest on the counter for a couple of minutes, and serve.

Pesto de Roquette

2 large handfuls arugula, rinsed and dried
3 tablespoons pine nuts
3 tablespoons Parmesan cheese
3 tablespoons olive oil
2 garlic cloves, peeled

1. Combine all ingredients in mortar (preferably) or a food processor. Pestle or mix until smooth.

2. Taste a bit, and add more of any of the ingredients to suit your taste. If using as a spread with the Fig and Mozzarella Warm Sandwich, the pesto should be thick and not too oily.

PESTO VARIATIONS: Start from the basic pesto recipe (basil, pine nuts, pecorino and/or parmesan cheese, olive oil, and garlic), and work from there, replacing some of the ingredients by their cousins, be they close or removed—another kind of herb, another kind of nut, another kind of cheese. You can prepare the pestos ahead of time and keep them on hand for an improvised minimeal.

Washington Apple Salad with Cougar Gold and Holmquist Hazelnuts

SERVES 4

Recipes courtesy of Chef Sean Hartley, Palace Kitchen,
tomdouglas.com/restaurants/palace-kitchen

2 Washington apples, such as Honeycrisp,
   cored and julienned
2 loosely packed cups friseé, trimmed, washed, and dried
2 Belgian endives, cored and chopped
¼ medium fennel bulb, cored and very thinly sliced
Hazelnut Cider Vinaigrette (see recipe below)
4 ounces Cougar Gold cheese (a sharp
   aged white cheddar), crumbled
½ cup toasted Holmquist hazelnuts, chopped

1. Put the apple, friseé, endive, and fennel in a large bowl.

2. Toss with as much Hazelnut Cider Vinaigrette as needed to lightly coat everything. Season the salad to taste with salt and pepper.

3. Divide the salad among 4 chilled plates and sprinkle each serving with cheese and hazelnuts. Serve.

Hazelnut Cider Vinaigrette

1½ teaspoons minced shallot
1½ teaspoons Dijon mustard
1 teaspoon honey
1 teaspoon chopped thyme
2 tablespoons cider vinegar
6 tablespoons hazelnut oil
kosher salt and freshly ground black pepper

1. Combine the shallot, mustard, honey, thyme, and vinegar in a bowl and gradually whisk in the oil. Season to taste with salt and pepper.

FROMAGE BY ANY OTHER NAME: Cheese making is an art form. It's usually made from the milk of cows, buffalo, goats, and sheep, but other varieties include milk from deer, llamas, and yaks. For optimum flavor, bring cold cheese to room temperature prior to eating. Cheese should not be stored with strong-smelling foods, as it will absorb the aroma of whatever is around it.

Bacon and Kale Gratin
SERVES 4

Recipe courtesy of Seattle food blogger Jess
Thomson, Hogwash, jessthomson.com

2 thick slices bacon or pancetta, diced into ¼-inch cubes
1¼ pounds chiffonade of Red Russian kale
    (approximately 1 big bundle)
salt and freshly ground pepper
1 cup chicken stock or broth
2 tablespoons all-purpose flour
1 tablespoon butter, cut into tiny cubes,
    plus more for buttering dish
¼ cup grated Parmesan cheese
½ cup heavy cream

1. Preheat the oven to 375° F.
2. Preheat a large, deep skillet or soup pot over medium heat. When hot, add the bacon, and cook for about 10 minutes, or until almost crispy.
3. Add the kale, season with salt and pepper, and cook 5 minutes, stirring, or until the kale turns bright green. Add the stock, cover the pot, and cook 10 minutes, stirring once or twice.
4. Take the lid off the kale and cook another 5 minutes or so, until no liquid remains at the bottom of the pot. (You want the kale to be fairly dry.)
5. Remove the pot from the heat, add the flour, and stir until no white remains.

6. Butter a medium oval gratin dish (a pie plate or several small crème brûlée dishes or large ramekins would work as well), and transfer the kale to the gratin dish in a roughly even layer.

7. Season the kale with salt and pepper, dot with the butter, and sprinkle the Parmesan evenly over the top.

8. Drizzle the cream over cheese, and bake for 30 minutes, until the cream is bubbling and the cheese is browned. Serve warm.

KALE 101: Red Russian Kale is gorgeous, with its deep emerald-green leaves and red ribs, but like most grown-up kale, it's most tender when it's cooked a long time. To prepare it for this hearty, warming side dish, chop the tough ends off right where the leaves begin to sprout out of the stalk. Arrange the kale in parallel bunches, and cut the kale into ¼-inch strips across the stalk, almost like cutting basil into chiffonade. Once the kale is cut, it's easier to soak and spin dry in a salad spinner.

—◀

Leek and Prosciutto Tart

SERVES 12

*Recipes courtesy of Chef Susan Kaplan, Boat
Street Kitchen, boatstreetkitchen.com*

3 slices or more prosciutto
1 large or 2 regular sized leeks, rinsed and patted dry
1 tablespoon butter
4 eggs
2 cups cream
1 tablespoon Dijon mustard
1 teaspoon freshly grated nutmeg
1 teaspoon salt
1 teaspoon black pepper
1 tart shell (see recipe below)
½ pound Emmenthaler cheese (or Swiss
    cheese), grated coarsely

1. Put prosciutto flat on baking pan and bake at 350° F until crispy.

2. Slice leeks crosswise into ¾-inch pieces. Include all edible bits of the leek, green or white, enough for 2 cups.

3. Place leeks in glass measuring cup, cover with plastic wrap, and microwave for 1-2 minutes.

4. Add 1 tablespoon butter, salt, and pepper to taste. Leeks can be firm.

5. Combine eggs, cream, Dijon mustard, nutmeg, salt, and pepper in bowl. Whisk well.

6. Cover bottom of tart shell with light layer of cheese

(enough to prevent bottom from getting too wet). Sprinkle leek and broken prosciutto crisps evenly over cheese. Pour on custard until almost to top of crust. You may have extra but don't overflow crust. Sprinkle on remaining cheese.

7. Bake at 350° F until custard is set but still jiggles slightly and top of tart is attractively brown. Wait until cool to slice. If you will want to cut it sooner, cook it until firm.

Tart Shell

2 cups sifted flour
1 teaspoon salt
½ pound butter
¼ cup cold water

1. Mix 1 cup flour, salt, and butter in mixer until well mixed.
2. Add second cup of flour and mix lightly.
3. Add water and mix until dough sticks in a large clump to beater blade.
4. Refrigerate dough for 1 hour or until firm. Do not let it get excessively hard. If it does get too hard, let the dough soften on counter before rolling.
5. Roll out dough to cover an 11-inch tart pan (ceramic or other straight-sided pan).
6. Line tart pan with dough, leaving an excess of about 1 inch around the top edge. Fold edge back toward center of pan and press against wall of pan so that shell is slightly higher than original pan. Prick bottom of tart shell with fork and blind bake with parchment paper and pastry weights at 400° F until shell is well set, about 12 minutes.
7. Remove parchment paper and pastry weights and bake

until bottom of crust is no longer translucent. If shell gets too dark, cover loosely with foil.

FROM THE KITCHEN: Leeks aren't green onions, but they're in the same family. Leeks are milder and sweeter, with a much gentler flavor than green onions, which can be pungent at times. You can use the dark green leaves for flavoring broth, but only the white and tender pale green portions are used as a vegetable. Leeks need to be well-cleaned; growers pile dirt around the shoots of the leek while it is growing so the white portion is not exposed to sunlight.

WHAT IS BLIND BAKING? Blind baking, also known as prebaking, refers to baking an empty pie or tart crust. Blind baking is necessary when the filling cannot be baked as long as the crust, or if the filling would make the crust too soggy when added. Oftentimes pastry weights are placed inside to help the pastry keep its shape when baking. If you don't have pastry weights, line the crust with parchment paper or a coffee filter and fill with beans or rice, taking care to push them up against the sides of the crust. Avoid using foil, which doesn't allow the pastry to breathe.

Summer Beef Bourguignonne Skewers

SERVES 8

Recipes courtesy of Chef Scott Harberts,
Chateau Ste. Michelle, ste-michelle.com

2 pounds beef top round or tenderloin
16 button mushrooms
16 pearl onions or cipollini onions, peeled
8 slices bacon, halved
16 cherry tomatoes
16 metal or bamboo skewers
Bourguignonne Marinade (see recipe below)

1. Cut beef into 16 2-ounce cubes; set aside.

2. Bring 2 quarts of salted water to a boil, and prepare an ice bath. Blanch mushrooms for 1 minute; remove with slotted spoon and place in ice bath to cool. Remove mushrooms from ice bath and set aside. Bring water back to a boil and blanch onions for 2 minutes; remove with slotted spoon and place in ice bath to cool. Remove onions from ice bath and set aside.

3. Preheat oven to 350° F. Lay bacon on parchment-lined baking sheet. Roast until fat is rendered but bacon is still pliable. Place bacon on paper-towel-lined plate and cool in refrigerator.

4. On each skewer assemble 1 piece beef, 1 piece bacon, 1 mushroom, 1 onion, and 1 tomato. Place finished skewers in baking dish and pour marinade over beef skewers, being sure

to coat pieces evenly. Marinate for at least 1 hour, and up to 4 hours.

5. Grill and serve.

Bourguignonne Marinade

2 cups Chateau Ste. Michelle merlot
2 cups olive oil
1 tablespoon Dijon mustard
1 tablespoon tomato paste
2 cloves garlic
1 medium shallot, chopped
¼ cup chopped parsley
2 tablespoons chopped thyme
2 tablespoons kosher salt
1 teaspoon freshly ground black pepper

1. Combine all ingredients in a blender; blend for 30 seconds.

ON FOOD AND WINE PAIRINGS: Wine is often called "nature's perfect condiment." When matched with the right food, it refreshes the palate and enhances a meal. Our taste buds perceive only four things: salt, sweet, bitter, and acid. When wine meets food, these components combine to create a variety of taste sensations. And while there are no absolute rules for matching wine and food, there is little question some pairings are more complementary than others are. Beef is best paired with a full-bodied red wine such as a merlot or cabernet sauvignon.

Pan-Seared Rainbow Trout with Warm Summer Tomato-Olive-Caper Salad

SERVES 4

*Recipe courtesy Chef Lisa Dupar, Pomegranate
Bistro, duparandcompany.com*

3 yellow heirloom tomatoes, diced
3 red or zebra stripe heirloom tomatoes, diced
½ cup kalamata olives, pitted and sliced in half
½ cup capers, drained
¼ cup chiffonade of fresh basil leaves
½ cup minced sweet summer onion (Walla Walla or Vidalia)
3 cloves of minced fresh garlic
¾ cup extra virgin olive oil
¼ cup balsamic vinegar
2 cups baby spinach (½ cup per trout) to toss just before serving
4 whole 6–8 ounce deboned trout, butterflied open
4 teaspoon seasoning salt blend
1 tablespoon extra virgin olive oil (to sauté fish)
1 tablespoon butter

1. For the warm tomato-olive-caper salad, mix tomatoes, olives, capers, basil, onion, garlic, oil, and vinegar. Let it sit at room temperature until you are ready to serve the trout. This is best served within 1 hour after mixing.

2. To prepare the trout, take one whole trout fillet per person and season evenly with a sprinkle of the seasoning salt blend.

3. In large 12-inch sauté pan, heat 1 tablespoon of olive oil and 1 tablespoon of butter together until just before the smoking point.

4. Sear the trout, starting with the skin side up, for about 2 minutes on each side. Repeat for each trout.

5. With a slotted spatula, place trout in the middle of a dinner plate. Toss the warm tomato-olive-caper salad with baby spinach leaves and spoon down the middle of the trout. Serve immediately.

YOU SAY TOMATO: Fresh tomatoes are most abundant at the end of the summer and are best when picked off the vine. Tomatoes purchased in grocery stores are picked early and even when ripened do not have the same taste or texture of a fresh tomato. Ripe tomatoes should be stored at room temperature, away from sunlight. Avoid storing them in the refrigerator, which will cause them to become pulpy and lose their flavor.

Hunan-Style Marinated Lamb Lollipops with Niçoise Vegetable Ragout

SERVES 4

Recipes courtesy of Chef Daniel Thiebaut, Daniel Thiebaut Restaurant, danielthiebaut.com

8 lamb chops, about 2-inches thick each
Hunan Lamb Marinade (see recipe below)
½ onion, diced
2 garlic cloves, chopped
1 tablespoon tomato paste
2 zucchini, diced
2 eggplants, diced
4 tomatoes, diced
¼ cup niçoise olives, diced
salt and pepper to taste
2 small red potatoes, cut in half with center removed
2 Roma tomatoes, cut in half with center removed

1. Marinate lamb chops in Hunan Lamb Marinade overnight.

2. Sauté onions and garlic in olive oil for 2 minutes. Add tomato paste and cook for one more minute.

3. Add zucchini and eggplant, cooking slowly for 10 to 15 minutes.

4. Add diced tomatoes (not Roma tomato halves) and olives. Cook until soft and season with salt and pepper to taste. Set aside.

5. Steam the potatoes for three minutes.

6. Fill the potato cups and Roma tomato cups with the vegetable mixture and bake in a 375° F oven for 5 minutes.

7. Grill lamb chops to desired doneness, about 4 to 6 minutes per side.

8. Place 1 potato cup and 1 tomato cup on plate with 2 lamb lollipops. Serve immediately.

Hunan Lamb Marinade

1 cup hoisin sauce
1 tablespoon brown sugar
¼ cup red wine
½ cup plum sauce
1 teaspoon sesame oil
½ teaspoon Chinese five-spice powder
½ teaspoon curry powder
¼ teaspoon chili garlic sauce
1 teaspoon soy sauce
¼ cup char siu mix

1. Mix all ingredients and store in refrigerator until ready to use.

THE YIN AND YANG OF COOKING: Five-spice powder is a seasoning in Chinese cuisine that incorporates the five basic flavors of Chinese cooking: sweet, sour, bitter, savory, and salty. It's based on the principle of balancing the yin (cooling elements) and yang (warming elements) in food. The elements are complementary rather than opposing, and are an added delight to most vegetables and stir-frys, and even baked goods. It is generally comprised of China Tung Hing cassia cinnamon, powdered cassia buds, powdered star anise and anise seed, ginger root, and ground cloves.

⟀

Ricotta Cheesecake with Fresh Seasonal Fruit

SERVES 6

Recipes courtesy of Seattle food blogger Peabody Rudd, Culinary Concoctions by Peabody, culinaryconcoctionsbypeabody.com

2 cups crushed vanilla Oreos or vanilla wafers
1¾ cups granulated sugar
¼ cup melted butter
1 pound cream cheese
1 pound ricotta cheese
2 cups sour cream
½ cup all-purpose flour
6 eggs
1 teaspoon lemon zest
1 tablespoon vanilla extract
Fresh fruit mixture (see recipe below)

1. Preheat oven to 350° F. Grease a 10-inch springform pan.
2. To make the crust, combine wafers, ¼ cup sugar, and melted butter in a food processor. This will make a thick crust; if you want less crust, halve the recipe.
3. Press mixture down flat into prepared springform pan.
4. Bake crust for 12 minutes. Set aside. Reduce oven heat to 325° F.

5. Cream the cheeses on medium speed until soft and blended. Add the remaining sugar and mix well, about 3 minutes.

6. Add the sour cream and mix for another minute. Reduce speed to low and add flour.

7. Add eggs one at a time, scraping down the bowl after each addition. Add lemon zest and vanilla extract.

8. Pour batter into prepared pan. Wrap the bottom and sides of the springform pan in aluminum foil to prevent any leaks, then bake in a water bath for 1 hour and 15 minutes. Check cheesecake after one hour.

9. When cake is removed from oven, remove it from water bath. Let cool on a wire rack for 20 minutes. Refrigerate for at least 4 hours; overnight works best.

Fresh Fruit Mixture

3 cups diced strawberries or fresh fruit
juice of one lime
⅓ cup sugar

1. Mix together and let macerate overnight. Place on top of cheesecake when ready to serve.

WHAT IS A WATER BATH? A water bath, or au bain-marie, is a cooking technique similar to double boiling that consists of placing food in a pan that is placed within another pan containing hot water. The hot water surrounds and protects delicate foods from direct heating, allowing it to cook slowly and evenly without burning or scorching.

Green Tea Tart with Lychees and Raspberries

SERVES 6

Recipes courtesy of Private Chef Stephane Lemagnen, Zencancook.com

½ cup sugar
3 tablespoons cornstarch
5 eggs
½ cup heavy cream
½ cup whole milk
1 tablespoon green tea powder (matcha)
1 tablespoon butter
a few drops green food coloring (optional)
Coconut Sable Crust (see recipe below)
⅓ cup seedless raspberry jam
2 cups drained lychees, cut in half
1 cup fresh raspberries
¼ cup chiffonade of fresh mint leaves

1. In a medium bowl, whisk together sugar and cornstarch, then whisk in the eggs until well combined.

2. In a small saucepan, combine the cream and the milk and bring to a boil. Whisk in green tea powder and remove from heat. Add half of cream mixture to eggs while whisking constantly. Whisk mixture back into remaining cream and place over medium heat, stirring constantly until mixture reaches a pudding-like consistency (if mixture gets lumpy, blend for 30 seconds).

3. Remove from heat, stir in butter, strain through fine mesh sieve and cool over ice bath. Whisk in a few drops of green food coloring (if using).

4. With small offset spatula, line the bottom of the coconut sable crust with an even layer of raspberry jam.

5. Fill the shell with the cool green tea cream and spread evenly.

6. Garnish with lychees, fresh raspberries, and mint. Keep in the refrigerator until ready to serve.

Coconut Sable Crust

2 tablespoons heavy cream
1 large egg yolk
1½ cups all-purpose flour
1 tablespoon sugar
1 pinch of salt
4 ounces butter
1¾ cups sweetened coconut flakes

1. Preheat oven to 400° F. Butter an 8-inch tart pan and set aside.

2. Whisk the cream and egg yolk together in a small bowl.

3. In a mixer fitted with the dough attachment, combine the flour, sugar, salt, and butter and mix on medium speed until the mixture looks like coarse meal. Add the coconut flakes and mix until just combined. Add the cream and yolk and mix until the dough comes together. Wrap the dough and chill for one hour.

4. When ready to proceed, place the dough on a lightly floured surface and roll it out into a ¼-inch circle. Roll and

wrap the dough around the rolling pin to pick it up and unroll over the tart pan. Gently fit the dough into the pan and cut out the excess. Prick the bottom with a fork and blind bake with parchment paper and pastry weights for 12 minutes. (For more on blind baking, see page 301).

5. Remove the parchment paper and pastry weights and bake another 12 minutes, until the crust is an even light golden brown. Set aside on a rack to cool completely.

———

Macarons Chocolat
SERVES 20

Recipes courtesy of Kristi Drake and Thierry Mougin, Le Panier Bakery, lepanier.com

1¼ cup powdered sugar
4 ounces (1 cup) ground almond powder
2 tablespoons unsweetened cocoa powder
4 egg whites
¼ cup granulated sugar
Chocolate Ganache (see recipe below)

1. Preheat oven to 350° F. Sift together powdered sugar, almond powder, and cocoa powder.

2. In a separate bowl, whip egg whites on medium speed until foamy. Increase speed to high and gradually add granulated sugar. Continue to whip to stiff peaks.

3. With rubber spatula, gently fold in powdered sugar mixture until completely combined.

4. Line baking sheets with parchment paper. Fit a piping bag with $7/16$-inch, number 8, stainless steel round tip. Pipe batter into 1-inch disks, 2 inches apart. Let them rest at room temperature for 20 minutes.

5. With oven door slightly ajar, bake for 15 minutes or until surface of the *macarons* is completely dry. Let *macarons* cool completely before gently peeling them off the parchment. The tops are very fragile, so be careful when removing from parchment.

6. Turn over all *macarons* so flat bottoms face up. On half of them, pipe out about 1 teaspoon chocolate ganache. Sandwich with remaining *macarons*, pressing slightly to spread filling to edges.

Chocolate Ganache

4 ounces bittersweet chocolate
1 cup heavy cream

1. Grate chocolate into small pieces. Place in heat-resistant bowl.

2. In a saucepan, bring cream to a light simmer.

3. Remove from stove and pour cream over chocolate. Gently whisk until chocolate is completely melted and smooth.

—❦—

Cassis Truffles
SERVES 30

Recipe courtesy of chocolatier Lan Wong,
Petits Noirs, petitsnoirs.com

1 pound of semisweet chocolate
1 cup heavy cream
8 ounces of cassis fruit purée (red currant is best, as it
    has a huge red berry flavor, but black currant purée
    or even raspberry purée would work as well)
2 tablespoons unsalted butter
1 tablespoon of Cointreau (or Crème de Cassis)
1 cup cocoa powder

1. Chop chocolate into coin-size chunks and place in a mixing bowl.

2. Heat cream and fruit purée together in a small saucepan and bring to a boil.

3. Pour mixture into the bowl with chocolate. Let stand for a minute and then whisk until smooth.

4. Add butter and then the Cointreau. Mix.

5. Cool the entire mixture so that the ganache can set, about 30 minutes in the refrigerator.

6. Once the ganache is set, scoop out little balls. Roll each ball between your palms and toss in cocoa powder.

7. For best results store at 55–60° F. Otherwise, store in an airtight container and place in refrigerator. Bring to room temperature before serving.

GOOD FOR YOU: Black currants, known in French as *cassis*, are chockfull of antioxidants and vitamins, with an extraordinarily high vitamin C content of almost 302 percent of the daily value. They also contain more potassium than bananas.

Dark Chocolate Truffles
SERVES 30

Recipe courtesy of chocolatier Ivy Chan,
Cocoa Chai Chocolates, cocoachai.com

100 grams (about 3½ ounces) heavy whipping cream
250 grams (about 8¾ ounces) dark chocolates, chopped
30 grams (about 1 ounce) sweet butter
cocoa powder for dusting

1. Heat whipping cream to just boiling and remove from heat.
2. Add chopped chocolates to the heated cream and swirl the pan until chocolates are melted, then add butter and mix until smooth.
3. Pour mixture into a shallow square container lined in plastic wrap and leave at room temperature for 24 to 36 hours until firm.
4. Lift the chocolates out and cut into 1-inch by 1-inch squares. Toss them with cocoa.
5. Serve them on a nice plate. These truffles are meant to be consumed within one day.

FROM THE KITCHEN: Buy the best quality chocolates you can when making truffles. You can also add a little spice into the mixture if you like (cinnamon, hot chili pepper powder, etc.).

—◄

Sparkling Pomegranate Lemonade
SERVES 6

From Mia's personal recipe collection, miaking.com

3 tablespoons sugar
½ cup fresh lemon juice
1 cup pomegranate juice
1 liter club soda or sparkling water
ice cubes
fresh mint sprigs, for garnish

1. Combine sugar and lemon juice. Stir until well dissolved.
2. In a tall pitcher, combine lemon mixture and pomegranate juice.
3. Add club soda and stir.
4. Pour into glasses filled with ice. Garnish with mint sprigs and serve.

JUICY LEMONS: To get the most from your lemons, soak them in hot water for 10 minutes and then roll each lemon firmly on the countertop to soften. If pressed for time you can heat them individually in the microwave on high for 20-30 seconds before rolling. It takes approximately 4 to 5 lemons to yield one cup of juice.

Lemongrass Green Tea
SERVES 1

Recipe courtesy of Bartender Jamie Boudreau,
spiritsandcocktails.wordpress.com

2 ounces iced green tea
2 ounces aloe vera juice
¼ ounce lime juice
2 lychees
¼ ounce lemongrass syrup
soda water

1. Muddle lychees in a cocktail shaker.
2. Add remaining ingredients (except for soda water) with ice and shake.
3. Strain into an iced Collins glass.
4. Top with soda water and serve.

DEFINITION, PLEASE: A muddler is a small wooden pestle shaped like a baseball bat. One end is large and rounded and is used to mash the ingredients. The other end is skinnier and flat and is used to mix ingredients. "To muddle" is to combine ingredients, usually in the bottom of a mixing glass, by pressing them with a muddler before adding the majority of the liquid ingredients.

William and Alain's Summertime Sake
SERVES 1

Recipe courtesy of Bartender Jamie Boudreau,
spiritsandcocktails.wordpress.com

¼ fresh peach
2 ounces Junmai Daiginjo sake
½ ounce gin
¼ ounce lemon juice
1 teaspoon lemongrass syrup
ice cubes

1. Muddle the peach in a cocktail shaker.
2. Add remaining ingredients with ice and shake.
3. Strain into a chilled cocktail glass and serve.

Lychee Martini with Crystallized Ginger
SERVES 2

From the author's personal recipe collection, miaking.com

6 ounces vodka
2 tablespoons lychee syrup or liqueur
splash vermouth
ice cubes
crystallized ginger, crushed, for garnish
2 fresh lychees, for garnish

1. Rim two martini glasses with crushed crystallized ginger.
2. In a cocktail shaker filled with ice, add vodka, lychee syrup (not the juice from canned lychees, which is cloudy and not very flavorful) and vermouth.
3. Shake until well chilled.
4. Pour into two martini glasses and garnish with lychees. Serve immediately.